PIRANHA TO SCURFY

Also by Ruth Rendell

Ruth Rendell

PIRANHA TO SCURFY

HUTCHINSON
London

Copyright © Kingsmarkham Enterprises 2000

The right of Ruth Rendell to be identified
as the author of this work has been asserted
by her in accordance with the
Copyright Designs and Patents Act, 1988

This novel is a work of fiction. Names
and characters are the product of the author's
imagination and any resemblance to actual persons,
living or dead, is entirely coincidental

First published in the United Kingdom in 2000 by Hutchinson

The Random House Group Limited
20 Vauxhall Bridge Road, London SW1V 2SA

Random House Australia (Pty) Limited
20 Alfred Street, Milsons Point, Sydney,
New South Wales 2061,
Australia

Random House New Zealand Limited
18 Poland Road, Glenfield, Auckland 10,
New Zealand

Random House (Pty) Limited
Endulini, 5a Jubilee Road, Parktown 2193, South Africa

The Random House Group Limited Reg. No. 954009
www.randomhouse.co.uk

A CIP catalogue record for this book is available from the British Library

Papers used by Random House are natural, recyclable
products made from wood grown in sustainable forests.
The manufacturing processes conform to the environmental regulations
of the country of origin

ISBN 0 09 179347 5 – Hardback
ISBN 0 09 179383 1 – Paperback

Typeset by Deltatype Ltd, Birkenhead, Merseyside
Printed and bound in Great Britain by
Mackays of Chatham PLC

Contents

Piranha to Scurfy

It was the first time he had been away on holiday without Mummy. The first time in his life. They had always gone to the Isle of Wight, to Ventnor or Totland Bay, so, going alone, he had chosen Cornwall for the change that people say is as good as a rest. Not that Ribbon's week in Cornwall had been entirely leisure. He had taken four books with him, read them carefully in the B and B's lounge, in his bedroom, on the beach and sitting on the clifftop, and made meticulous notes in the loose-leaf notebook he had bought in a shop in Newquay. The results had been satisfactory, more than satisfactory. Allowing for the anger and disgust-making these discoveries invariably aroused, he felt he could say he had had a relaxing time. To use a horrible phrase much favoured by Eric Owlberg in his literary output, he had recharged his batteries.

Coming home to an empty house would be an ordeal. He had known it would be and it was. Instead of going out into the garden, he gave it careful scrutiny from the dining room window. Everything outside and indoors was as he had left it. In the house, all the books in their places. Every room contained books. Ribbon was not one to make jokes but he considered it witty to remark that while other people's walls were papered his were booked. No one knew what he meant for hardly anyone except himself ever entered 21 Grove Green Avenue, Leytonstone, and those to whom he uttered his little joke smiled uneasily. He had put up the shelves himself, buying them from IKEA. As they filled he bought more, until the shelves extended from floor to ceiling. A strange appearance was given to the house by this superfluity of books as the shelves necessarily reduced the size of the rooms, so that the living room, originally fifteen feet by twelve, shrank to thirteen feet by ten. The hall and landing were 'booked' as densely as the rooms. The place looked like a library, but one mysteriously divided into small sections. His windows appeared as alcoves set deep in the walls, affording a view at the front of the house of a rather gloomy suburban street, thickly treed. The back gave on to the yellow brick rears of other houses and, in the foreground, his garden which was mostly lawn, dotted about with various drab shrubs. At the far end was a wide flowerbed the sun never reached and in which grew creeping ivies and dark-leaved flowerless plants which like the shade.

He had got over expecting Mummy to come downstairs or walk into a room. She had been gone five months now. He sighed, for he was a long way from recovering from his loss and his regrets. Work was in some ways easier without her and in others immeasurably harder. She had reassured him, sometimes she had made him strong. But he had to press on, there was really no choice. Tomorrow things would be back to normal.

He began by ranging before him on the desk in the study – though was not the whole house a study? – the book review pages from the newspapers which had arrived while he was away. As he had expected, Owlberg's latest novel, *Paving Hell*, appeared this very day in paperback, one year after hardcover publication. It was priced at £6.99 and by now would be in all the shops. Ribbon made a memo about it on one of the plain cards he kept for this purpose. But before continuing he let his eyes rest on the portrait of Mummy in the plain silver frame that stood on the table where used, read and dissected books had their temporary home. It was Mummy who had first drawn his attention to Owlberg. She had borrowed one of his books from the public library and pointed out to Ribbon with indignation the mass of errors, solecisms and abuse of the English language to be found in its pages. How he missed her! Wasn't it principally to her that he owed his choice of career as well as the acumen and confidence to pursue it?

He sighed anew. Then he returned to his newspapers and noted down the titles of four more novels currently published in paperback as well as the new Kingston Marle, *Demogorgon*, due to appear this coming Thursday in hardcover with the maximum hype and fanfares of metaphorical trumpets, but almost certainly already in the shops. A sign of the degeneracy of the times, Mummy had said, that a book whose publication was scheduled for May appeared on sale at the end of April. No one could wait these days, everyone was in a hurry. It certainly made his work harder. It increased the chances of his missing a vitally important novel which might have sold out before he knew it was in print.

Ribbon switched on his computer and checked that the printer was linked to it. It was only nine in the morning. He had at least an hour before he need make his trip to the bookshop. Where should it be today? Perhaps the City or the West End of London. It would be unwise to go back to his local shop so soon and attract too much attention to himself. Hatchards, perhaps then, or Books Etc or Dillons, or even all three. He opened the notebook he had bought in Cornwall, reread what he had written and with the paperback open on the desk, reached for the *Shorter Oxford Dictionary*, Brewer's *Dictionary of Phrase and Fable* and *Whittaker's Almanack*. Referring to the first two and noting down his finds, he began his letter.

21 *Grove Green Avenue,*
London E11 4ZH

Dear Joy Anne Fortune,
I have read your new novel Dreadful Night *with very little pleasure and great disappointment. Your previous work has seemed to me, while being without any literary merit whatsoever, at least to be*

3

fresh, occasionally original and largely free from those errors of fact and slips in grammar which, I may say, characterise Dreadful Night.

Look first at page 24. Do you really believe 'desiccated' has two 's's and one 'c'? And if you do, have your publishers no copy editor whose job it is to recognise and correct these errors? On page 82 you refer to the republic of Guinea as being in East *Africa and as a former British possession, instead of being in West Africa and formerly French, and on page 103 to the late General Sikorski as a one-time prime minister of Czechoslovakia rather than of Poland. You describe, on page 139, 'hadith' as being the Jewish prayers for the dead instead of what it correctly means, the body of tradition and legend surrounding the Prophet Mohammed and his followers, and on the following page 'tabernacle' as an entrance to a temple. Its true meaning is a portable sanctuary in which the Ark of the Covenant was carried.*

Need I go on? I am weary of underlining the multifarious mistakes in your book. Needless to say, I shall buy no more of your work, and shall advise my highly literate and discerning friends to boycott it.

Yours sincerely,

Ambrose Ribbon

The threat in the last paragraph was an empty one. Ribbon had no friends and could hardly say he missed having any. He was on excellent, at least speaking, terms with his neighbours and various managers of bookshops. There was a cousin in Gloucestershire he saw occasionally. Mummy had been his friend. There was no one he had ever met who could approach replacing her. He wished, as he did every day, she were back there beside him and able to read and appreciate his letter.

He addressed an envelope to Joy Anne Fortune care of her publishers – she was not one of 'his' authors unwise enough to reply to him on headed writing paper – put the letter inside it and sealed it up. Two more must be written before he left the house, one to Graham Prink pointing out mistakes in *Dancing Partners*, 'lay' for 'lie' in two instances and 'may' for 'might' in three, and the other to Jeanne Pettle to tell her that the plot and much of the dialogue in *Southern Discomfort* had been blatantly lifted from *Gone With the Wind*. He considered it the most flagrant plagiarism he had seen for a long while. In both he indicated how distasteful he found the authors' frequent use of obscenities, notably those words beginning with an 'f' and a 'c' and the taking of the Deity's name in vain.

At five to ten Ribbon took his letters, switched off the computer and closed the door behind him. Before going downstairs, he paid his second visit of the day to Mummy's room. He had been there for the first time since his return from Cornwall at seven the previous evening, again before he went to bed and once more at seven this morning. While he was away his second greatest worry had been that something would be disturbed in there, an object removed or its position changed, for, though he did his own housework, Glenys Next-door had a key and often in his absence, in her own words, 'popped in to see that everything was OK'.

But nothing was changed. Mummy's dressing table was exactly as she had left it, the two cut-glass scent bottles with silver stoppers set one on each side of the lace-edged mat, the silver-backed hairbrush on its glass tray alongside the hair tidy and the pink pincushion. The wardrobe door he always left ajar so that her clothes could be seen inside, those dear garments, the afternoon dresses, the coats and skirts – Mummy had never possessed a pair of trousers – the warm winter coat, the neatly placed pairs of court shoes. Over the door, because he had seen this in an interiors magazine, he had hung, folded in two, the beautiful white and cream tapestry bedspread he had once given her but which she said was too good for daily use. On the bed lay the dear old one her own mother had worked, and on its spotless if worn bands of lace, her pink silk nightdress. He lingered, looking at it.

After a moment or two he opened the window two inches at the top. It was a good idea to allow a little fresh air to circulate. He

5

closed Mummy's door behind him and, carrying his letters, went downstairs. A busy day lay ahead. His tie straightened, one button only out of the three on his linen jacket done up, he set the burglar alarm. Eighteen fifty-two was the code, one-eight, five-two, the date of the first edition of *Roget's Thesaurus*, a compendium Ribbon had found useful in his work. He opened the front door and closed it just as the alarm started braying. While he was waiting on the doorstep, his ear to the keyhole, for the alarm to cease until or unless an intruder set it off again, Glenys Next-door called out a cheery 'Hiya!'.

Ribbon hated this mode of address, but there was nothing he could do to stop it, any more than he could stop her calling him Amby. He smiled austerely and said good morning. Glenys Next-door – this was her own description of herself, first used when she moved into 23 Grove Green Avenue fifteen years before, 'Hiya, I'm Glenys Next-door' – said it was the window cleaner's day and should she let him in.

'Why does he have to come in?' Ribbon said rather testily.

'It's his fortnight for doing the back, Amby. You know how he does the front on a Monday and the back on the Monday fortnight and inside and out on the last Monday in the month.'

Like any professional with much on his mind, Ribbon found these domestic details almost unbearably irritating. Nor did he like the idea of a strange man left free to wander about his back garden. 'Well, yes, I suppose so.' He had never called Glenys Next-door by her given name and did not intend to begin. 'You know the code, Mrs Judd.' It was appalling that she had to know the code but since Mummy passed on and no one was in the house it was inevitable. 'You do know the code, don't you?'

'Eight one five two.'

'No, no, no.' He must not lose his temper. Glancing up and down the street to make sure there was no one within earshot, he whispered, 'One eight five two. You can remember that, can't you? I really don't want to write it down. You never know what happens to something once it has been put in writing.'

Glenys Next-door had started to laugh. 'You're a funny old fusspot you are, Amby. D'you know what I saw in your garden last night? A fox. How about that? In *Leytonstone*.'

'Really?' Foxes dig, he thought.

'They're taking refuge, you see. Escaping the hunters. Cruel, isn't it? Are you off to work?'

'Yes and I'm late,' Ribbon said, hurrying off. 'Old fusspot' indeed. He was a good ten years younger than she.

Glenys Next-door had no idea what he did for a living and he intended to keep her in ignorance. 'Something in the media, is it?' she had once said to Mummy. Of course, 'for a living' was not strictly true, implying as it did that he was paid for his work. That he was not was hardly for want of trying. He had written to twenty major publishing houses, pointing out to them that what he did, by uncovering errors in their authors' works and showing them to be unworthy of publication, was potentially saving the publishers hundreds of thousands of pounds a year. The least they could do was offer him some emolument. He wrote to four national newspapers as well, asking for his work to receive publicity in their pages, and to the Department of Culture, Media and Sport, in the hope of recognition of the service he performed. A change in the law was what he wanted, providing something for him in the nature of the Public Lending Right (he was vague about this) or the Value Added Tax. None of them replied, with the exception of the Department, who sent a card saying that his communication had been noted, not signed by the Secretary of State, though, but by some underling with an indecipherable signature.

It was the principle of the thing, not that he was in need of money. Thanks to Daddy, who, dying young, had left all the income from his royalties to Mummy and thus, of course, to him. No great sum but enough to live on if one was frugal and managing as he was. Daddy had written three textbooks before death came for him at the heartbreaking age of forty-one, and all were still in demand for use in business schools. Ribbon, because he could not help himself, in great secrecy and far from Mummy's sight, had gone through those books after his usual fashion, looking for errors. The compulsion to do this was irresistible, though he had tried to resist it, fighting against the need, conscious of the disloyalty, but finally succumbing, as another man might ultimately yield to some ludicrous auto-eroticism. Alone, in the night, his bedroom door locked, he had perused Daddy's books and found – nothing.

The search was the most shameful thing he had ever done. And this not only on account of the distrust in Daddy's expertise and acumen that it implied, but also because he had to confess to himself that he did not understand what he read and would not have known a mistake if he had seen one. He put Daddy's books away in a cupboard after that and, strangely enough, Mummy had never commented on their absence. Perhaps, her eyesight failing, she hadn't noticed.

Ribbon walked to Leytonstone tube station and sat on the seat to wait for a train. He had decided to change at Holborn and take the Piccadilly Line to Piccadilly Circus. From there it was only a short walk to Dillons and a further few steps to Hatchards. He acknowledged that Hatchards was the better shop but Dillons guaranteed a greater anonymity to its patrons. Its assistants seemed indifferent to the activities of customers, ignoring their presence most of the time and not apparently noticing whether they stayed five minutes or half an hour. Ribbon liked that. He liked to describe himself as reserved, a private man, one who minded his own business and lived quietly. Others, in his view, would do well to be the same. As far as he was concerned, a shop assistant was there to take your money, give you your change and say thank you. The displacement of the high street or corner shop by vast impersonal supermarkets was one of few modern innovations he could heartily approve.

The train came. It was three-quarters empty, as was usually so at this hour. He had read in the paper that London Transport was thinking of introducing Ladies Only carriages in the tube. Why not Men Only carriages as well? Preferably, when you considered what some young men were like, Middle-aged Scholarly Gentlemen Only carriages. The train stopped for a long time in the tunnel between Mile End and Bethnal Green. Naturally, passengers were offered no explanation for the delay. He waited a long time for the Piccadilly Line train, due apparently to some signalling failure outside Cockfosters, but eventually arrived at his destination just before eleven thirty.

The sun had come out and it was very hot. The air smelt of diesel and cooking and beer, very different from Leytonstone on the verges of Epping Forest. Ribbon went into Dillons, where no one showed the slightest interest in his arrival, and the first thing to assault his senses was an enormous pyramidal display of Kingston Marle's *Demogorgon*. Each copy was as big as the average-sized dictionary and encased in a jacket printed in silver and two shades of red. A hole in the shape of a pentagram in the front cover revealed beneath it the bandaged face of some mummified corpse. The novel had already been reviewed and the poster on the wall above the display quoted the *Sunday Express's* encomium in exaggeratedly large type: *Readers will have fainted with fear before page 10.*'

The price, at £18.99, was a disgrace but there was no help for it. A legitimate outlay, if ever there was one. Ribbon took a copy and, from what a shop assistant had once told him were called 'dump bins', helped himself to two paperbacks of books he had already examined and commented on in hardcover. There was no sign in the whole shop of Eric Owlberg's *Paving Hell*. Ribbon's dilemma was to ask or not to ask. The young woman behind the counter put his purchases in a bag and he handed her Mummy's direct debit Visa card. Lightly, as if it were an afterthought, the most casual thing in the world, he asked about the new Owlberg. 'Already sold out, has it?' he said with a little laugh.

Her face was impassive. 'We're expecting them in tomorrow.'

He signed the receipt B. J. Ribbon and passed it to the girl without a smile. She need not think he was going to make this trip all over again tomorrow. He made his way to Hatchards, on the way depositing the Dillons bag in a litter bin and transferring the books into the plain plastic holdall he carried rolled up in his pocket. If the staff at Hatchards had seen Dillons' name on the bag he would have felt rather awkward. Now they would think he was carrying his purchases from a chemist or a photographic store.

One of them came up to him the minute he entered Hatchards. He recognised her as the marketing manager, a tall, good-looking dark woman. She recognised him too and to his astonishment and displeasure addressed him by his name. 'Good morning, Mr Ribbon.'

Inwardly he groaned, for he remembered having had forebodings about this at the time. On one occasion he had ordered a book, he was desperate to see an early copy, and had been obliged to say who he was and give them his phone number. He said good morning in a frosty sort of voice.

'How nice to see you,' she said. 'I rather think you may be in search of the new Kingston Marle, am I right? *Demogorgon?* Copies came in today.'

Ribbon felt terrible. The plastic of his carrier was translucent rather than transparent but he was sure she must be able to see the silver and the two shades of red glowing through the cloudy film that covered it. He held it behind his back in a manner he hoped looked natural. 'It was *Paving Hell* I actually wanted,' he muttered, wondering what rule of life or social usage made it necessary for him to explain his wishes to marketing managers.

'We have it, of course,' she said with a radiant smile and picked the paperback off a shelf. He was sure she was going to point out to him in schoolmistressy fashion that he had already had it in hardcover, she quite distinctly remembered, and why on earth did he want another copy. Instead she said, 'Mr Owlberg is here at this moment, signing stock for us. It's not a public signing but I'm sure he'd love to meet such a constant reader as yourself. And be happy to sign a copy of his book for you.'

Ribbon hoped his shudder hadn't been visible. No, no, he was in a hurry, he had a pressing engagement at 12.30 on the other side of town, he couldn't wait, he'd pay for his book . . . Thoughts raced through his mind of the things he had written to Owlberg about his work, all of it perfectly justified, of course, but galling to the author. His name would have lodged in Owlberg's mind as firmly as Owlberg's had in his. Imagining the reaction of *Paving Hell*'s author when he looked up from his signing, saw the face and heard the name of his stern judge made him shudder again. He almost ran out of the shop. How fraught with dangers visits to the West End of London were! Next time he came up he'd stick to the City or Bloomsbury. There was a very good Waterstone's in the Gray's Inn Road. Deciding to walk up to Oxford Circus tube station and thus obviate a train change, he stopped on the way to draw money out from a cash dispenser. He punched in Mummy's pin number, her birth date, 1-5-27, and drew from the slot one hundred pounds in crisp new notes.

Most authors to whom Ribbon wrote his letters of complaint either did not reply at all or wrote back in a conciliatory way to admit their mistakes and promise these would be rectified for the paperback edition. Only one, out of all the hundreds, if not thousands, who had had a letter from him, reacted violently and with threats. This was a woman called Selma Gunn. He had written to her, care of her publishers, criticising, but quite mildly, her novel *A Dish of Snakes*, remarking how irritating it was to read so many verbless sentences and pointing out the absurdity of her premiss that Shakespeare, far from being a sixteenth-century English poet and dramatist, was in fact an Italian astrologer born in Verona and a close friend of Leonardo da Vinci. Her reply came within four days, a vituperative response in which she several times used the 'f' word, called him an ignorant swollen-headed nonentity and threatened legal action. Sure enough, on the following day a letter arrived from Ms Gunn's solicitors, suggesting that many of his remarks were actionable, all were indefensible and they awaited his reply with interest.

Ribbon had been terrified. He was unable to work, incapable of thinking of anything but Ms Gunn's letter and the one from Evans Richler Sabatini. At first he said nothing to Mummy, though she, of course, with her customary sensitive acuity, could tell something was wrong. Two days later he received another letter from Selma Gunn. This time she drew his attention to certain astrological predictions in her book, told him that he was one of those Nostradamus had predicted would be destroyed when the world came to an end next year and that she herself had occult powers. She ended by demanding an apology.

Ribbon did not, of course, believe in the supernatural but, like most of us, was made to feel deeply uneasy when cursed or menaced by something in the nature of necromancy. He sat down at his computer and composed an abject apology. He was sorry, he wrote, he had intended no harm, Ms Gunn was entitled to express her beliefs; her theory as to Shakespeare's origins was just as valid as identifying him with Bacon or Ben Jonson. It took it out of him, writing that letter, and when Mummy, observing his pallor and trembling hands, finally asked him what was wrong, he told her everything. He showed her the letter of apology.

Masterful as ever, she took it from him and tore it up. 'Absolute nonsense,' she said. He could tell she was furious. 'On what grounds can the stupid woman bring an action, I should like to know? Take no notice. Ignore it. It will soon stop, you mark my words.'

'But what harm can it do, Mummy?'

'You coward,' Mummy said witheringly. 'Are you a man or a mouse?'

Ribbon asked her, politely but as manfully as he could, not to talk to him like that. It was almost their first quarrel – but not their last.

He had bowed to her edict and stuck it out in accordance with her instructions, as he did in most cases. And she had been right, for he heard not another word from Selma Gunn or from Evans Richler Sabatini. The whole awful business was over and Ribbon felt he had learned something from it – to be brave, to be resolute, to soldier on. But this did not include confronting Owlberg in the flesh, even though the author of *Paving Hell* had promised him in a letter responding to Ribbon's criticism of the hardcover edition of his book that the errors of fact he had pointed out would all be rectified in the paperback. His publishers, he wrote, had also received Ribbon's letter of complaint and were as pleased as he to have had such informed critical comment. Pleased, my foot! What piffle! Ribbon had snorted over this letter, which was a lie from start to finish. The man wasn't pleased, he was aghast and humiliated, as he should be.

Ribbon sat down in his living room to check in the paperback edition for the corrections so glibly promised. He read down here and wrote upstairs. The room was almost as Mummy had left it. The changes were only in that more books and bookshelves had been added and in the photographs in the silver frames. He had taken out the picture of himself as a baby and himself as a schoolboy and replaced them with one of his parents' wedding, Daddy in Air Force uniform, Mummy in cream costume and small cream hat, and one of Daddy in his academic gown and mortarboard. There had never been one of Ribbon himself in similar garments. Mummy, for his own good, had decided he would be better off at home with her, leading a quiet sheltered life, than at a university. Had he regrets? A degree would have been useless to a man with a private income, as Mummy had pointed out, a man who had all the resources of an excellent public library system to educate him.

He opened *Paving Hell*. He had a foreboding, before he had even turned to the middle of chapter one where the first mistake occurred, that nothing would have been put right. All the errors would be still there, for Owlberg's promises meant nothing, he had probably never passed Ribbon's comments on to the publishers; and they, if they had received the letter he wrote them, had never answered it. For all that, he was still enraged when he found he was right. Didn't the man care? Was money and a kind of low notoriety, for you couldn't call it fame, all he was interested in? None of the errors had been corrected. No, that wasn't quite true; one had. On page 99 Owlberg's ridiculous statement that the One World Trade Center tower in New York was the world's tallest building had been altered. Ribbon noted down the remaining mistakes, ready to write to Owlberg next day. A vituperative letter it would be, spitting venom, catechising illiteracy, carelessness and a general disregard (contempt?) for the sensibilities of readers. And Owlberg would reply to it in his previous pusillanimous way, making empty promises, for he was no Selma Gunn.

Ribbon fetched himself a small whisky and water. It was six o'clock. A cushion behind his head, his feet up on the footstool Mummy had embroidered, but covered now with a plastic sheet, he opened *Demogorgon*. This was the first book by Kingston Marle he had ever read but he had some idea of what Marle wrote about. Murder, violence, crime, but instead of a detective detecting and reaching a solution, supernatural interventions, demonic possession, ghosts, as well as a great deal of unnatural or perverted sex, cannibalism and torture. Occult manifestations occurred side by side with rational, if unedifying, events. Innocent people were caught up in the magical dabblings, frequently going wrong, of so-called adepts. Ribbon had learned this from the reviews he had read of Marle's books, most of which, surprisingly to him, received good notices in periodicals of repute. That is, the serious and reputable critics engaged by literary editors to comment on his work praised the quality of the prose as vastly superior to the general run of thriller writing. His characters, they said, convinced and he induced in the reader a very real sense of terror, while a deep vein of moral theology underlay his plot. They also said that his serious approach to mumbo-jumbo and such nonsense as evil spirits and necromancy was ridiculous, but they said it *en passant* and without much enthusiasm. Ribbon read the blurb inside the front cover and turned to chapter one.

Almost the first thing he spotted was an error on page 2. He made a note of it. Another occurred on page 7. Whether Marle's prose was beautiful or not he scarcely noticed, he was too incensed by errors of fact, spelling mistakes and grammatical howlers. For a while, that is. The first part of the novel concerned a man living alone in London, a man in his own situation whose mother had died not long before. There was another parallel: the man's name was Charles Ambrose. Well, it was common enough as surname, much less so as baptismal name, and only a paranoid person would think any connection was intended.

Charles Ambrose was rich and powerful, with a house in London, a mansion in the country and a flat in Paris. All these places seemed to be haunted in various ways by something or other but the odd thing was that Ribbon could see what that reviewer meant by readers fainting with terror before page 10. He wasn't going to faint but he could feel himself growing increasingly alarmed. 'Frightened' would be too strong a word. Every few minutes he found himself glancing up towards the closed door or looking into the dim and shadowy corners of the room. He was such a reader, so exceptionally well read, that he had thought himself proof against this sort of thing. Why, he had read hundreds of ghost stories in his time. As a boy he had inured himself by reading first Dennis Wheatley, then Stephen King, not to mention M. R. James. And this *Demogorgon* was so absurd, the supernatural activity the reader was supposed to accept so pathetic, that he wouldn't have gone on with it but for the mistakes he kept finding on almost every page.

After a while he got up, opened the door and put the hall light on. He had never been even mildly alarmed by Selma Gunn's *A Dish of Snakes*, nor touched with disquiet by any effusions of Joy Anne Fortune's. What was the matter with him? He came back into the living room, put on the central light and an extra table lamp, the one with the shade Mummy had decorated with pressed flowers. That was better. Anyone passing could see in now, something he usually disliked, but for some reason he didn't feel like drawing the curtains. Before sitting down again he fetched himself some more whisky.

This passage about the mummy Charles Ambrose brought back with him after the excavations he had carried out in Egypt was very unpleasant. Why had he never noticed before that the diminutive by which he had always addressed his mother was the same word as that applied to embalmed bodies? Especially nasty was the paragraph where Ambrose's girlfriend Kaysa reaches in semi-darkness for a garment in her wardrobe and her wrist is grasped by a scaly paw. This was so upsetting that Ribbon almost missed noticing that Marle spelt the adjective 'scaley'. He had a sense of the room being less light than a few moments before, as if the bulbs in the lamps were weakening before entirely failing. One of them did indeed fail while his eyes were on it, flickered, buzzed and went out. Of course, Ribbon knew perfectly well this was not a supernatural phenomenon but simply the result of the bulb coming to the end of its life after a thousand hours or whatever it was. He switched off the lamp, extracted the bulb when it was cool, shook it to hear the rattle that told him its usefulness was over, and took it outside to the waste bin. The kitchen was in darkness. He put on the light and the outside light which illuminated part of the garden. That was better. A siren wailing on a police car going down Grove Green Road made him jump. He helped himself to more whisky, a rare indulgence for him. He was no drinker.

Supper now. It was almost eight. Ribbon always set the table for himself, either here or in the dining room, put out a linen table napkin in its silver ring, a jug of water and a glass, and the silver pepper pot and salt cellar. This was Mummy's standard and if he had deviated from it he would have felt he was letting her down. But this evening, as he made toast and scrambled two large free-range eggs in a buttered pan, filled a small bowl with mandarin oranges from a can and poured evaporated milk over them, he found himself most unwilling to venture into the dining room. It was at the best of times a gloomy chamber, its rather small window set deep in bookshelves, its furnishing largely a reptilian shade of brownish-green Mummy always called 'crocodile'. Poor Mummy only kept the room like that because the crocodile-green had been Daddy's choice when they were first married. There was only a central light, a bulb in a parchment shade, suspended above the middle of the mahogany table. Books covered as yet only two sides of the room, but new shelves had been bought and were waiting for him to put them up. One of the pictures on the wall facing the window had been most distasteful to Ribbon when he was a small boy, a lithograph of some Old Testament scene and entitled *Saul Encounters the Witch of Endor*. Mummy, saying he should not fear painted devils, refused to take it down. He was in no mood tonight to have that lowering over him while he ate his scrambled eggs.

Nor did he much fancy the kitchen. Once or twice, while he was sitting there, Glenys Next-door's cat had looked through the window at him. It was a black cat, totally black all over, its eyes large and of a very pale crystalline yellow. Of course he knew what it was and had never in the past been alarmed by it but somehow he sensed it would be different tonight. If Tinks Next-door pushed its black face and yellow eyes against the glass it might give him a serious shock. He put the plates on a tray and carried it back into the living room with the replenished whisky glass.

It was both his job and his duty to continue reading *Demogorgon* but there was more to it than that, Ribbon admitted to himself in a rare burst of honesty. He *wanted* to go on, he wanted to know what happened to Charles Ambrose and Kaysa de Floris, whose the embalmed corpse was and how it had been liberated from its arcane and archaic (writers always muddled up those adjectives) sarcophagus, and whether the mysterious and saintly rescuer was in fact the reincarnated Joseph of Arimathea and the vessel he carried the Holy Grail. By the time Mummy's grandmother clock in the hall struck eleven, half an hour past his bedtime, he had read half the book and would no longer have described himself as merely alarmed. He was frightened. So frightened that he had to stop reading.

Twice during the course of the past hour he had refilled his whisky glass, half in the hope that strong drink would induce sleep when, finally at a quarter past eleven, he went to bed. He passed a miserable night, worse even than those he experienced in the weeks after Mummy's death. It was, for instance, a mistake to take *Demogorgon* upstairs with him. He hardly knew why he had done so, for he certainly had no intention of reading any more of it that night, if ever. The final chapter he had read – well, he could scarcely say what had upset him most, the orgy in the middle of the Arabian desert in which Charles and Kaysa had both enthusiastically taken part, wallowing in perverted practices, or the intervention, disguised as a Bedouin tribesman, of the demon Kabadeus, later revealing in his nakedness his hermaphrodite body with huge female breasts and trifurcated member.

As always, Ribbon placed his slippers by the bed. He pushed the book a little under the bed but he couldn't forget that it was there. In the darkness he seemed to hear sounds he had never heard, or never noticed, before: a creaking as if a foot trod first on one stair, then the next; a rattling of the window-pane, though it was a windless night; a faint rustling on the bedroom door as if a thing in grave clothes had scrabbled with its decaying hand against the panelling. He put on the bed lamp. Its light was faint, showing him deep wells of darkness in the corners of the room. He told himself not to be a fool. Demons, ghosts, evil spirits had no existence. If only he hadn't brought the wretched book up with him! He would be better, he would be able to sleep, he was sure, if the book weren't there, exerting a malign influence. Then something dreadful occurred to him. He couldn't take the book outside, downstairs, away. He hadn't the nerve. It would not be possible for him to open the door, go down the stairs, carrying that book.

The whisky, asserting itself in the mysterious way it had, began a banging in his head. A flicker of pain ran from his eyebrow down his temple to his ear. He climbed out of bed, crept across the floor, his heart pounding, and put on the central light. That was a little better. He drew back the bedroom curtains and screamed. He actually screamed aloud, frightening himself even more with the noise he made. Tinks Next-door was sitting on the windowsill, staring impassively at curtain linings, now into Ribbon's face. It took no notice of the scream but lifted a paw, licked it and began washing its face.

Ribbon pulled the curtains back. He sat down on the end of the bed, breathing deeply. It was two in the morning, a pitch-black night, ill-lit by widely spaced yellow chemical lamps. What he would really have liked to do was rush across the passage – do it quickly, don't think about it – into Mummy's room, burrow down into Mummy's bed and spend the night there. If he could only do that he would be safe, would sleep, be comforted. It would be like creeping back into Mummy's arms. But he couldn't do it, it was impossible. For one thing it would be a violation of the sacred room, the sacrosanct bed, never to be disturbed since Mummy spent her last night in it. And for another, he dared not venture out on to the landing.

Trying to court sleep by thinking of himself and Mummy in her last years helped a little. The two of them sitting down to an evening meal in the dining room, a white candle alight on the table, its soft light dispelling much of the gloom and ugliness. Mummy had enjoyed television when a really good programme was on, *Brideshead Revisited*, for instance, or something from Jane Austen. She had always liked the curtains drawn, even before it was dark, and it was his job to do it, then fetch each of them a dry sherry. Sometimes they read aloud to each other in the gentle lamplight, Mummy choosing to read her favourite Victorian writers to him, he picking a book from his work, correcting the grammar as he read. Or she would talk about Daddy and her first meeting with him in a library, she searching the shelves for a novel whose author's name she had forgotten, he offering to help her and finding – triumphantly – Mrs Henry Wood's *East Lynne*.

But all these memories of books and reading pulled Ribbon brutally back to *Demogorgon*. The scaly hand was the worst thing and, second to that, the cloud or ball of visible darkness that arose in the lighted room when Charles Ambrose cast salt and asafoetida into the pentagram. He reached down to find the lead on the bed lamp where the switch was and encountered something cold and leathery. It was only the tops of his slippers, which he always left just beside his bed, but he had once again screamed before he remembered. The lamp on, he lay still, breathing deeply. Only when the first light of morning, a grey trickle of dawn, came creeping under and between the curtains at about six did he fall into a troubled doze.

Morning makes an enormous difference to fear and to depression. It wasn't long before Ribbon was castigating himself for a fool and blaming the whisky and the scrambled eggs for his disturbed night rather than Kingston Marle. However, he would read no more of *Demogorgon*. No matter how much he might wish to know the fate of Charles and Kaysa or the identity of the bandaged reeking thing, he preferred not to expose himself any longer to this distasteful rubbish or Marle's grammatical lapses.

A hot shower, followed by a cold one, did a lot to restore him. He breakfasted, but in the kitchen. When he had finished he went into the dining room and had a look at *Saul Encounters the Witch of Endor*. It was years since he had even glanced at it, which was no doubt why he had never noticed how much like Mummy the witch looked. Of course, Mummy would never have worn diaphanous grey draperies and she had all her own teeth, but there was something about the nose and mouth, the burning eyes and the pointing finger, this last particularly characteristic of Mummy, that reminded him of her. He dismissed the disloyal thought but, on an impulse, took the picture down and put it on the floor, its back towards him, to lean against the wall. It left behind it a paler rectangle on the ochre-coloured wallpaper but the new bookshelves would cover that. Ribbon went upstairs to his study and his daily labours. First, the letter to Owlberg.

21 *Grove Green Avenue,*
London E11 4ZH

Dear Sir,

In spite of your solemn promise to me as to the correction of errors in your new paperback publication, I find you have fulfilled this undertaking only to the extent of making one single amendment.

This, of course, in anyone's estimation, is a gross insult to your readers, displaying as it does your contempt for them and for the TRUTH. I am sending a copy of this letter to your publishers and await an explanation both from you and them.

Yours faithfully,
Ambrose Ribbon

Letting off steam always put him in a good mood. He felt a joyful adrenalin rush and inspired to write a congratulatory letter for a change. This one was addressed to: The Manager, Dillons Bookshop, Piccadilly, London W1.

21 *Grove Green Avenue,*
London E11 4ZH

Dear Sir or Madam [there were a lot of women taking men's jobs these days, poking their noses in where they weren't needed].

I write to congratulate you on your excellent organisation, management and the, alas, now old-fashioned attitude you have to your book buyers. I refer, of course, to the respectful distance and detachment maintained between you and them. It makes a refreshing change from the over-familiarity displayed by many of your competitors.

    Yours faithfully,

      Ambrose Ribbon

Before writing to the author of the novel which had been directly responsible for his loss of sleep, Ribbon needed to look something up. A king of Egypt of the seventh century BC called Psamtik I he had come across before in someone else's book. Marle referred to him as Psammetichus I and Ribbon was nearly sure this was wrong. He would have to look it up and the obvious place to do this was the *Encyclopaedia Britannica*.

Others might have recourse to the Internet. Because Mummy had despised such electronic devices, Ribbon did so too. He wasn't even on the Net and never would be. The present difficulty was that Psamtik I would be found in volume VIII of the Micropaedia, the one that covered subjects from *Piranha to Scurfy*. This volume he had had no occasion to use since Mummy's death, though his eyes sometimes strayed fearfully in its direction. There it was placed, in the bookshelves to the left of where he sat facing the window, bound in its black, blue and gold, its position between *Montpel to Piranesi* and *Scurlock to Tirah*. He was very reluctant to touch it but he *had to*. Mummy might be dead but her injunctions and instructions lived on. Don't be deterred, she had often said, don't be deflected by anything from what you know to be right, not by weariness, nor indifference nor doubt. Press on, tell the truth, shame these people.

There would not be a mark on *Piranha to Scurfy*, he knew that, nothing but his fingerprints and they, of course, were invisible. It had been used and put back, and was unchanged. Cautiously he advanced upon the shelf where the ten volumes of the Micro-paedia and the nineteen of the Macropaedia were arranged and put out his hand to volume VIII. As he lifted it down he noticed something different about it, different, that is, from the others.

Not a mark, not a stain or scar, but a slight loosening of the 1002 pages as if at some time it had been mistreated, violently shaken or in some similar way abused. It had. He shivered a little but he opened the book and turned the pages to the 'P's. It was somewhat disappointing to find that Marle had been right. Psamtik was right and so was the Greek form, Psammetichus I, it was optional. Still, there were enough errors in the book, a plethora of them, without that. Ribbon wrote as follows, saying nothing about his fear, his bad night and his interest in *Demogorgon* characters:

21 Grove Green Avenue,
London E11 4ZH

Sir,

Your new farrago of nonsense (I will not dignify it with the name of 'novel' or even 'thriller') is a disgrace to you, your publishers and those reviewers corrupt enough to praise your writing. As to the market you serve, once it has sampled this revolting affront to English literary tradition and our noble language, I can hardly imagine its members will remain your readers for long. The greatest benefit to the fiction scene conceivable would be for you to retire, disappear, and take your appalling effusions with you into outer darkness.

The errors you have made in the text are numerous. On page 30 alone there are three. You cannot say 'less people'. 'Fewer people' is correct. Only the illiterate would write: 'He gave it to Charles and I.' By 'mitigate against' I suppose you mean 'militate against'. More howlers occur on pages 34, 67 and 103. It is unnecessary to write 'meet with'. 'Meet' alone will do. 'A copy' of something is sufficient. 'A copying' is a nonsense.

Have you any education at all? Or were you one of these children who somehow missed schooling because their parents were neglectful or itinerant? You barely seem able to understand the correct location of an apostrophe, still less the proper usage of a colon. Your book has wearied me too much to allow me to write more. Indeed, I have not finished it and shall not. I am too fearful of its corrupting my own prose.

He wrote 'Sir' without the customary endearment so that he could justifiably sign himself 'yours truly'. He reread his letters and paused a while over the third one. It was very strong and uncompromising. But there was not a phrase in it he didn't sincerely mean (for all his refusing to end with that word) and he told himself that he who hesitates is lost. Often when he wrote a really vituperative letter he allowed himself to sleep on it, not posting it till the following day and occasionally, though seldom, not sending it at all. But he quickly put all three into envelopes and addressed them, Kingston Marle's care of his publishers. He would take them to the box at once.

While he was upstairs his own post had come. Two envelopes lay on the mat. The direction on one was typed, on the other he recognised the handwriting of his cousin Frank's wife Susan. He opened that one first. Susan wrote to remind him that he was spending the following weekend with herself and her husband at their home in the Cotswolds, as he did at roughly this time every year. Frank or she herself would be at Kingham station to pick him up. She supposed he would be taking the one-fifty train from Paddington to Hereford which reached Kingham at twenty minutes past three. If he had other plans perhaps he would let her know.

Ribbon snorted quietly. He didn't want to go, he never did, but they so loved having him he could hardly refuse after so many years. This would be his first visit without Mummy or Auntie Bee as they called her. No doubt they too desperately missed her. He opened the other letter and had a pleasant surprise. It was from Joy Anne Fortune and she gave her own address, a street in Bournemouth, not her publishers' or agents'. She must have written by return of post.

Her tone was humble and apologetic. She began by thanking him for pointing out the errors in her novel *Dreadful Night*. Some of them were due to her own carelessness but others she blamed on the printer. Ribbon had heard that one before and didn't think much of it. Ms Fortune assured him that all the mistakes would be corrected if the book ever went into paperback, though she thought it unlikely that this would happen. Here Ribbon agreed with her. However, this kind of letter – though rare – was always gratifying. It made all his hard work worthwhile.

He put stamps on the letters to Eric Owlberg, Kingston Marle and Dillons, and took them to the postbox. Again he experienced a quiver of dread in the pit of his stomach when he looked at the envelope addressed to Marle and recalled the words and terms he had used. But he drew strength from remembering how stalwartly he had withstood Selma Gunn's threats and defied her. There was no point in being in his job if he was unable to face resentful opposition. Mummy was gone but he must soldier on alone and he repeated to himself Paul's words about fighting the good fight, running a straight race and keeping the faith. He held the envelope in his hand for a moment or two after the Owlberg and Dillons letters had fallen down inside the box. How much easier it would be, what a lightening of his spirits would take place, if he simply dropped that envelope into a litter bin rather than this postbox! On the other hand, he hadn't built up his reputation for uncompromising criticism and stern incorruptible judgement by being cowardly. In fact, he hardly knew why he was hesitating now. His usual behaviour was far from this. What was wrong with him? There in the sunny street, a sudden awful dread took hold of him that when he put his hand to that aperture in the postbox and inserted the letter a scaly paw would reach out of it and seize hold of his wrist. How stupid could he be? How irrational? He reminded himself of his final quarrel with Mummy, those awful words she had spoken, and quickly, without more thought, he dropped the letter into the box and walked away.

At least they hadn't to put up with that ghastly old woman, Susan Ribbon remarked to her husband as she prepared to drive to Kingham station. Old Ambrose was a pussy cat compared to Auntie Bee.

'You say that,' said Frank. 'You haven't got to take him down the pub.'

'I've got to listen to him moaning about being too hot or too cold or the bread being wrong or the tea or the birds singing too early or us going to bed too late.'

'It's only two days,' said Frank. 'I suppose I do it for my Uncle Charlie's sake. He was a lovely man.'

'Considering you were only four when he died I don't see how you know.'

Susan got to Kingham at twenty-two minutes past three and found Ambrose standing in the station approach, swivelling his head from left to right, up the road and down, a peevish look on his face. 'I was beginning to wonder where you were,' he said. 'Punctuality is the politeness of princes, you know. I expect you heard my mother say that. It was a favourite dictum of hers.'

In her opinion Ambrose appeared far from well. His face, usually rather full and flabby, had a pasty, sunken look. 'I haven't been sleeping,' he said as they drove through Moreton-in-Marsh. 'I've had some rather unpleasant dreams.'

'It's all those highbrow books you read. You've been overtaxing your brain.' Susan didn't exactly know what it was Ambrose did for a living. Some sort of freelance editing, Frank thought. The kind of thing you could do from home. It wouldn't bring in much, but Ambrose didn't need much, Auntie Bee being in possession of Uncle Charlie's royalties. 'And you've suffered a terrible loss. It's only a few months since your mother died. But you'll soon feel better down here. Good fresh country air, peace and quiet, it's a far cry from London.'

They would go into Oxford tomorrow, she said, do some shopping, visit Blackwell's, perhaps do a tour of the colleges and then have lunch at the Randolph. She had asked some of her neighbours in for drinks at six, then they would have a quiet supper and watch a video. Ambrose nodded, not showing much interest. Susan told herself to be thankful for small mercies. At least there was no Auntie Bee. On that old witch's last visit with Ambrose, the year before she died, she had told Susan's friend from Stow that her skirt was too short for someone with middle-aged knees, and at ten thirty informed the people who had come to dinner that it was time they went home.

When he had said hallo to Frank she showed Ambrose up to his room. It was the one he always had but he seemed unable to remember the way to it from one year to the next. She had made a few alterations. For one thing, it had been redecorated and for another, she had changed the books in the shelf by the bed. A great reader herself, she thought it rather dreary always to have the same selection of reading matter in the guest bedroom.

Ambrose came down to tea, looking grim. 'Are you a fan of Mr Kingston Marle, Susan?'

'He's my favourite author,' she said, surprised.

'I see. Then there's no more to be said, is there?' Ambrose proceeded to say more. 'I rather dislike having a whole shelfful of his works by my bed. I've put them out on the landing.' As an afterthought, he added, 'I hope you don't mind.'

After that, Susan decided against telling her husband's cousin the prime purpose of their planned visit to Oxford next day. She poured him a cup of tea and handed him a slice of Madeira cake. Manfully, Frank said he would take Ambrose to see the horses and then they might stroll down to the Cross Keys for a nourishing glass of something.

'Not whisky, I hope,' said Ambrose.

'Lemonade, if you like,' said Frank in an out-of-character sarcastic voice.

When they had gone Susan went upstairs and retrieved the seven novels of Kingston Marle which Ambrose had stacked on the floor outside his bedroom door. She was particularly fond of *Evil Incarnate* and noticed that its dust jacket had a tear in the front on the bottom right-hand side. That tear had certainly not been there when she put the books on the shelf two days before. It looked, too, as if the jacket of *Wickedness in High Places* had been removed, screwed up in an angry fist and later replaced. Why on earth would Ambrose do such a thing?

She returned the books to her own bedroom. Of course, Ambrose was a strange creature. You could expect nothing else with that monstrous old woman for a mother, his sequestered life and, whatever Frank might say about his being a freelance editor, the probability that he subsisted on a small private income and had never actually worked for his living. He had never married nor even had a girlfriend, as far as Susan could make out. What did he do all day? These weekends, though only occurring annually, were terribly tedious and trying. Last year he had awakened her and Frank by knocking on their bedroom door at three in the morning to complain about a ticking clock in his room. Then there had been the business of the dry-cleaning spray. A splash of olive oil had left a pinpoint spot on the (already not very clean) jacket of Ambrose's navy-blue suit. He had averred that the stain remover Susan had in the cupboard left it untouched, though Susan and Frank could see no mark at all after it had been applied, and insisted on their driving him into Cheltenham for a can of a particular kind of dry-cleaning spray. By then it was after five and by the time they got there all possible purveyors of the spray were closed till Monday. Ambrose had gone on and on about that stain on his jacket right up to the moment Frank dropped him at Kingham station on Sunday afternoon.

The evening passed uneventfully and without any real problems. It was true that Ambrose remarked on the silk trousers she had changed into, saying on a slightly acrimonious note that reminded Susan of Auntie Bee what a pity it was that skirts would soon go entirely out of fashion. He left most of his pheasant *en casserole*, though without comment. Susan and Frank lay awake a long while, occasionally giggling and expecting a knock at their door. None came. The silence of the night was broken only by the melancholy hooting of owls.

It was a fine morning, though not hot, and Oxford looked particularly beautiful in the sunshine. When they had parked the car they strolled up the High and had coffee in a small select café outside which tables and chairs stood on the wide pavement. The Ribbons, however, went inside where it was rather gloomy and dim. Ambrose deplored the adoption by English restaurants of Continental habits totally unsuited to what he called 'our island climate'. He talked about his mother and the gap in the company her absence caused, interrupting his own monologue to ask in a querulous tone why Susan kept looking at her watch. 'We have no particular engagement, do we? We are, as might be said, free as air?'

'Oh, quite,' Susan said. 'That's exactly right.'

But it wasn't *exactly* right. She resisted glancing at her watch again. There was, after all, a clock on the café wall. So long as they were out of there by ten to eleven they would be in plenty of time. She didn't want to spend half the morning standing in a queue. Ambrose went on talking about Auntie Bee, how she lived in a slower-paced and more gracious past, how, much as he missed her, he was glad for her sake she hadn't survived to see the dawn of a new, and doubtless worse, millennium.

They left at eight minutes to eleven and walked to Blackwell's. Ambrose was in his element in bookshops, which was partly, though only partly, why they had come. The signing was advertised in the window and inside, though there was no voice on a public address system urging customers to buy and get the author's signature. And there he was, sitting at the end of a table loaded with copies of his new book. A queue there was but only a short one. Susan calculated that by the time she had selected her copy of *Demogorgon* and paid for it she would be no further back than eighth in line, a matter of waiting ten minutes.

She hadn't counted on Ambrose's extraordinary reaction. Of course, she was well aware – he had seen to that – of his antipathy to the works of Kingston Marle, but not that it should take such a violent form. At first, the author and perhaps also the author's name, had been hidden from Ambrose's view by her own back and Frank's, and the press of people around him. But as that crowd for some reason melted away, Frank turned round to say a word to his cousin and she went to collect the book she had reserved, Kingston Marle lifted his head and seemed to look straight at Frank and Ambrose.

He was a curious-looking man, tall and with a lantern-shaped but not unattractive face, his chin deep and his forehead high. A mass of long, dark, womanish hair sprang from the top of that arched brow, flowed straight back and descended to his collar in full, rather untidy curves. His mouth was wide and with the sensitive look lips shaped like this usually give to a face. Dark eyes skimmed over Frank, then Ambrose, and came to rest on her. He smiled. Whether it was this smile or the expression in Marle's eyes that had the effect on Ambrose it apparently did Susan never knew. Ambrose let out a little sound, not quite a cry, more a grunt of protest. She heard him say to Frank, 'Excuse me – must go – stuffy in here – can't breathe – just pop out for some fresh air,' and he was gone, running faster than she would have believed him capable of.

When she was younger she would have thought it right to go after him, ask what was wrong, could she help and so on. She would have left her book, given up the chance of getting it signed and given all her attention to Ambrose. But she was older now and no longer believed it was necessary inevitably to put others first. As it was, Ambrose's hasty departure had lost her a place in the queue and she found herself at number ten. Frank joined her.

'What was all that about?'

'Some nonsense about not being able to breathe. The old boy gets funny ideas in his head, just like his old mum. You don't think she's been reincarnated in him, do you?'

Susan laughed. 'He'd have to be a baby for that to have happened, wouldn't he?'

She asked Kingston Marle to inscribe the book on the title page: *For Susan Ribbon*. While he was doing so and adding, *with best wishes from the author, Kingston Marle*, he told her hers was a very unusual name. Had she ever met anyone else called Ribbon?

'No, I haven't. I believe we're the only ones in this country.'

'And there aren't many of us,' said Frank. 'Our son is the last of the Ribbons but he's only sixteen.'

'Interesting,' said Marle politely.

Susan wondered if she dared. She took a deep breath. 'I admire your work very much. If I sent you some of my books – I mean, your books – and if I put in the postage, would you – would you sign those for me too?'

'Of course. It would be a pleasure.'

Marle gave her a radiant smile. He rather wished he could have asked her to have lunch with him at the Lemon Tree instead of having to go to the Randolph with this earnest bookseller. Susan, of course, had no inkling of this and, clutching her signed book in its Blackwell's bag, she went in search of Ambrose. He was standing outside on the pavement, staring at the roadway, his hands clasped behind his back. She touched his arm and he flinched.

'Are you all right?'

He spun round, nearly cannoning into her. 'Of course I'm all right. It was very hot and stuffy in there, that's all. What have you got in there? Not his latest?'

Susan was getting cross. She asked herself why she was obliged to put up with this year after year, perhaps until they all died. In silence, she took *Demogorgon* out of the bag and handed it to him. Ambrose took it in his fingers as someone might pick up a package of decaying refuse prior to dropping it in an incinerator, his nostrils wrinkling and his eyebrows raised. He opened it. As he looked at the title page his expression and his whole demeanour underwent a violent change. His face had gone a deep mottled red and a muscle under one eye began to twitch. Susan thought he was going to hurl the book in among the passing traffic. Instead he thrust it back at her and said in a very curt, abrupt voice, 'I'd like to go home now. I'm not well.'

Frank said, 'Why don't we all go into the Randolph – we're lunching there anyway – have a quiet drink and a rest, and I'm sure you'll soon feel better, Ambrose. It *is* a warm day and there was a quite a crowd in there. I don't care for crowds myself, I know how you feel.'

'You don't know how I feel at all. You've just made that very plain. I don't want to go to the Randolph, I want to go home.'

There was little they could do about it. Susan, who seldom lunched out and sometimes grew very tired of cooking, was disappointed. But you can't force an obstinate man to go into an hotel and drink sherry if he is unwilling to do so. They went back to the car park and Frank drove home. When she and Frank had a single guest, it was usually Susan's courteous habit to sit in the back of the car and offer the visitor the passenger seat. She had done this on the way to Oxford but this time she sat next to Frank and left the back to Ambrose. He sat in the middle of the seat, obstructing Frank's view in the rear mirror. Once, when Frank stopped at a red light, she thought she felt Ambrose trembling, but it might only have been the engine which was inclined to judder.

On their return he went straight up to his room without explanation and remained there, drinkless, lunchless and, later on, tealess. Susan read her new book and was soon totally absorbed in it. She could well understand what the reviewer had meant when he wrote about readers fainting with fear, though in fact she herself had not fainted but only felt pleasurably terrified. Just the same, she was glad Frank was there, a large, comforting presence, intermittently reading *The Times* and watching the golf on television. Susan wondered why archaeologists went on excavating tombs in Egypt when they knew the risk of being laid under a curse or bringing home a demon. Much wiser to dig up a bit of

Oxfordshire as a party of archaeology students were doing down the road. But Charles Ambrose – how funny he should share a name with such a very different man! – was nothing if not brave and Susan felt total empathy with Kaysa de Floris when she told him one midnight, smoking *kif* on Mount Ararat, '*I could never put my body and soul into the keeping of a coward.*'

The bit about the cupboard was almost too much for her. She decided to shine a torch into her wardrobe that night before she hung up her dress. And make sure Frank was in the room. Frank's roaring with laughter at her she wouldn't mind at all. It was terrible, that chapter where Charles first sees the small dark *curled-up* shape in the corner of the room. Susan had no difficulty in imagining her hero's feelings. The trouble (or the wonderful thing) was that Kingston Marle wrote so well. Whatever people might say about only the plot and the action and suspense being of importance in this sort of book, there was no doubt that good literary writing made threats, danger, terror, fear and a dark nameless dread immeasurably more real. Susan had to lay the book down at six; their friends were coming in for a drink at half past.

She put on a long skirt and silk sweater, having first made Frank come upstairs with her, open the wardrobe door and demonstrate, while shaking with mirth, that there was no scaly paw inside. Then she knocked on Ambrose's door. He came at once, his sports jacket changed for a dark-grey, almost black suit, which he had perhaps bought new for Auntie Bee's funeral. That was an occasion she and Frank had not been asked to. Probably Ambrose had attended it alone.

'I hadn't forgotten about your party,' he said in a mournful tone.

'Are you feeling better?'

'A little.' Downstairs, his eye fell at once on *Demogorgon*. 'Susan, I wonder if you would oblige me and put that book away. I hope I'm not asking too much. It is simply that I would find it extremely distasteful if there were to be any discussion of that book in my presence among your friends this evening.'

Susan took the book upstairs and put it on her bedside cabinet. 'We are only expecting four people, Ambrose,' she said. 'It's hardly a party.'

'A gathering,' he said. 'Seven is a gathering.'

For years she had been trying to identify the character in fiction of whom Ambrose Ribbon reminded her. A children's book, she thought it was. *Alice in Wonderland*? *The Wind in the Willows*? Suddenly she knew. It was Eeyore, the lugubrious donkey in *Winnie the Pooh*. He even looked rather like Eeyore, with his melancholy grey face and stooping shoulders. For the first time, perhaps the first time ever, she felt sorry for him. Poor Ambrose, prisoner of a selfish mother. Presumably, when she died, she had left those royalties to him, after all. Susan distinctly remembered one unpleasant occasion when the two of them had been staying and Auntie Bee had suddenly announced her intention of leaving everything she had to the Royal National Lifeboat Institute. She must have changed her mind.

Susan voiced these feelings to her husband in bed that night, their pillow talk consisting of a review of the 'gathering', the low-key, rather depressing supper they had eaten afterwards and the video they had watched failing to come up to expectations. Unfortunately, in spite of the novel's absence from the living room, Bill and Irene had begun to talk about *Demogorgon* almost as soon as they arrived. Apparently, this was the first day of its serialisation in a national newspaper. They had read the instalment with avidity, as had James and Rosie. Knowing Susan's positive addiction to Kingston Marle, Rosie wondered if she happened to have a copy to lend to them. When Susan had finished reading it, of course.

Susan was afraid to look at Ambrose. Hastily she promised a loan of the novel and changed the subject to the less dangerous one of the archaeologists' excavations in Haybury Meadow and the protests it occasioned from local environmentalists. But the damage was done. Ambrose spoke scarcely a word all evening. It was as if he felt Kingston Marle and his book underlying everything that was said and threatening always to break through the surface of the conversation, as in a later chapter in *Demogorgon* the monstrous Dragosoma, with the head and breasts of a woman and the body of a manatee, rises slowly out of the Sea of Azov. At one point a silvery sheen of sweat covered the pallid skin of Ambrose's face.

'Poor devil,' said Frank. 'I suppose he was very cut up about his old mum.'

'There's no accounting for people, is there?'

They were especially gentle to him next day, without knowing exactly why gentleness was needed. Ambrose refused to go to church, treating them to a lecture on the death of God and atheism as the only course for enlightened mankind. They listened indulgently. Susan cooked a particularly nice lunch, consisting of Ambrose's favourite foods, chicken, sausages, roast potatoes and peas. It had been practically the only dish on Auntie Bee's culinary repertoire, Ambrose having been brought up on sardines on toast and tinned spaghetti, the chicken being served on Sundays. He drank more wine than was usual with him and had a brandy afterwards.

They put him on an early afternoon train for London. Though she had never done so before, Susan kissed him. His reaction was very marked. Seeing what was about to happen, he turned his head abruptly as her mouth approached and the kiss landed on the bristles above his right ear. They stood on the platform and waved to him.

'That was a disaster,' said Frank in the car. 'Do we have to do it again?'

Susan surprised herself. 'We have to do it again.' She sighed. 'Now I can go back and have a nice afternoon reading my book.'

A letter from Kingston Marle, acknowledging the errors in *Demogorgon* and perhaps offering some explanation of how they came to be there, with a promise of amendment in the paperback edition, would have set everything to rights. The disastrous weekend would fade into oblivion and those stupid guests of Frank's with it. Frank's idiot wife, good-looking, they said, though he had never been able to see it, but a woman of neither education nor discernment, would dwindle away into the mists of the past. Above all, that lantern-shaped face, that monstrous jaw and vaulted forehead, looming so shockingly above its owner's blood-coloured works, would lose its menace and assume a merely arrogant cast. But before he reached home, while he was still in the train, Ambrose, thinking about it – he could think of nothing else – knew with a kind of sorrowful resignation that no such letter would be waiting for him. No such letter would come next day or the next. By his own foolhardy move, his misplaced *courage*, by doing his duty, he had seen to that.

And yet it had scarcely been all his own doing. If that retarded woman, his cousin's doll-faced wife, had only had the sense to ask Marle to incribe the book 'to Susan', rather than 'to Susan Ribbon', little harm would have been done. Ribbon could hardly understand why she had done so, unless from malice, for these days it was the custom, and one he constantly deplored, to call everyone from the moment you met them, or even if you only talked to them on the phone, by their first names. Previously, Marle would have known his address but not his appearance, not seen his face, not established him as a real and therefore vulnerable person.

No letter had come. There were no letters at all on the doormat, only a flyer from a pizza takeaway company and two hire car cards. It was still quite early, only about six. Ribbon made himself a pot of real tea – that woman used *teabags* – and decided to break with tradition and do some work. He never worked on a Sunday evening but he was in need of something positive to distract his mind from Kingston Marle. Taking his tea into the front room, he saw Marle's book lying on the coffee table. It was the first thing his eye lighted on. The Book. The awful book that had been the ruin of his weekend. He must have left *Demogorgon* on the table when he abandoned it in a kind of queasy disgust halfway through. Yet he had no memory of leaving it there. He could have sworn he had put it away, tucked it into a drawer to be out of sight and therefore of mind. The dreadful face, fish-belly white between the bandages, leered at him out of the star-shaped hole in the red and silver jacket. He opened the drawer in the cabinet where he thought he had put it. There was nothing there but what had been there before, a few sheets of writing paper and an old diary of Mummy's. Of course there was nothing there, he didn't possess two copies of the horrible thing, but it was going in there now ...

The phone rang. This frequent event in other people's homes happened seldom in Ribbon's. He ran out into the hall where the phone was and stood looking at it while it rang. Suppose it should be Kingston Marle? Gingerly he lifted the receiver. If it was Marle he would slam it down fast. That woman's voice said, 'Ambrose? Are you all right?'

'Of course I'm all right. I've just got home.'

'It was only that we've been rather worried about you. Now I know you're safely home that's fine.'

Ribbon remembered his manners and recited Mummy's rubric. 'Thank you very much for having me, Susan. I had a lovely time.'

He would write to her, of course. That was the proper thing. Upstairs in the office he composed three letters. The first was to Susan.

21 Grove Green Avenue,
London E11 4ZH

Dear Susan,
I very much enjoyed my weekend with you and Frank. It was very enjoyable to take a stroll with Frank and take in 'the pub' on the way.

The ample food provided was tip-top. Your friends seemed charming
people, though I cannot commend their choice of reading matter!

All is well here. It looks as if we may be in for another spell of hot
weather.

With kind regards to you both,
Yours affectionately,
Ambrose

Ribbon wasn't altogether pleased with this. He took out 'very much' and put in 'enormously', and for 'very enjoyable' substituted 'delightful'. That was better. It would have to do. He was rather pleased with that acid comment about those ridiculous people's reading matter and hoped it would get back to them.

During the weekend, particularly during those hours in his room on Saturday afternoon, he had gone carefully through the two paperbacks he had bought at Dillons. Lucy Grieves, author of *Cottoning On*, had meticulously passed on to her publishers all the errors he had pointed out to her when the novel appeared in hardcover down to 'on to' instead of 'onto'. Ribbon felt satisfied. He was pleased with Lucy Grieves, though not to the extent of writing to congratulate her. The second letter he wrote was to Channon Scott Smith, the paperback version of whose novel *Carol Conway* contained precisely the same mistakes and literary howlers as it had in hardcover. That completed, a scathing paean of contempt if ever there was one, Ribbon sat back in his chair and thought long and hard.

Was there some way he could write to Kingston Marle and *make things all right* without grovelling, without apologising? God forbid that he should apologise for boldly telling truths that needed to be told. But could he compose something, without saying he was sorry, that would mollify Marle, better still that would make him understand? He had a notion that he would feel easier in his mind if he wrote to Marle, would sleep better at night. The two nights he had passed at Frank's had been very wretched, the second one almost sleepless.

What was he afraid of? Afraid of writing and afraid of not writing? Just afraid? Marle couldn't do anything to him. Ribbon acknowledged to himself that he had no absurd fears of Marle's setting some hit man on to him or stalking him or even attempting to sue him for libel. It wasn't that. What was it then? The cliché came into his head unbidden, the definition of what he felt: a nameless dread. If only Mummy were here to advise him! Suddenly he longed for her and tears pricked the backs of his eyes. Yet he knew what she would have said. She would have said what she had that last time.

That *Encyclopaedia Britannica* Volume VIII had been lying on the table. He had just shown Mummy the letter he had written to Desmond Erb, apologising for correcting him when he wrote about 'the quinone structure'. Of course he should have looked the word up but he hadn't. He had been so sure it should have been 'quinine'. Erb had been justifiably indignant, as writers tended to be, when he corrected an error in their work that was in fact not an error at all. He would never forget Mummy's anger, nor anything of that quarrel, come to that; how, almost of their own volition, his hands had crept across the desk towards the black, blue and gold volume . . .

She was not here now to stop him and after a while he wrote this:

Dear Mr Marle,

*   With reference to my letter of June 4th, in which I pointed out certain errors of fact and of grammar and spelling in your recent novel, I fear I may inadvertently have caused you pain. This was far from my intention. If I have hurt your feelings I must tell you that I very much regret this. I hope you will overlook it and forgive me.*

*   Yours sincerely,*

Reading this over, Ribbon found he very much disliked the bit about overlooking and forgiving. 'Regret' wasn't right either. Also he hadn't actually named the book. He ought to have put in its title but, strangely, he found himself reluctant to type the word *Demogorgon*. It was as if, by putting it into cold print, he would set something in train, spark off some reaction. Of course, this was mad. He must be getting tired. Nevertheless, he composed a second letter.

Dear Mr Marle,

With reference to my letter to yourself of June 4th, in which I pointed out certain errors in your recent and highly acclaimed novel, I fear I may inadvertently have hurt your feelings. It was not my intention to cause you pain. I am well aware – who is not? – of the high position you enjoy in the ranks of literature. The amendments I suggested you make to the novel when it appears in paperback – in many hundreds of thousand copies, no doubt – were meant in a spirit of assistance, not criticism, simply so that a good book might be made better.

Yours sincerely,

Sycophantic. But what could be more mollifying than flattery? Ribbon endured half an hour's agony and self-doubt, self-recrimination and self-justification too, before writing a third and final letter.

Dear Mr Marle,

With reference to my letter to your good self, dated June 4th, in which I presumed to criticise your recent novel, I fear I may inadvertently have been wanting in respect. I hope you will believe me when I say it was not my intention to offend you. You enjoy a high and well-deserved position in the ranks of literature. It was gauche and clumsy of me to write to you as I did.

With best wishes,
Yours sincerely,

To grovel in this way made Ribbon feel actually sick. And it was all lies too. Of course it had been his intention to offend the man, to cause him pain and to make him angry. He would have given a great deal to recall that earlier letter but this – he quoted silently to himself those hackneyed but apt words about the moving finger that writes and having writ moves on – neither he nor anyone else could do. What did it matter if he suffered half an hour's humiliation when by sending this apology he would end his sufferings? Thank heavens only that Mummy wasn't here to see it.

Those letters had taken him hours and it had grown quite dark. Unexpectedly dark, he thought, for nine in the evening in the middle of June with the longest day not much more than a week away. But still he sat there, in the dusk, looking at the backs of houses, yellow brick punctured by the bright rectangles of windows, at the big shaggy trees, his own garden, the square of grass dotted with dark shrubs, big and small. He had never previously noticed how unpleasant ordinary privets and cypresses can look in deep twilight when they are not clustered together in a shrubbery or copse; when they stand individually on an otherwise open space, strange shapes, tall and slender or round and squat, or with a branch here and there protruding like a limb, and casting elongated shadows.

He got up abruptly and put on the light. The garden and its gathering of bushes disappeared. The window became dark, shiny, opaque. He switched off the light almost immediately and went downstairs. Seeing *Demogorgon* on the coffee table made him jump. What was it doing there? How did it get there? He had put it in the drawer. And there was the drawer standing open to prove it.

It couldn't have got out of the drawer and returned to the table on its own. Could it? *Of course not.* Ribbon put on every light in the room. He left the curtains open so that he could see the street lights as well. He must have left the book on the table himself. He must have intended to put it into the drawer and for some reason not done so. Possibly he had been interrupted. But nothing ever interrupted what he was doing, did it? He couldn't remember. A cold teapot and a cup of cold tea stood on the tray on the coffee table beside the book. He couldn't remember making tea.

After he had taken the tray and the cold teapot away and poured the cold tea down the sink, he sat down in an armchair with Chambers dictionary. He realised that he had never found out what the word Demogorgon meant. Here was the definition: *A mysterious infernal deity first mentioned about* AD *450. [Appar Gr* daimon *deity, and* gorgo *Gorgon, from* gorgos *terrible.]* He shuddered, closed the dictionary and opened the second Channon Scott Smith paperback he had bought. This novel had been published four years before but Ribbon had never read it, nor indeed any of the works of Mr Scott Smith before the recently published one, but he thought this fat volume might yield a rich harvest, if *Carol Conway* were anything to go by. But instead of opening *Destiny's Suzerain*, he found that the book in his hands was *Demogorgon*, open one page past where he had stopped a few days before.

In a kind of horrified wonder he began to read. It was curious how he was compelled to go on reading, considering how every line was like a faint pinprick in his equilibrium, a tiny physical tremor through his body, reminding him of those things he had written to Kingston Marle and the look Marle had given him in Oxford on Saturday. Later he was to ask himself why he had read any more of it at all, why he hadn't just stopped, why indeed he hadn't put the book in the rubbish for the refuse collectors to take away in the morning.

The dark shape in the corner of Charles Ambrose's tent was appearing for the first time: in his tent, then his hotel bedroom, his mansion in Shropshire, his flat in Mayfair. A small curled-up shape like a tiny huddled person or small monkey. It sat or simply *was*, amorphous but for faintly visible hands or paws and uniformly dark but for pinpoint malevolent eyes that stared and glinted. Ribbon looked up from the page for a moment. The lights were very bright. Out in the street a couple went by, hand in hand, talking and laughing. Usually, the noise they made would have angered him but tonight he felt curiously comforted. They made him feel he wasn't alone. They drew him, briefly, into reality. He would post the letter in the morning and once it had gone all would be well.

He read two more pages. The unravelling of the mystery began on page 423. The demogorgon was Charles Ambrose's own mother who had been murdered and whom he had buried in the grounds of his Shropshire house. Finally, she came back to tell him the truth, came in the guise of a cypress tree which walked out of the pinetum. Ribbon gasped out loud. It was his own story. How had Marle known? What was Marle – some kind of god or magus that he knew such things? The dreadful notion came to him that *Demogorgon* had not always been like this, that the ending had originally been different, but that Marle, seeing him in Oxford and immediately identifying him with the writer of that defamatory letter, *had by some remote control or sorcery altered the end of the copy that was in his, Ribbon's, possession.*

He went upstairs and rewrote his letter, adding to the existing text: *Please forgive me. I meant you no harm. Don't torment me like this. I can't stand any more.* It was a long time before he went to bed. Why go to bed when you know you won't sleep? With the light on – and all the lights in the house were on now – he couldn't see the garden, the shrubs on the lawn, the flowerbed, but he drew the curtains just the same. At last he fell uneasily asleep in his chair, waking four or five hours later to the horrid thought that his original letter to Marle was the first really vituperative criticism he had sent to anyone since Mummy's death. Was there some significance in this? Did it mean he couldn't get along without Mummy? Or, worse, that he had killed all the power and confidence in himself he had once felt?

He got up, had a rejuvenating shower but was unable to face breakfast. The three letters he had written the night before were in the postbox by nine and Ribbon on the way to the tube station. Waterstone's in Leadenhall Market was his destination. He bought Clara Jenkins's *Tales My Lover Told Me* in hardcover as well as Raymond Kobbo's *The Nomad's Smile* and Natalya Dreadnought's *Tick* in paperback. Copies of *Demogorgon* were everywhere, stacked in piles or displayed in fanciful arrangements. Ribbon forced himself to touch one of them, to pick it up. He looked over his shoulder to see if any of the assistants was watching him and, having established that they were not, opened it at page 423. It was as he had thought, as he had hardly dared put into words. Charles Ambrose's mother made no appearance, there was nothing about a burial in the grounds of Montpellier Hall or a cypress tree walking. The end was quite different. Charles Ambrose, married to Kaysa in a ceremony conducted in a balloon above the Himalayas, awakens on his wedding night and sees in the corner of the honeymoon bedroom the demon curled up, hunched and small, staring at him with gloating eyes. It had followed him from Egypt to Shropshire, from London to Russia, from Russia to New Orleans and from New Orleans to Nepal. It would never leave him, it was his for life and perhaps beyond.

Ribbon replaced the book, took up another copy. The same thing, no murder, no burial, no tree walking, only the horror of the demon in the bedroom. So he had been right. Marle had infused this alternative ending into *his* copy alone. It was part of the torment, part of the revenge for the insults Ribbon had heaped on him. On the way back to Liverpool Street Station a shout and a thump made him look over his shoulder – a taxi had clipped the rear wheel of a motorbike – and he saw, a long way behind, Kingston Marle following him.

Ribbon thought he would faint. A great flood of heat washed over him, to be succeeded by shivering. Panic held him still for a moment. Then he dived into a shop, a sweetshop it was, and it was like entering a giant chocolate box. The scent of chocolate swamped him. Trembling, he stared at the street through a window draped with pink frills. Ages passed before Kingston Marle went by. He paused, turned his head to look at the chocolates and Ribbon, again almost fainting, saw an unknown man, lantern-jawed but not monstrously so, long-haired but the hair sparse and brown, the blue eyes mild and wistful. Ribbon's heartbeat slowed, the blood withdrew from the surface of his skin. He muttered, 'No, no thank you,' to the woman behind the counter and went back into the street. What a wretched state his nerves were in! He'd be encountering a scaly paw in the wardrobe next. Clasping his bag of books, he got thoughtfully into the train.

What he really should have done was add a PS to the effect that he would appreciate a prompt acknowledgement of his letter. Just a line saying something like *Please be kind enough to acknowledge receipt*. However, it was too late now. Kingston Marle's publishers would get his letter tomorrow and send it straight on. Ribbon knew publishers did not always do this but surely in the case of so eminent an author and one of the most profitable on their list . . .

Sending the letter should have allayed his fears but they seemed to crowd in upon him more urgently, jostling each other for preeminence in his mind. The man who had followed him along Bishopsgate, for instance. Of course, he knew it had not been Kingston Marle, yet the similarity of build, of feature, of height, between the two men was too great for coincidence. The most likely explanation was that his stalker was Marle's younger brother, and now, as he reached this reasonable conclusion, Ribbon no longer saw the man's eyes as mild but sly and crafty. When his letter came Marle would call his brother off but, in the nature of things, the letter could not arrive at Marle's home before Wednesday at the earliest. Then there was the matter of The Book itself. The drawer in which it lay failed to hide it adequately. It was part of a mahogany cabinet (one of Mummy's wedding presents, Ribbon believed), well polished but of course opaque. Yet sometimes the wood seemed to become transparent and the harsh reds and glaring silver of *Demogorgon* shone through it as he understood a block of radium would appear as a glowing cuboid behind a wall of solid matter. Approaching closely, creeping up on it, he would see the bright colours fade and the woodwork reappear, smooth, shiny and *ordinary* once more.

In the study upstairs on Monday evening he tried to do some work but his eye was constantly drawn to the window and what lay beyond. He became convinced that the bushes on the lawn had moved. That small thin one had surely stood next to the pair of tall fat ones, not several yards away. Since the night before it had shifted its position, taking a step nearer to the house. Drawing the curtains helped but after a while he got up and pulled them apart a little to check on the big round bush, to see if it had taken a step further or had returned to its previous position. It was where it had been ten minutes before. All should have been well but it was not. The room itself had become uncomfortable and he resolved not to go back there, to move the computer downstairs, until he had heard from Kingston Marle.

The doorbell ringing made him jump so violently he felt pain travel through his body and reverberate. Immediately he thought of Marle's brother. Suppose Marle's brother, a strong young man, was outside the door and, when it was opened, would force his way in? Or, worse, was merely checking that Ribbon was at home and when footsteps sounded inside, intended to disappear? Ribbon went down. He took a deep breath and threw the door open. His caller was Glenys Next-door.

Marching in without being invited, she said 'Hiya, Amby' and that Tinks Next-door was missing. The cat had not been home since the morning when he was last seen by Sandra On-the-other-side, sitting in Ribbon's front garden eating a bird.

'I'm out of my mind with worry, as you can imagine, Amby.'

As a matter of fact, he couldn't. Ribbon cared very little for songbirds but he cared for feline predators even less. 'I'll let you know if I come across him. However –' he laughed lightly '– he knows he's not popular with me so he makes himself scarce.'

This was the wrong thing to say. In the works of his less literate authors Ribbon sometimes came upon the expression 'to bridle' – 'she bridled' or even 'the young woman bridled'. At last he understood what it meant.

Glenys Next-door tossed her head, raised her eyebrows and looked down her nose at him. 'I'm sorry for you, Amby, I really am. You must find that attitude problem of yours a real hang-up. I mean socially. I've tried to ignore it all these years but there comes a time when one has to speak one's mind. No, don't bother, please, I can see myself out.'

This was not going to be a *good* night. He knew that before he switched the bedside light off. For one thing, he always read in bed before going to sleep. Always had and always would. But for some reason he had forgotten to take *Destiny's Suzerain* upstairs with him and though his bedroom was full of reading matter, shelves and shelves of it, he had read all the books before. Of course, he could have gone downstairs and fetched himself a book, or even just gone into the study which was lined with books. Booked, not papered, indeed. He *could* have done so, in theory he could have, but on coming into his bedroom he had locked the door. Why? He was unable to answer that question, though he put it to himself several times. It was a small house, potentially brightly lit, in a street of a hundred and fifty such houses, all populated. A dreadful feeling descended upon him as he lay in bed that if he unlocked that door, if he turned the key and opened it, something would come in. Was it the small thin bush that would come in? These thoughts, ridiculous, unworthy of him, puerile, frightened him so much that he put the bedside lamp on and left it on till morning.

Tuesday's post brought two letters. Eric Owlberg called Ribbon 'a little harsh' and informed him that printers do not always do as they are told. Jeanne Pettle's letter was from a secretary who wrote that Ms Pettle was away on an extended publicity tour but would certainly attend to his 'interesting communication' when she returned. There was nothing from Dillons. It was a bright, sunny day. Ribbon went into the study and contemplated the garden. The shrubs were, of course, where they had always been. Or where they had been before the large round bush stepped back into its original position?

'Pull yourself together,' Ribbon said aloud.

Housework day. He started, as he always did, in Mummy's room, dusting the picture rail and the central lamp with a bunch of pink and blue feathers attached to a rod, and the ornaments with a clean fluffy yellow duster. The numerous books he took out and dusted on alternate weeks but this was not one of those. He vacuumed the carpet, opened the window wide and replaced the pink silk nightdress with a pale-blue one. He always washed Mummy's nightdresses by hand once a fortnight. Next his own room and the study, then downstairs to the dining and front rooms. Marle's publishers would have received his letter by the first post this morning and the department which looked after this kind of thing would, even at this moment probably, be readdressing the envelope and sending it on. Ribbon had no idea where the man lived. London? Devonshire? Most of those people seemed to live in the Cotswolds, its green hills and lush valleys must be chock-full of them. But perhaps Shropshire was more likely. He had written about Montpellier Hall as if he really knew such a house.

Ribbon dusted the mahogany cabinet and passed on to Mummy's little sewing table, but he couldn't quite leave things there and he returned to the cabinet; to stand, duster in hand, staring at that drawer. It was not transparent on this sunny morning and nothing could be seen glowing in its depths. He pulled it open suddenly and snatched up The Book. He looked at its double redness and at the pentagram. After his experiences of the past days he wouldn't have been surprised if the bandaged face inside had changed its position, closed its mouth or moved its eyes. Well, he would have been surprised, he'd have been horrified, aghast. But the demon was the same as ever, The Book was just the same, an ordinary, rather tastelessly jacketed, cheap thriller.

'What on earth is the matter with me?' Ribbon said to The Book.

He went out shopping for food. Sandra On-the-other-side appeared behind him in the queue at the check-out. 'You've really upset Glenys,' she said. 'You know me, I believe in plain speaking, and in all honesty I think you ought to apologise.'

'When I want your opinion I'll ask for it, Mrs Wilson,' said Ribbon.

Marle's brother got on the bus and sat behind him. It wasn't actually Marle's brother, he only thought it was, just for a single frightening moment. It was amazing, really, what a lot of people there were about who looked like Kingston Marle, men and women too. He had never noticed it before, had never had an inkling of it until he came face to face with Marle in that bookshop. If only it were possible to go back. For the moving finger, having writ, not to move on but to retreat, retrace its strokes, white them out with correction fluid and begin writing again. He would have guessed why that silly woman, his cousin's wife, was so anxious to get to Blackwell's, her fondness for Marle's works – distributed so tastelessly all over his bedroom – would have told him, and he would have cried off the Oxford trip, first warning her on no account to let Marle know her surname. Yet – and this was undeniable – Marle had Ribbon's home address, the address was on the letter. The moving finger would have to go back a week and erase *21 Grove Green Avenue, London E11 4ZH* from the top right-hand corner of his letter. Then, and only then, would he have been safe . . .

Sometimes a second post arrived on a weekday but none came that day. Ribbon took his shopping bags into the kitchen, unpacked them, went into the front room to open the window – and saw *Demogorgon* lying on the coffee table. A violent trembling convulsed him. He sat down, closed his eyes. He *knew* he hadn't taken it out of the drawer. Why on earth would he? He hated it. He wouldn't touch it unless he had to. There was not much doubt now that it had a life of its own. Some kind of kinetic energy lived inside its covers, the same sort of thing as moved the small thin bush across the lawn at night. Kingston Marle put that energy into objects, he infused them with it, he was a sorcerer whose powers extended far beyond his writings and his fame. Surely that was the only explanation why a writer of such appallingly bad books, misspelt, the grammar non-existent, facts awry, should enjoy such a phenomenal success, not only with an ignorant illiterate public but among the cognoscenti. He practised sorcery or was himself one of the demons he wrote about, an evil spirit living inside that hideous lantern-jawed exterior.

Ribbon reached out a slow, wavering hand for The Book and found that, surely by chance, he had opened it at page 423. Shrinking while he did so, holding The Book almost too far away from his eyes to see the words, he read of Charles Ambrose's wedding night, of his waking in the half-dark with Kaysa sleeping beside him and seeing the curled-up shape of the demon in the corner of the room . . . So Marle had called off his necromancer's power, had he? He had restored the ending to what it originally was. Nothing about Mummy's death and burial, nothing about the walking tree. Did that mean he had already received Ribbon's apology? It might mean that. His publishers had hardly had time to send the letter on, but suppose Marle, for some reason – and the reason would be his current publicity tour – had been in his publishers' office and the letter had been handed to him. It was the only explanation, it fitted the facts. Marle had read his letter, accepted his apology and, perhaps with a smile of triumph, whistled back whatever dogs of the occult carried his messages.

Ribbon held The Book in his hands. Everything might be over now but he still didn't want it in the house. Carefully, he wrapped it up in newspaper, slipped the resulting parcel into a plastic carrier, tied the handles together and dropped it in the waste bin.

'Let it get itself out of that,' he said aloud. 'Just let it try.' Was he imagining that a fetid smell came from it, swathed in plastic though it was? He splashed disinfectant into the waste bin, opened the kitchen window.

He sat down in the front room and opened *Tales My Lover Told Me* but he couldn't concentrate. The afternoon grew dark, there was going to be a storm. For a moment he stood at the window, watching the clouds gather, black and swollen. When he was a little boy Mummy had told him a storm was the clouds fighting. It was years since he had thought of that and now, remembering, for perhaps the first time in his life he questioned Mummy's judgement. Was it quite right so to mislead a child?

The rain came, sheets of it blown by the huge gale which arose. Ribbon wondered if Marle, among his many accomplishments, could raise a wind, strike lightning from some diabolical tinder-box and, like Jove himself, beat the drum of thunder. Perhaps. He would believe anything of that man now. He went around the house closing all the windows. The one in the study he closed and fastened the catches. From his own bedroom window he looked at the lawn, where the bushes stood as they had always stood, unmoved, immovable, lashed by rain, whipping and twisting in the wind. Downstairs, in the kitchen, the window was wide open, flapping back and forth, and the waste bin had fallen on its side. The parcel lay beside it, the plastic bag that covered it, the newspaper inside, torn as if a scaly paw had ripped it. Other rubbish, food scraps, a sardine can, were scattered across the floor.

Ribbon stood transfixed. He could see the red and silver jacket of The Book gleaming, almost glowing, under its torn wrappings. What had come through the window? Was it possible the demon, unleashed by Marle, was now beyond his control? He asked the question aloud, he asked Mummy, though she was long gone. The sound of his own voice, shrill and horror-stricken, frightened him. Had whatever it was come in to retrieve the – he could hardly put it even into silent words – the *chronicle of its exploits*? Nonsense,

nonsense. It was Mummy speaking, Mummy telling him to be strong, not to be a fool. He shook himself, gritted his teeth. He picked up the parcel, dropped it into a black rubbish bag and took it into the garden, getting very wet in the process. In the wind the biggest bush of all reached out a needly arm and lashed him across the face.

He left the black bag there. He locked all the doors and even when the storm had subsided and the sky cleared he kept all the windows closed. Late that night, in his bedroom, he stared down at the lawn, The Book in its bag was where he had left it but the small thin bush had moved, in a different direction this time, stepping to one side so that the two fat bushes, the one that had lashed him and its twin, stood close together and side by side like tall heavily built men gazing up at his window. Ribbon had saved half a bottle of Mummy's sleeping pills. For an emergency, for a rainy day. All the lights blazing, he went into Mummy's room, found the bottle and swallowed two pills. They took effect rapidly. Fully clothed, he fell on to his bed and into something more like a deep trance than sleep. It was the first time in his life he had ever taken a soporific.

In the morning he looked through the Yellow Pages and found a firm of tree fellers, operating locally. Would they send someone to cut down all the shrubs in his garden? They would, but not before Monday. On Monday morning they would be with him by nine. In the broad daylight he asked himself again what had come through the kitchen window, come in and taken That Book out of the waste bin and, sane again, wondered if it might have been Glenys Next-door's fox. The sun was shining, the grass gleaming wet after the rain. He fetched a spade from the shed and advanced upon the wide flowerbed. Not the right-hand side, not there, avoid that at all costs. He selected a spot on the extreme left, close by the fence dividing his garden from that of Sandra On-the-other-side. While he dug he wondered if it was a commonplace with people, this burying of unwanted or hated or threatening objects in their back gardens. Maybe all the gardens in Leyton-stone, in London suburbs, in the United Kingdom, in the world, were full of such concealed things, hidden in the earth, waiting . . .

He laid *Demogorgon* inside. The wet earth went back over the top of it, covering it, and Ribbon stamped the surface down viciously. If whatever it was came back and dug The Book out he thought he would die.

Things were better now *Demogorgon* was gone. He wrote to Clara Jenkins at her home address – for some unaccountable reason she was in *Who's Who* – pointing out that in chapter one of *Tales My Lover Told Me* Humphry Nemo had blue eyes and in chapter twenty-one brown eyes, Thekla Pattison wore a wedding ring on page 20 but denied, on page 201, that she had ever possessed one, and on page 245 Justin Armstrong was taking part in an athletics contest, in spite of having broken his leg on page 223, a mere five days before. But Ribbon wrote with a new gentleness, as if she had caused him pain rather than rage.

Nothing had come from Dillons. He wondered bitterly why he had troubled to congratulate them on their service if his accolade was to go unappreciated. And more to the point, nothing had come from Kingston Marle by Friday. He had the letter of apology, he must have, otherwise he wouldn't have altered the ending of *Demogorgon* back to the original plot line. But that hardly meant he had recovered from all his anger. He might still have other revenges in store. And, moreover, he might intend never to answer Ribbon at all.

The shrubs seemed to be back in their normal places. It would be a good idea to have a plan of the garden with the bushes all accurately positioned so that he could tell if they moved. He decided to make one. The evening was mild and sunny, though damp and, of course, at not long past midsummer, still broad daylight at eight. A deckchair was called for, a sheet of paper and, better than a pen, a soft lead pencil. The deckchairs might be up in the loft or down here, he couldn't remember, though he had been in the shed on Wednesday evening to find a spade. He looked through the shed window. In the far corner, curled up, was a small dark shape.

Ribbon was too frightened to cry out. A pain seized him in the chest, ran up his left arm, held him in its grip before it slackened and released him. The black shape opened its eyes and looked at him, just as the demon in The Book looked at Charles Ambrose. Ribbon hunched his back and closed his eyes. When he opened them and looked again he saw Tinks Next-door get up, stretch, arch its back and begin to walk in leisurely fashion towards the door. Ribbon flung it open. 'Scat! Get out! Go home!' he screamed.

Tinks fled. Had the wretched thing slunk in there when he opened the door to get the spade? Probably. He took out a deckchair and sat on it, but all heart had gone out of him for drawing a plan of the garden. In more ways than one, he thought, the pain receding and leaving only a dull ache. You could have mild heart attacks from which you recovered and were none the worse. Mummy said she had had several, some of them brought on – he sadly recalled – by his own defections from her standards. It could be hereditary. He must take things easy for the next few days, not *worry*, try to put stress behind him.

Kingston Marle had signed all the books she sent him and returned them with a covering letter. Of course she had sent postage and packing as well, and had put in a very polite little note, repeating how much she loved his work and what a great pleasure meeting him in Blackwell's had been. But still she had hardly expected such a lovely long letter from him, nor one of quite that nature. Marle wrote how very different she was from the common run of fans, not only in intellect but in appearance too. He hoped she wouldn't take it amiss when he told her he had been struck by her beauty and elegance among that dowdy crowd.

It was a long time since any man had paid Susan such a compliment. She read and reread the letter, sighed a little, laughed and showed it to Frank.

'I don't suppose he writes his own letters,' said Frank, put out. 'Some secretary will do it for him.'

'Well, hardly.'

'If you say so. When are you seeing him again?'

'Oh, don't be silly,' said Susan.

She covered each individual book Kingston Marle had signed for her with cling film and put them all away in a glass-fronted bookcase from which, to make room, she first removed Frank's *Complete Works of Shakespeare*, Tennyson's *Poems*, *The Poems of Robert Browning* and Kobbé's *Complete Opera Book*. Frank appeared not to notice. Admiring through the glass, indeed gloating over, her wonderful collection of Marle's works with the secret inscriptions hidden from all eyes, Susan wondered if she should respond to the author. On the one hand a letter would keep her in the forefront of his mind but on the other it would be in direct contravention of the playing-hard-to-get principle. Not that Susan had any intention of being 'got', of course not, but she was not averse to inspiring thoughts about her in Kingston Marle's mind or even a measure of regret that he was unable to know her better.

Several times in the next few days she surreptitiously took one of the books out and looked at the inscription. Each had something different in it. In *Wickedness in High Places* Marle had written, 'To Susan, met on a fine morning in Oxford' and in *The Necromancer's Bride*, 'To Susan, with kindest of regards', but on the title page of *Evil Incarnate* appeared the inscription Susan liked best. 'She was a lady sweet and kind, ne'er a face so pleased my mind – ever yours, Kingston Marle.'

Perhaps he would write again, even if she didn't reply. Perhaps he would be *more likely* to write if she didn't reply.

On Monday morning the post came early, soon after eight, delivering just one item. The computer-generated address on the envelope made Ribbon think for one wild moment that it might be from Kingston Marle. But it was from Clara Jenkins, and it was an angry, indignant letter, though containing no threats. Didn't he understand her novel was fiction? You couldn't say things were true or false in fiction, for things were as the author, who was all-powerful, wanted them to be. In a magic realism novel, such as *Tales My Lover Told Me*, only an ignorant fool would expect facts (and these included spelling, punctuation and grammar) to be as they were in the dreary reality he inhabited. Ribbon took it into the kitchen, screwed it up and dropped it in the waste bin.

He was waiting for the tree fellers who were due at nine. Half past nine went by, ten went by. At ten past the front doorbell rang. It was Glenys Next-door.

'Tinks turned up,' she said. 'I was so pleased to see him I gave him a whole can of red sockeye salmon.' She appeared to have forgiven Ribbon for his 'attitude'. 'Now don't say what a wicked waste, I can see you were going to. I've got to go and see my mother, she's fallen over, broken her arm and bashed her face, so would you be an angel and let the washing machine man in?'

'I suppose so.' The woman had a mother! She must be getting on for seventy herself.

'You're a star. Here's the key and you can leave it on the hall table when he's been. Just tell him it's full of pillowcases and water, and the door won't open.'

The tree fellers came at eleven thirty. The older one, a joker, said, 'I'm a funny feller and he's a nice feller, right?'

'Come this way,' Ribbon said frostily.

'What d'you want them lovely Leylandiis down for then? Not to mention that lovely flowering currant?'

'Them currants smell of cat's pee, Damian,' said the young one. 'Whether there's been cats peeing on them or not.'

'Is that right? The things he knows, guv. He's wasted in this job, ought to be fiddling with computers.'

Ribbon went indoors. The computer and printer were downstairs now, in the dining room. He wrote first to Natalya Dreadnought, author of *Tick*, pointing out in a mild way that 'eponymous' applies to a character or object which gives a work its name, not to the name derived from the character. Therefore it was the large blood-sucking mite of the Acarina order which was eponymous, not her title. The letter he wrote to Raymond Kobbo would correct just two mistakes in *The Nomad's Smile*, but for both Ribbon needed to consult *Piranha to Scurfy*. He was pretty sure the Libyan caravan centre should be spelt 'Sabha', not 'Sebha', and he was even more certain that 'qalam', meaning a reed pen used in Arabic calligraphy, should start with a K. He went upstairs and lifted the heavy tome off the shelf. Finding that Kobbo had been right in both instances – 'Sabha' and 'Sebha' were optional spellings and 'qalam' perfectly correct – unsettled him. Mummy would have known, Mummy would have set him right in her positive, no-nonsense way, before he had set foot on the bottom stair. He asked himself if he could live without her and could have sworn he heard her sharp voice say, 'You should have thought of that before.'

Before what? That day in February when she had come up here to – well, oversee him, supervise him. She frequently did so and in later years he hadn't been as grateful to her as he should have been. By the desk here she had stood and told him it was time he earned some money by his work, by a man's fifty-second year it was time. She had made up her mind to leave Daddy's royalties to the lifeboat people. But it wasn't this which finished things for him, or triggered things off, however you liked to put it. It was the sneering tone in which she told him, her right index finger pointing at his chest, that he was no good, he had failed. She had kept him in comfort and luxury for decade after decade, she had instructed him, taught him everything he knew, yet in spite of this, his literary criticism had not had the slightest effect on authors' standards or effected the least improvement in English fiction. He had wasted his time and his life through cowardice and pusillanimity, through mousiness instead of manliness.

It was that word 'mousiness' which did it. His hands moved across the table to rest on *Piranha to Scurfy*, he lifted it in both hands and brought it down as hard as he could on her head. Once, twice, again and again. The first time she screamed but not again after that. She staggered and sank to her knees and he beat her to the ground with Volume VIII of the *Encyclopaedia Britannica*. She was an old woman, she put up no struggle, she died quickly. He very much wanted not to get blood on the book – she had taught him books were sacred – but there was no blood. What was shed was shed inside her.

Regret came immediately. Remorse followed. But she was dead. He buried her in the wide flowerbed at the end of the garden that night, in the dark without a torch. The widows on either side slept soundly, no one saw a thing. The ivies grew back and the flowerless plants that liked shade. All summer he had watched them slowly growing. He told only two people she was dead, Glenys Next-door and his cousin Frank. Neither showed any inclination to come to the 'funeral', so when the day he had appointed came he left the house at ten in the morning, wearing the new dark suit he had bought, a black tie that had been Daddy's and carrying a bunch of spring flowers. Sandra On-the-other-side spotted him from her front room window and, approving, nodded sombrely while giving him a sad smile. Ribbon smiled sadly back. He put the flowers on someone else's grave and strolled round the cemetery for half an hour.

From a material point of view, living was easy. He had more money now than Mummy had ever let him have. Daddy's royalties were paid into her bank account twice a year and would continue to be paid in. Ribbon drew out what he wanted on her direct debit card, his handwriting being so like hers that no one could tell the difference. He had been collecting her retirement pension for years, and he went on doing so. It occurred to him that the Department of Social Security might expect her to die some time and the bank might expect it too, but she had been very young when he was born and might in any case have been expected to outlive him. He could go on doing this until what would have been her hundredth birthday and even beyond. But could he live without her? He had 'made it up to her' by keeping her bedroom as a shrine, keeping her clothes as if one day she would come back and wear them again. Still he was a lost soul, only half a man, a prey to doubts and fears and self-questioning and a nervous restlessness.

Looking down at the floor, he half expected to see some mark where her small, slight body had lain. There was nothing, any more than there was a mark on Volume VIII of *Britannica*. He went downstairs and stared out into the garden. The cypress he had associated with her, had been near to seeing as containing her spirit, was down, was lying on the grass, its frondy branches already wilting in the heat. One of the two fat shrubs was down too. Damian and the young one were sitting *on Mummy's grave*, drinking something out of a vacuum flask and smoking cigarettes. Mummy would have had something to say about that, but he lacked the heart. He thought again how strange it was, how horrible and somehow wrong, that the small child's name for its mother was the same as that for an embalmed Egyptian corpse.

In the afternoon, after the washing machine man had come and been let into Glenys Next-door's, Ribbon plucked up the courage to phone Kingston Marle's publishers. After various people's voice mail, instructions to press this button and that and requests to leave messages, he was put through to the department which sent on authors' letters. A rather indignant young woman assured him that all mail was sent on within a week of the publishers receiving it. Recovering a little of Mummy's spirit, he said in the strongest tone he could muster that a week was far too long. What about readers who were waiting anxiously for a reply? The young woman told him she had said 'within a week' and it might be much sooner. With that he had to be content. It was eleven days now since he had apologised to Kingston Marle, ten since his publishers had received the letter. He asked tentatively if they ever handed a letter to an author in person. For a while she hardly seemed to understand what he was talking about, then she gave him a defiant 'no', such a thing could never happen.

So Marle had not called off his dogs because he had received the apology. Perhaps it was only that the spell, or whatever it was, lasted no more than, say, twenty-four hours. It seemed, sadly, a more likely explanation. The tree fellers finished at five, leaving the wilted shrubs stacked on the flowerbed, not on Mummy's grave but on the place where The Book was buried. Ribbon took two of Mummy's sleeping pills and passed a good night. No letter came in the morning, there was no post at all. Without any evidence as to the truth of this, he became suddenly sure that no letter would come from Marle now, it would never come.

He had nothing to do, he had written to everyone who needed reproving, he had supplied himself with no more new books and had no inclination to go out and buy more. Perhaps he would never write to anyone again. He unplugged the link between computer and printer and closed the computer's lid. The new shelving he had bought from IKEA to put up in the dining room would never be used now. In the middle of the morning he went into Mummy's bedroom, tucked the nightdress under the pillow and quilt, removed the bedspread from the wardrobe door and closed the door. He couldn't have explained why he did these things, it simply seemed time to do them. From the window he saw a taxi draw up and Glenys Next-door get out of it. There was someone else inside the taxi she was helping out but Ribbon didn't stay to see who it was.

He contemplated the back garden from the dining room. Somehow he would have to dispose of all those logs, the remains of the cypresses, the flowering currant, the holly and the lilac bush. For a ten-pound note the men would doubtless have taken them away but Ribbon hadn't thought of this at the time. The place looked bleak and characterless now, an empty expanse of grass with a stark ivy-clad flowerbed at the end of it. He noticed, for the first time, over the wire dividing fence, the profusion of flowers in Glenys Next-door's, the bird table, the little fish pond (both hunting grounds for Tinks), the red-leaved Japanese maple. He would burn that wood, he would have a fire.

Of course he wasn't supposed to do this. In a small way it was against the law, for this was a smokeless zone and had been for nearly as long as he could remember. By the time anyone complained – and Glenys Next-door and Sandra On-the-other-side would both complain – the deed would have been done and the logs consumed. But he postponed it for a while and went back into the house. He felt reasonably well, if a little weak and dizzy. Going upstairs made him breathless in a way he never had been before, so he postponed that for a while too and had a cup of tea, sitting in the front room with his feet up. What would Marle do next? There was no knowing. Ribbon thought that when he was better he would find out where Marle lived, go to him and apologise in person. He would ask what he could do to make it up to Marle and whatever the answer was he would do it. If Marle wanted him to be his servant he would do that, or kneel at his feet and kiss the ground or allow Marle to flog him with a whip. Anything Marle wanted he would do, whatever it was.

Of course, he shouldn't have buried the book. That did no good. It would be ruined now and the best thing, the *cleanest* thing, would be to cremate it. After he was rested he made his way upstairs, crawled really, his hands on the stairs ahead of him, took *Piranha to Scurfy* off the shelf and brought it down. He'd burn that too. Back in the garden he arranged the logs on a bed of screwed-up newspaper, rested Volume VIII of *Britannica* on top of them and, fetching the spade, unearthed *Demogorgon*. Its plastic covering had been inadequate to protect it and it was sodden as well as very dirty. Ribbon felt guilty for treating it as he had. The fire would purify it. There was paraffin in a can somewhere, Mummy had used it for the little stove that heated her bedroom. He went back into the house, found the can and sprinkled paraffin on newspaper, logs and books, and applied a lighted match.

The flames roared up immediately, slowed once the oil had done its work. He poked at his fire with a long stick. A voice started shouting at him but he took no notice, it was only Glenys Next-door complaining. The smoke from the fire thickened, grew dense and grey. Its flames had reached The Book's wet pages, the great thick wad of 427 of them, and as the smoke billowed in a tall whirling cloud an acrid smell poured from it. Ribbon stared at the smoke for, in it now, or behind it, something was taking shape, a small, thin and very old woman swathed in a mummy's bandages, her head and arm bound in white bands, the skin between fish-belly white. He gave a small choking cry and fell, clutching the place where his heart was, holding on to the overpowering pain.

'The pathologist seems to think he died of fright,' the policeman said to Frank. 'A bit fanciful, that, if you ask me. Anyone can have a heart attack. You have to ask yourself what he could have been frightened *of*. Nothing, unless it was of catching fire. Of course, strictly speaking, the poor chap had no business to be having a fire. Mrs Judd and her mother saw it all. It was a bit of a shock for the old lady, she's over ninety and not well herself, she's staying with her daughter while recovering from a bad fall.'

Frank was uninterested in Glenys Judd's mother and her problems. He had a severe summer cold, could have done without any of this and doubted if he would be well enough to attend Ambrose Ribbon's funeral. In the event, Susan went to it alone. Someone had to. It would be too terrible if no one was there.

She expected to find herself the only mourner and she was very surprised to find she was not alone. On the other side of the aisle from her in the crematorium chapel sat Kingston Marle. At first she could hardly believe her eyes, then he turned his head, smiled and came to sit next to her. Afterwards, as they stood admiring the two wreaths, his, and hers and Frank's, he said that he supposed some sort of explanation would be in order.

'Not really,' Susan said. 'I just think it's wonderful of you to come.'

'I saw the announcement of his death in the paper with the date and place of the funeral,' Marle said, turning his wonderful deep eyes from the flowers to her. 'A rather odd thing had happened. I had a letter from your cousin – well, your husband's cousin. It was a few days after we met in Oxford. His letter was an apology, quite an abject apology, saying he was sorry for having written to me before, asking me to forgive him for criticising me for something or other.'

'What sort of something or other?'

'That I don't know. I never received his previous letter. But what he said reminded me that I *had* received a letter intended for Dillons bookshop in Piccadilly and signed by him. Of course I sent it on to them and thought no more about it. But now I'm wondering if he put the Dillons letter into the envelope intended for me and mine into the one for Dillons. It's easily done. That's why I prefer e-mail myself.'

Susan laughed. 'It can't have had anything to do with his death, anyway.'

'No, certainly not. I didn't really come here because of the letter, that's not important, I came because I hoped I might see you again.'

'Oh.'

'Will you have lunch with me?'

Susan looked around her, as if spies might be about. But they were alone. 'I don't see why not,' she said.

Computer Seance

Sophia de Vasco (Sheila Vosper on her birth certificate) was waiting at the bus stop when she saw her brother coming out of a side turning. Her brother looked a lot younger than he had before he died seven years before, but any doubts she might have had as to his identity were dispelled when he came up to her and asked her for money. 'Price of a cup of tea, missus?'

'You haven't changed, Jimmy,' said Sophia with a little laugh.

He didn't reply but continued to hold out his hand.

Sophia said roguishly, 'Now how would I know the price of a cup of tea, eh?'

'Fifty pee,' said Jimmy's ghost. 'A couple of quid for a cuppa and a butty.'

'I think you've been following my career from the Other Side, Jimmy. You know I've done rather well for myself since you passed over. You've seen how I've been responsible for London's spiritualist renaissance, haven't you? But you have to realise that I am no more made of money than I have ever been. If you're thinking Mother and Father left me anything you're quite wrong.'

'You some sort of loony tune?' He was looking at her fake fur, her high-heeled boots, the two large carriers and small leather case she carried. 'What's in the bag?'

'That is my computer. An indispensable tool of my trade, Jimmy. You could call it a symbol of the electronic advances spiritualism has made in recent years. My bus is coming now so I'll say goodbye.'

She went upstairs. She thought he might follow her but when she was sitting down she looked behind her and he was nowhere to be seen. Encounters with her dead relatives were not unusual events in Sophia's life. Only last week her aunt Lily had walked into her bedroom at midnight – she had always been a nocturnal type – and brought her a lot of messages from her mother, mostly warnings to Sophia to be on her guard in matters of men and money. Then, two evenings ago, an old woman came through the wall while Sophia was eating her supper. They manifested themselves so confidently, Sophia thought, because she never showed fear, she absolutely wasn't frightened. The old woman didn't stay long but flitted about the flat, peering at everything, and disappeared after telling Sophia that she was her maternal grandmother who had died in the Spanish flu epidemic of 1919.

So it was no great surprise to have seen Jimmy. In life he had always been feckless, unable to hold down a job, chronically short of money, with a talent for nothing but sponging off his relations. Few tears had been shed when his body was found floating in the Grand Union Canal, into which he had fallen after two or three too many in the Hero of Maida. Sophia devoutly hoped he wouldn't embarrass her by manifesting himself at the seance she was about to hold in half an hour's time at Mrs Paget-Brown's.

But, in fact, he was to make a more positive, almost concrete, appearance before that. As she descended the stairs from the top of the bus she saw him waiting for her at the stop. A less sensitive woman than Sophia might have assumed that he too had come on the bus and had sat downstairs, but she knew better. Why go on a bus when, in the manner of spirits, he could travel through space in no time and be wherever he wished in the twinkling of an eye?

Sophia decided that the only wise course was to ignore him. She shook her head in his direction and set off at a brisk pace along Kendal Street. Outside the butcher's she looked round and saw him following her. There was nothing to be done about it, she could only hope he wasn't going to attach himself to her, even take up residence in her flat, for that might mean all the trouble and expense of an exorcism.

Mrs Paget-Brown lived in Hyde Park Square. Before she rang the bell Sophia looked behind her once more. It was growing dark and she could no longer see Jimmy, but it might only be that he was already inside, in the drawing room, waiting for her. It couldn't be helped. Mrs Paget-Brown opened the door promptly. She had everything prepared, the long rectangular table covered by a dark-brown chenille cloth, Sophia's chair, the semicircle of chairs behind it. Five guests were expected, of whom two had already arrived. They were in the dining room, having a cup of herb tea, for Sophia discouraged the consumption of alcohol before encounters with denizens of the Other Side.

When Mrs Paget-Brown had gone back to her guests, Sophia took her laptop out of its case and set it on the table. She raised its lid so that the keyboard and screen could be seen. Then she took a large screen out of one of her carriers and plugged its cable into one of the computer ports. Glancing over her shoulder to check that Mrs Paget-Brown was really gone and the door shut, she took a big keyboard out of the other carrier and plugged its cable into a second port.

The doorbell rang, and rang again five minutes afterwards. That probably meant everyone had arrived, for two of the expected guests were a husband and wife, a Mr and Mrs Jameson, hoping for an encounter with their dead daughter. Mrs Paget-Brown had told her a lot about this daughter, how she had been called Deirdre, had had a husband and two small children and had been a harpist. Sophia sometimes felt a warm glow of happiness when she reflected how often she was able to bring relief and hope to such people as the Jamesons by putting them in touch with those who had gone before.

The computer was switched on, the small screen dark, the big screen alight but blank. She had settled herself into the big chair with the keyboard on her lap and it and her hands covered by the overhang of the chenille cloth, when someone tapped on the door and asked if she was ready. In a fluting voice Sophia asked them to come in.

She wouldn't have been at all surprised if Jimmy had been among them. They wouldn't have been able to see him, of course, but she would. Still, only six people entered the room, including Mrs Paget-Brown herself, the couple called Jameson who had the dead daughter, a very fat man who wheezed and two elderly women, one very smartly dressed in a turquoise suit, the other dowdy with untidy hair.

Sophia said a gracious, 'Good evening' and then, 'Please take a seat behind me where you can see the screen. In a moment we shall turn out the lights but before that I want to explain what will happen. What *may* happen. Of course, I can guarantee nothing if the spirits are unwilling.'

They sat down. The asthmatic man breathed noisily. Turquoise suit took off her hat. Sophia could see their faces reflected in the screen, Mrs Jameson's eyes bright with hope and yearning. The dowdy woman said could she ask a question and when Sophia said, certainly, my pleasure, asked if they would see anything or would it only be a matter of table raps and ectoplasm.

Sophia couldn't help laughing at the idea of ectoplasm. These people were so incredibly behind the times. But her laughter was kindly and she explained that there would be no table-rapping. The spirits, who were very advanced about such things, made their feelings and their messages known through the computer. Those seekers after truth who sat behind her would see answers appear on the screen.

Of course, everyone's eyes went to the laptop's small integral keyboard. And when the lights were lowered it was possible to imagine those keys moving. Sophia kept her hands under the cloth, her fingers on the big keyboard. She was ceaselessly thankful that she had taken that touch-typing course all those years ago when she was a girl.

The asthmatic man's wife was the first spirit to present herself.

Her husband asked her if she was happy and YES appeared in green letters on the screen. He asked her if she missed him and WAITING FOR YOU TO FOLLOW DEAR appeared. Very much impressed, Mrs Paget-Brown summoned up her father. She said in an awed voice that she could see the keys very faintly moving on the integral keyboard as his spirit fingers touched them. Her father answered YES when she asked if he was with her mother and NO when she enquired if death had been a painful experience. Sophia leaned back a little and closed her eyes. Communing with the spirits took it out of her.

But she supplied the dowdy woman with a fairly satisfactory dead fiancé, her dead husband's predecessor. In answer to a rather timid question he replied that he had always regretted not marrying her and his life had been a failure. When the dowdy woman reminded him that he had fathered five children, owned three houses, been a junior minister in Margaret Thatcher's administration and later on chairman of a multinational company, Sophia told herself to be more careful.

She was more successful with Deirdre Jameson. The Jamesons were transfixed with joy when Deirdre declared her happiness on the screen and intimated that she watched over her husband and children from afar. Where she now was she had ample opportunity to play the harp and did so for all the company of heaven. For a moment Sophia wondered if she had gone too far but Mr and Mrs Jameson accepted everything and when the lights went on again, thanked her, as they put it, from the bottom of their hearts. 'Thank you, thank you, you have done a wonderful thing for us, you've transformed our lives.'

As she packed everything up again, Sophia reflected on something she had occasionally thought of in the past. It wasn't possible for her to go too far, it wasn't possible for her to deceive. Although she might conceal from these seekers after truth the hidden keyboard and the busy activity of her hands, the truth must be that these spirits were present and waiting to communicate. She was a true medium and her hands were the means they entered in order to transmit their messages. The world wasn't ready yet to have the keyboard and the moving fingers exposed, there was too much ignorance and prejudice, but one day . . .

One day, Sophia believed, everyone would be attuned to seeing and speaking to the dead, as she had seen and spoken to Jimmy. One day, when the earth was filled with the glory of the supernatural.

Carrying her bags and her laptop in its case, she tapped on the dining room door, was admitted and given a small glass of sherry. Discreetly, Mrs Paget-Brown slipped an envelope containing her cheque into her hand. Turquoise suit wanted to know if she would hold a seance for herself and some personal friends in Westbourne Terrace next week and the Jamesons asked for more revelations from Deirdre. Sophia graciously accepted both invitations.

She was always the first to leave. It was wiser not to engage in too much conversation with the guests but to preserve the vague air of mystery that surrounded her. By now it was very dark and there were so many trees in this neighbourhood that the street lights failed to make much of a show. But there was enough light for her to see her brother. He was waiting for her on the corner of Hyde Park Street and Connaught Street.

No one else was about, the Edgware Road wasn't a very pleasant area for a woman to be alone in at night, and Sophia thought that, nuisance though Jimmy was, she wouldn't be altogether averse to a man's escort until her bus came. Then, of course, she realised how absurd this was. Jimmy's presence at her side would be no deterrent to a mugger who would be unable to see him. 'It's time you went back to wherever you came from, Jimmy,' she said rather severely. 'I must say I doubt if it's the pleasantest of places but you should have thought of that while you were on earth.'

'Loony tune,' said Jimmy. 'I want the bag. I want all the bags. You give them to me and you'll be OK.'

'Give you my computer? What an idea. You couldn't even carry it. The handle would pass right through your hand.'

As if to demonstrate her error, Jimmy made a grab for the laptop in its case. Sophia snatched it back and held it above her head. She didn't cry out. It was all too absurd. She didn't see the knife either. In fact, she never saw it, only felt it like a blow that robbed her first of breath, then of life. She dropped the carriers. The secret keyboard made a litle clatter when it struck the pavement.

Jimmy, or Darren Palmer, picked up the bags and retrieved the case. Next morning he sold the lot to a man he knew in Leather Lane market and spent the money on crack cocaine.

Fair Exchange

'You're looking for Tom Dorchester, aren't you?' Penelope said.

I nodded. 'How did you know?'

'I've been expecting you to ask. I mean, he's always been at this conference in the past. Quite a fixture. This must be the first he hasn't come to in – what? Fifteen years? Twenty?'

'He's not here, then?'

'He's dead.'

I wanted to say, 'He can't be!' But that's absurd. Anyone can be dead. Here today and gone tomorrow, as the saying goes. Still, the more full of vitality a person is the more you feel he has a firmer grasp on life than the rest of us. Only violence, some appalling accident, could prise him loose. And Tom was – had been, I should say – more vital, more enthusiastic and more interested in everything than most people. He seemed to love and hate more intensely, specially to love. I remember him once saying he needed no more than five hours' sleep a night, there was too much to do, to learn, to appreciate, to waste time sleeping. And then his wife had become ill, very ill. Much of his abundant energy he devoted to finding a cure for her particular kind of cancer. Or trying to find it.

I said, stupidly, I suppose, 'But it was Frances who was going to die.'

Penelope gave me a strange, indecipherable look. 'I'll tell you

73

about it, if you like. It's an odd story. Of course, I don't know how much you know.'

'About what? I wouldn't have called Tom a close friend but I'd known him for years. I know he adored Frances. I mean, I adore Marian but – well, you know what I mean. He was like a young lover. To say he worshipped the ground she trod on wouldn't be an exaggeration.'

Penelope took her cigarettes out of her handbag and offered me one.

'I've given it up.'

'I wish I could but I know my limitations. Now, d'you want the story?' I nodded. 'You may not like it. It's pretty awful one way and another. He killed himself, you know.'

'He *what? Tom Dorchester?*'

'Did away with himself, committed suicide, whatever.'

There was only one possible event that could make this believable. 'Ah, you mean Frances did die?'

Penelope shook her head. She took a sip of her drink. 'It was June or July of last year, about a month after the conference. You'll remember Tom only came for two days because he felt he couldn't leave Frances any longer than that, though their younger daughter was with her. They had two daughters, both married, and the older one has three children. The eldest child was twelve at the time.'

'I had dinner with Tom,' I said. 'There were a couple of other people there but he mostly talked to me. He was telling me about some miracle cure they'd tried on Frances but it hadn't worked.'

'It was at a clinic in Switzerland. They dehydrate you and give you nothing but walnuts to eat, something like that. When she came back and she was worse than ever, Tom found a healer. I actually met her. Chris and I went round to Tom's one evening and this woman was there. Very weird she was, very weird indeed.'

'What do you mean, weird?'

'Well, you think of a healer as laying on hands, don't you? Or reciting mantras while using herbal remedies, something like that. This woman wasn't like that. She did it all by talk and the power of thought. That's what she said, the power of thought. Her name was Davina Tarsis and she was quite young. Late thirties, early forties, very strangely dressed. Not that sort of floaty hippy look, oriental garments and beads and whatever, not like that at all. She was very thin, only a very thin woman could have got away with wearing skin-tight white leggings and a white tunic with a great orange sun printed on the front of it. Her hair was long and dyed a deep purplish red. I don't know why I say "was". I expect she's still got purple hair. No make-up, of course, a scrubbed face and a ring in one nostril – not a stud, a ring.

'Tom thought she was wonderful. He claimed she'd cured a woman who had been having radiotherapy at the same time as Frances. Now the odd thing was that she didn't talk much to Frances at all – I had a feeling Frances didn't altogether care for her. She talked to Tom. Not while we were there, I don't mean that. I mean in private. Apparently they had long sessions, like a kind of mad form of psychotherapy. Chris said maybe she was making a play for Tom but I don't think it was that. I think she really believed in what she was doing and so did he. So, my God, did he.

'She taught him to believe that anything you wished for hard enough you could have. He told me that – not at the time, when it was all over.'

'What do you mean,' I said, 'when it was all over?'

'When Tom had got what he wanted.'

'Presumably, that was for Frances to be cured.'

'That's right. He got very emotional with me one night – Chris was out somewhere – and he started crying and sobbing. I know men do cry these days but I've never known a man cry like Tom did that night. The tears poured out of his eyes. There was quite a long time when he couldn't speak, he choked on the words. It was dreadful, I didn't know what to do. I gave him some brandy but he'd only take a sip of it because he was driving and he had to go back to Frances before his daughter and *her* daughter had to go home. That's the nine-year-old, Emma she's called. Anyway, he calmed down after a bit and then he said he couldn't live without Frances, he couldn't imagine life without her, he'd kill himself . . .'

'Ah,' I said.

'Ah, nothing. That had nothing to do with it. Frances went back into hospital soon after that. They were trying some new kind of chemotherapy on her. Tom hadn't any faith in it. By then he only had faith in Tarsis. He was having daily talk sessions with her. He'd taken leave from his job and he'd spend an entire morning talking to Tarsis, mostly about his feelings for Frances, I gather, and how he felt about the rest of his family, and how he and Frances had met and so on. She'd make him go over and over it and the more he repeated himself the more approving she was.

'Frances came home and she was very ill, thin, with no appetite. Her hair began to fall out. She could barely walk. The side effects from the chemo were the usual ghastly thing, nausea and faintness and ringing in the ears and all that. Tarsis came round and took a look at her, said the chemo was a mistake but in spite of it, she thought she could heal Frances completely. Then came the crunch. I didn't know this at the time, Tom didn't tell me until – oh, I don't know, two or three months afterwards. But this is what Tarsis said to him.

'They talked while Frances was asleep. Tarsis said, "What would you give to make Frances live?" Well, of course, Tom asked what she meant and she said, "Whose life would you give in exchange for Frances's life?" Tom said that was nonsense, you couldn't trade one person's life for another and Tarsis said, oh yes, you could. The power of thought could do that for you. She'd trained Tom in practising the power of thought and now all he had to do was wish for Frances to live. Only he had to offer someone else up in her place.

'That was when he started to see her for what she was. A charlatan. But he played along, he said. He wanted to see what she'd do. Called her bluff, was what he said, but he was deceiving himself in that. He still half believed. Who would he offer up, she asked him. "Oh, anyone you like," he said and he laughed. She was deadly serious. That day she'd met Tom's elder daughter and the granddaughter Emma. Tom said – he hated telling me this but on the other hand he was really past caring what he told anyone – he said Emma hadn't been very polite to Davina Tarsis. She'd sort of stared at her, at the tight leggings and the sun on her tunic and sneered a bit, I suppose, and then she'd said it wasn't Tarsis but the chemo that was doing her grandmother good, it stood to reason that was what it was.'

I interrupted her. 'What do you mean, he hated telling you?'

'Wait and see. He had good reason. It was after Emma and her mother had gone and Frances was resting that they had this talk. When Tom said it could be anyone she liked, Tarsis said it wasn't what she liked but what Tom wanted, and then she said, "How about that girl Emma?" Tom told her not to be ridiculous but she persisted and at last he said that, well, yes, he supposed so, he would give Emma, only the whole thing was absurd. The fact was that he'd give anyone to save Frances's life if it were possible to do that, so of course, yes, he'd give Emma.'

'It must have put him off this Davina Tarsis, surely?'

'You'd think so. I'm not sure. All this was about nine or ten months ago. Frances started to get better. Oh, yes, she did. You needn't look like that. It was just an amazing thing. The doctors were amazed. But it wasn't unheard-of, it wasn't a miracle, though people said it was. Presumably, the chemo worked. All the things that should get right got right. I mean, her blood count got to be normal, she put on weight, the pain went, the tumours shrivelled up. She simply got a bit better every day. It wasn't a remission, it was a recovery.'

'Tom must have been over the moon,' I said.

Penelope made a face. 'He was. For a while. And then Emma died.'

'*What?*'

'In a road crash. She died.'

'You're not saying this witch woman, this Davina Tarsis . . . ?'

'No, I'm not. Of course I'm not. At the time of the crash Tarsis and Tom were together in Tom's house with Frances. Besides, there was no mystery about the accident. It *was* indisputably an accident. Emma was on a school bus coming back from a visit with the rest of her class to some stately home. There was ice on the road, the bus skidded and overturned, and three of the pupils were killed, Emma among them. You must have read about it, it was all over the media.'

'I think I did,' I said. 'I can't remember.'

'It affected Tom – well, profoundly. I don't mean in the way the death of a grandchild would affect any grandparent. I mean he was racked with guilt. He had such faith in Tarsis that he really believed he'd done it. He believed he'd given Emma's life in exchange for Frances's. And another awful thing was that his love for Frances simply vanished, all that great love, that amazing devotion that was an example to us all, really, it disappeared. He came to dislike her. He told me it wasn't that he had no feeling for her any more, he actively disliked her.

'So there was nothing for him to live for. He believed he'd ruined his own life and ruined his daughter's and destroyed his love for Frances. One night after Frances was asleep he drank a whole bottle of liquid morphia she'd had prescribed but hadn't used and twenty paracetomol and a few brandies. He died quite quickly, I believe.'

'That's terrible,' I said. 'The most awful tragedy. I'd no idea. And poor Frances. One's heart goes out to Frances.'

Penelope looked at me and took another cigarette. 'Don't feel too sorry for her,' she said. 'She's as fit as a fiddle now and about to start a new life. Her GP lost his wife about the time he diagnosed her cancer and he and Frances are getting married next month. So you could say that all's well that ends well.'

'I wouldn't go as far as that,' I said.

The Wink

The woman in reception gave her directions. Go through the day room, then the double doors at the back, turn left and Elsie's in the third room on the right. Unless she's in the day room.

Elsie wasn't but the Beast was. Jean always called him that, she had never known his name. He was sitting with the others watching television. A semicircle of chairs was arranged in front of the television, mostly armchairs but some wheelchairs, and some of the old people had fallen asleep. He was in a wheelchair and he was awake, staring at the screen where celebrities were taking part in a game show.

Ten years had passed since she had last seen him but she knew him, changed and aged though he was. He must be well over eighty. Seeing him was always a shock but seeing him in here was a surprise. A not unpleasant surprise. He must be in that chair because he couldn't walk. He had been brought low, his life was coming to an end.

She knew what he would do when he saw her. He always did. But possibly he wouldn't see her, he wouldn't turn round. The game show would continue to hold his attention. She walked as softly as she could, short of tiptoeing, round the edge of the semicircle. Her mistake was to look back just before she reached the double doors. His eyes were on her and he did what he always did. He winked.

Jean turned sharply away. She went down the corridor and found Elsie's room, the third on the right. Elsie too was asleep, sitting in an armchair by the window. Jean put the flowers she had brought on the bed and sat down on the only other chair, an upright one without arms. Then she got up again and drew the curtain a little way across to keep the sunshine off Elsie's face.

Elsie had been at Sweetling Manor for two weeks and Jean knew she would never come out again. She would die here – and why not? It was clean and comfortable, and everything was done for you and probably it was ridiculous to feel, as Jean did, that she would prefer anything to being here, including being helpless and old and starving and finally dying alone.

They were the same age, she and Elsie, but she felt younger and thought she looked it. They had always known each other, had been at school together, had been each other's bridesmaids. Well, Elsie had been her matron of honour, having been married a year by then. It was Elsie she had gone to the pictures with that evening, Elsie and another girl whose name she couldn't remember. She remembered the film, though. It had been Deanna Durbin in *Three Smart Girls*. Sixty years ago.

When Elsie woke up she would ask her what the other girl was called. Christine? Kathleen? Never mind. Did Elsie know the Beast was in here? Jean remembered then that Elsie didn't know the Beast, had never heard what happened that night, no one had, she had told no one. It was different in those days, you couldn't tell because you would get the blame. Somehow, ignorant though she was, she had known that even then.

Ignorant. They all were, she and Elsie and the girl called Christine or Kathleen. Or perhaps they were just afraid. Afraid of what people would say, would think of them. Those were the days of blame, of good behaviour expected from everyone, of taking responsibility, and often punishment, for one's own actions. You put up with things and you got on with things. Complaining got you nowhere.

Over the years there had been extraordinary changes. You were no longer blamed or punished, you got something called empathy. In the old days what the Beast did would have been her fault. She must have led him on, encouraged him. Now it was a crime, *his* crime. She read about it in the papers, saw about things called helplines on television, and counselling and specially trained women police officers. This was to avoid your being marked for life, traumatised, though you could never forget.

That was true, that last part, though she had forgotten for weeks on end, months. And then, always, she had seen him again. It came of living in the country, in a small town, it came of her living there and his going on living there. Once she saw him in a shop, once out in the street, another time he got on a bus as she was getting off it. He always winked. He didn't say anything, just looked at her and winked.

Elsie had looked like Deanna Durbin. The resemblance was quite marked. They were about the same age, born in the same year. Jean remembered how they had talked about it, she and Elsie and Christine–Kathleen, as they left the cinema and the others walked with her to the bus stop. Elsie wanted to know what you had to do to get a screen test and the other girl said it would help to be in Hollywood, not Yorkshire. Both of them lived in the town, five minutes' walk away, and Elsie said she could stay the night if she wanted. But there was no way of letting her parents know. Elsie's had a phone but hers didn't.

Deanna Durbin was still alive, Jean had read somewhere. She wondered if she still looked like Elsie or if she had had her face lifted and her hair dyed and gone on diets. Elsie's face was plump and soft, very wrinkled about the eyes, and her hair was white and thin. She smiled faintly in her sleep and gave a little snore. Jean moved her chair closer and took hold of Elsie's hand. That made the smile come back but Elsie didn't wake.

The Beast had come along in his car about ten minutes after the girls had gone and Jean was certain the bus wasn't coming. It was the last bus and she hadn't known what to do. This had happened before, the driver just hadn't turned up and had got the sack for it, but that hadn't made the bus come. On that occasion she had gone to Elsie's and Elsie's mother had phoned her parents' next-door neighbours. She thought that if she did that a second time and put Mr and Mrs Rawlings to all that trouble, her dad would probably stop her going to the pictures ever again.

It wasn't dark. At midsummer it wouldn't get dark till after ten. If it had been she mightn't have gone with the Beast. Of course, he didn't seem like a Beast then but young, a boy, really, and handsome and quite nice. And it was only five miles. Mr Rawlings was always saying five miles was nothing, he used to walk five miles to school every day and five miles back. But she couldn't face the walk and, besides, she wanted a ride in a car. It would only be the third time she had ever been in one. Still, she would have refused his offer if he hadn't said what he had when she told him where she lived.

'You'll know the Rawlings then. Mrs Rawlings is my sister.'

It wasn't true but it sounded true. She got in beside him. The car wasn't really his, it belonged to the man he worked for, he was a chauffeur, but she found that out a lot later.

'Lovely evening,' he said. 'You been gallivanting?'

'I've been to the pictures,' she said.

After a couple of miles he turned a little way down a lane and stopped the car outside a derelict cottage. It looked as if no one could possibly live there but he said he had to see someone, it would only take a minute and she could come too. By now it was dusk but there were no lights on in the cottage. She remembered he was Mrs Rawlings's brother. There must have been a good ten years between them but that hadn't bothered her. Her own sister was ten years older than she was.

She followed him up the path, which was overgrown with weeds and brambles. Instead of going to the front door, he led her round the back where old apple trees grew among waist-high grass. The back of the house was a ruin, half its rear wall tumbled down.

'There's no one here,' she said.

He didn't say anything. He took hold of her and pulled her down in the long grass, one hand pressed hard over her mouth. She hadn't known anyone could be so strong. He took his hand away to pull her clothes off and she screamed, but the screaming was just a reflex, a release of fear, and otherwise useless. There was no one to hear. What he did was rape. She knew that now – well, had known it soon after it happened, only no one called it that then. Nobody spoke of it. Nowadays the word was on everyone's lips. Nine out of ten television series were about it. Rape, the crime against women. Rape, that these days you went into court and talked about. You went to self-defence classes to stop it happening to you. You attended groups and shared your experience with other victims.

At first she had been most concerned to find out if he had injured her. Torn her, broken bones. But there was nothing like that. Because she was all right and he was gone, she stopped crying. She heard the car start up and then move away. Walking home wasn't exactly painful, more a stiff, achy business, rather the way she had felt the day after she and Elsie had been learning to do the splits. She had to walk anyway, she had no choice. As it was, her father was in a rage, wanting to know what time she thought this was.

'Anything could have happened to you,' her mother said.

Something had. She had been raped. She went up to bed so they wouldn't see she couldn't stop shivering. She didn't sleep at all that night. In the morning she told herself it could have been worse, at least she wasn't dead. It never crossed her mind to say anything to anyone about what had happened, she was too ashamed, too afraid of what they would think. It was past, she kept telling herself, it was all over.

One thing worried her most. A baby. Suppose she had a baby. Never in all her life was she so relieved about anything, so happy, as when she saw that first drop of blood run down the inside of her leg a day early. She shouted for joy. She was all right! The blood cleansed her and now no one need ever know.

Trauma? That was the word they used nowadays. It meant a scar. There was no scar that you could see and no scar she could feel in her body, but it was years before she would let a man come near her. Afterwards she was glad about that, glad she had waited, that she hadn't met someone else before Kenneth. But at the time she thought about what had happened every day, she relived what had happened, the shock and the pain and the dreadful fear, and in her mind she called the man who had done that to her the Beast.

Eight years went by and she saw him again. She was out with Kenneth, he had just been demobbed from the Air Force and they were walking down the High Street arm in arm. Kenneth had asked her to marry him and they were going to buy the engagement ring. It was a big jewellers they went to, with several aisles. The Beast was in a different aisle, quite a long way away, on some errand for his employer, she supposed, but she saw him and he saw her. He winked.

He winked, just as he had ten minutes ago in the day room. Jean shut her eyes. When she opened them again Elsie was awake.

'How long have you been there, dear?'

'Not long,' Jean said.

'Are those flowers for me? You know how I love freesias. We'll get someone to put them in water. I don't have to do a thing in here, don't lift a finger. I'm a lady of leisure.'

'Elsie,' said Jean, 'what was the name of that girl we went to the pictures with when we saw *Three Smart Girls*?'

'What?'

'It was nineteen thirty-eight. In the summer.'

'I don't know, I shall have to think. My memory's not what it was. Bob used to say I looked like Deanna Durbin.'

'We all said you did.'

'Constance, her name was. We called her Connie.'

'So we did,' said Jean.

Elsie began talking of the girls they had been at school with. She could remember all their Christian names and most of their surnames. Jean found a vase, filled it with water and put the freesias into it because they showed signs of wilting. Her engagement ring still fitted on her finger, though it was a shade tighter. How worried she had been that Kenneth would be able to tell she wasn't a virgin! They said men could always tell. But of course, when the time came, he couldn't. It was just another old wives' tale.

Elsie, who already had her first baby, had worn rose-coloured taffeta at their wedding. And her husband had been Kenneth's best man. John was born nine months later and the twins eighteen months after that. There was a longer gap before Anne arrived but still she had had her hands full. That was the time, when the children were little, that she thought less about the Beast and what had happened than at any other time in her life. She forgot him for months on end. Anne was just four when she saw him again.

She was meeting the other children from school. They hadn't got a car then, it was years before they got a car. On the way to the school they were going to the shop to buy Anne a new pair of shoes. The Red Lion was just closing for the afternoon. The Beast came out of the public bar, not too steady on his feet, and he almost bumped into her. She said, 'Do you mind?' before she saw who it was. He stepped back, looked into her face and winked. She was outraged. For two pins she'd have told Kenneth the whole tale that evening. But of course she couldn't. Not now.

'I don't know what you mean about your memory,' she said to Elsie. 'You've got a wonderful memory.'

Elsie smiled. It was the same pretty teenager's smile, only they didn't use that word teenager then. You were just a person between twelve and twenty. 'What do you think of this place, then?'

'It's lovely,' said Jean. 'I'm sure you've done the right thing.'

Elsie talked some more about the old days and the people they'd known and then Jean kissed her goodbye and said she'd come back next week.

'Use the short cut next time,' said Elsie. 'Through the garden and in by the french windows next door.'

'I'll remember.'

She wasn't going to leave that way, though. She went back down the corridor and hesitated outside the day room door. The last time she'd seen the Beast, before *this* time, they were both growing old. Kenneth was dead. John was a grandfather himself, though a young one, the twins were joint directors of a prosperous business in Australia and Anne was a surgeon in London. Jean had never learned to drive and the car was given up when Kenneth died. She was waiting at that very bus stop, the one where he had picked her up all those years before. The bus came and he got off it, an old man with white hair, his face yellowish and wrinkled. But she knew him, she would have known him anywhere. He gave her one of his rude stares and he winked. That time it was an exaggerated, calculated wink, the whole side of his face screwed up and his eye squeezed shut.

She pushed open the day room door. The television was still on but he wasn't there. His wheelchair was empty. Then she saw him. He was being brought back from the bathroom, she supposed. A nurse held him tightly by one arm. The other rested heavily on the padded top of a crutch. His legs, in pyjama trousers, were half buckled and on his face was an expression of agony as, wincing with pain, he took small tottering steps.

Jean looked at him. She stared into his tormented face and his eyes met hers. Then she winked. She winked at him as he had winked at her that last time, and she saw what she had never thought to see happen to an old person. A rich, dark blush spread across his withered face. He turned away his eyes. Jean tripped lightly across the room towards the exit, like a sixteen-year-old.

Catamount

The sky was the biggest she had ever seen. They said the skies of Suffolk were big and the skies of Holland, but those were small, cosy, by comparison. It might belong on another planet, covering another world. Mostly a pale soft azure or a dark hard blue, it was sometimes overcast with huge rolling cumulus, swollen and edged with sharp white light, from which rain roared without warning.

Chuck's and Carrie's house was only the second built up there, under that sky. The other was what they called a modular home and Nora a prefab, a frame bungalow standing on a bluff between the dirt road and the ridge. The Johanssons who lived there kept a few cows and fattened white turkeys for Thanksgiving. It was – thank God, said Carrie – invisible from her handsome log house, built of yellow Montana pine. She and Chuck called it Elk Valley Ranch, a name Nora had thought pretentious when she read it on their headed notepaper but not when she saw it. The purpose of the letter was to ask her and Gordon to stay and she could hardly believe it, it seemed too glorious, the idea of a holiday in the Rocky Mountains, though she and Carrie had been best friends for years. That was before she married a captain in the US Air Force stationed at Bentwaters and went back home to Colorado with him.

It was August when they went the first time. The little plane from Denver took them to the airport at Hogan and Carrie met them in the Land Cruiser. The road ran straight and long, parallel with the Crystal river that was also straight, like a canal, with willows and cottonwood trees along its banks. Beyond the flat flowery fields the mountains rose, clothed in pine and scrub oak and aspen, mountains that were dark, almost black, but with green sunlit meadows bright between the trees. The sun shone and it was hot but the sky looked like a winter sky in England, the blue very pale and the clouds stretched across it like torn strips of chiffon.

There were a few small houses, many large barns and stables. Horses were in the fields, one chestnut mare with a new-born foal. Carrie turned in towards the western mountains and through a gateway with Elk Valley Ranch carved on a board. It was still a long way to the house. The road wound through curves and hairpin bends, and as they went higher the mountain slopes and the green canyons opened out below them, mountain upon mountain and valley upon valley, a herd of deer in one deep hollow, a golden eagle perched on a spar. By the roadside grew yellow asters and blue Michaelmas daisies, wild delphiniums, pale-pink geraniums and the bright-red Indian paintbrush, and above the flowers brown and yellow butterflies hovered.

'There are snakes,' Carrie said. 'Rattlesnakes. You have to be a bit careful. One of them was on the road last night. We stopped to look at it and it lashed against our tyres.'

'I'd like to see a porcupine.' Gordon had his Rocky Mountains wildlife book with him, open on his knees. 'But I'd settle for a raccoon.'

'You'll very likely see both,' Carrie said. 'Look, there's the house.'

It stood on the crown of a wooded hill, its log walls a dark gamboge, its roof green. A sheepdog came down to the five-barred gate when it saw the Land Cruiser.

'You must have spectacular views,' Gordon said.

'We do. If you wake up early enough you see fabulous things from your window. Last week I saw the cougar.'

'What's a cougar?'

'Mountain lion. I'll just get out and open the gate.'

It wasn't until she was home again in England that Nora had looked up the cougar in a *Mammals of North America* book. That night and for the rest of the fortnight she had forgotten it. There were so many things to do and see. Walking and climbing in the mountains, fishing in the Crystal river, picking a single specimen of each flower and pressing it in the book she bought for the purpose, photographing hawks and eagles, watching the chipmunks run along the fences. Driving down to the little town of Hogan (where on their way to Telluride, Butch Cassidy and Sundance had stopped to rob the bank), visiting the hotel where the Clanton Gang had left bullets from their handguns in the bathroom wall, shopping, sitting in the hot springs and swimming in the cold pool. Eating in Hogan's restaurant where elk steaks and rattlesnake burgers were specialities, and drinking in the Last Frontier Bar.

Carrie and Chuck said to come back next year or come in the winter when the skiing began. That was at the time when Hogan Springs was emerging as a ski resort. Or come in the spring when the snows melted and the alpine meadows burst into bloom, miraculous with gentians and avalanche lilies. And they did go again, but in late summer, a little later than in the previous year. The aspen leaves were yellowing, the scrub oak turning bronze.

'We shall have snow in a month,' Carrie said.

A black bear had come with her cubs and eaten Lily Johansson's turkeys. 'Like a fox at home,' Gordon said. They went up to the top of Mount Opie in the new ski lift and walked down. It was five miles through fields of blue flax and orange gaillardias. The golden ridge and the pine-covered slopes looked serene in the early autumn sunshine, the skies were clear until late afternoon when the clouds gathered and the rain came. The rain was torrential for ten minutes and then it was hot and sunny again, the grass and wild flowers steaming. A herd of elk came close up to the house and one of them pressed its huge head and stubby horns against the window. They saw the black bear and her cubs through Chuck's binoculars, loping along down in the green canyon.

'One day I'll see the cougar,' Nora said and Gordon asked if cougars were an endangered species.

'I wouldn't think so. There are supposed to be mountain lions in every state of the United States, but I guess most of them are here. You ought to talk to Lily Johansson, she's often seen them.'

'There was a boy got killed by one last fall,' Carrie said. 'He was cycling and the thing came out of the woods, pulled him off his bike and well – ate him, I suppose. Or started to eat him. It was scared off. They're protected, so there was nothing to be done.'

Cougar stories abounded. Everyone had one. Some of them sounded like urban – rural, rather – myths. There was the one about the woman out walking with her little boy in Winter Park and who came face to face with a cougar on the mountain. She put the child on her shoulders and told him to hold up his arms so that, combined, they made a creature eight feet tall, which was enough to frighten the animal off. The boy in the harness shop in Hogan had one about the man out with his dog. To save himself he had to let the cougar kill and eat his dog while he got away. In the town Nora bought a reproduction of Audubon's drawing of a cougar, graceful, powerful, tawny, with a cat's mysterious closed-in face.

'I thought they were small, like a lynx,' Gordon said.

'They're the size of an African lion – well, lioness. That's what they look like, a lioness.'

'I shall frame my picture,' Nora said, 'and one day I'll see the real thing.'

They came back to Hogan year after year. More houses were built but not enough to spoil the place. Once they came in winter but, at their age, it was too late to learn to ski. Seventeen feet of snow fell. The snowplough came out on to the roads on Christmas Eve and cleared a passage for cars, making ramparts of snow where the flowers had been. Nora wondered about the animals. What did they live on, these creatures? The deer ate the bark of trees. Chuck put cattle feed out for them and hay.

'The herds have been reduced enough by mountain lions,' he said. 'You once asked if they were endangered. There are tens of thousands of them now, more than there have ever been.'

Nora worried about the golden eagle. What could it find to feed on in this white world? The bears were hibernating. Were the cougars also? No one seemed to know. She would never come again in winter when everything was covered, sleeping, waiting, buried. It was one thing for the skiers, another for a woman, elderly now, afraid to go out lest she slip on the ice. The few small children they saw had coloured balloons tied to them on long strings so that their parents could see and rescue them if they sank too deep down in the snow. All Christmas Day the sun blazed, melting the snow on the roof, and by night frost held the place in its grip, so that the guttering round the house grew a fringe of icicles.

The following spring Gordon died. Lily Johansson wrote a letter of sympathy and when Jim Johansson died next Christmas Nora wrote one to her. She delayed going back to the mountains for a year, two years. Driving from the airport with Carrie, she noticed for the first time something strange. It was a beautiful landscape but not a comfortable one, not easeful, not conducive to peace and tranquillity. There was no lushness and, even in the heat, no warmth. Lying in bed at night or sitting in a chair at dawn, watching for elk or the cougar, she tried to discover what was not so much wrong, it was far from wrong, but what made this feeling. The answer came to her uncompromisingly. It was fear. The countryside was full of fear, and the fear, while it added to the grandeur and in a strange way to the beauty, denied peace to the observer. Danger informed it, it threatened while it smiled. Always something lay in wait for you round the corner, though it might be only a beautiful butterfly. It never slept, it never rested even under snow. It was alive.

Lily Johansson came round for coffee. She was a large, heavy woman with calloused hands who had had a hard life. Six children had been born to her, two husbands had died. She was alone, struggling to make a living from hiring out horses, from a dozen cows and turkeys. Every morning she got up at dawn, not because she had so much to do but because she couldn't sleep after dawn. The cougar, passing the night high up in the mountains, came down many mornings past Lily's fence to hunt along the green valley. It might be days before she came back to her mountain hideout but she would come back, and next morning lope down the rocky path between the asters and the Indian paintbrush past Lily's fence.

'Why do you call it "she"?' Nora asked. Was this an unlikely statement of feminist principles?

Lily smiled. 'I guess on account of knowing she's a mother. There was weeks went by when I never saw her, and then one morning she comes down the trail and she's two young ones with her. Real pretty kittens they was.'

'Do you ever speak to her?'

'Me? I'm scared of her. She'd kill me as soon as look at me. Sometimes I says to her, "Catamount, catamount", but she don't pay me no attention. You want to see her, you come down and stop over and maybe we'll see her in the morning.'

Nora went a week later. They sat together in the evening, the two old widows, drinking Lily's root beer, and talking of their dead husbands. Nora slept in a tiny bedroom, with linen sheets on the narrow bed and a picture on the wall of (appropriately) Daniel in the lion's den. At dawn Lily came in with a mug of tea and told her to get up, put on her 'robe' and they'd watch.

The eastern sky was black with stripes of red between the mountains. The hidden sun had coloured the snow on the peaks rosy pink. All the land lay still. Along the path where the cougar passed the flowers were still closed up for the night.

'What makes her come?' Nora whispered. 'Does she see the

dawn or feel it? What makes her get up from her bed and stretch, and maybe wash her paws and her face, and set off?'

'Are you asking me? I don't know. Who does? It's a mystery.'

'I wish we knew.'

'Catamount, catamount,' said Lily. 'Come, come, catamount.'

But the cougar didn't come. The sun rose, a magnificent spectacle, almost enough to bring tears to your eyes, Nora thought, all that purple and rose and orange and gold, all those miles and miles of serene blue. She had coffee and bread and blueberry jam with Lily and then she went back to Elk Valley Ranch.

'One day I'll see her,' she said to herself as she stroked the sheepdog and went to let herself in by the yard door.

But would she? She had almost made up her mind not to come back next year. This was young people's country and she was getting too old for it. It was for climbers and skiers and mountain bikers, it was for those who could withstand the cold and enjoy the heat. Sometimes when she stood in the sun, its power frightened her, it was too strong for human beings. When rain fell it was a wall of water, a cascade, a torrent, and it might drown her. Snakes lay curled up in the long grass and spiders were poisonous. If anything could be too beautiful for human beings to bear, this was. Looking at it for long made her heart ache, filled her with strange undefined longings. At home once more in the mild and gentle English countryside, she looked at her Audubon and thought how this drawing of the cougar symbolised for her all that landscape, all that vast green and gold space, yet she had never seen it in the flesh, the bones, the sleek tawny skin.

Two years passed before she went back. It would be the last time. Chuck was ill and Elk Valley was no place for an old, sick man. He and Carrie were moving to an apartment in Denver. They no longer walked in the hills or skied on the slopes or ate barbecue on the bluff behind the house. Chuck's heart was bad and Carrie had arthritis. Nora, who had always slept soundly at Elk Valley Ranch, now found that sleep eluded her; she lay awake for hours with the curtains drawn back, gazing at the black velvet starry sky and listening to the baying of the coyotes at the mountain's foot. Sleepless, she began getting up earlier and earlier, and on the second morning, tiptoeing to the kitchen, she found that Carrie got up early too. They sat together, drinking coffee and watching the dawn.

The night of the storm she slept and awoke, and slept till the thunder woke her at four. The storm was like nothing she had ever known and she, who had never been frightened by thunder and lightning, was afraid now. The lightning lit the room with searchlight brilliance and while it lingered, dimming and brightening, for a moment too bright to look at, the thunder rolled and cracked as if the mountains themselves moved and split. Into the ensuing silence the rain broke. If you were out in it, you couldn't defend yourself against it, it would beat you to the ground.

Carrie's calling fetched her out of her room. No lights were on. Carrie was feeling her way about in the dark.

'What is it?'

'Chuck's sick,' Carrie said. 'I mean, very sick. He's lying in bed on his back with his mouth all drawn down to one side and when he speaks his voice isn't like his voice, it's slurred; he can't form the words.'

'How do you phone the emergency services? I'll do it.'

'Nora, you can't. I've tried calling them. The phone's down. Why do you think I've no lights on? The power's gone.'

'What shall we do? I don't suppose you want to leave him but I could do something.'

'Not in this rain,' Carrie said. 'When it stops, could you take the Land Cruiser and drive into Hogan?'

Then Nora had to admit she had never learned to drive. They both went to look at Chuck. He seemed to be asleep, breathing noisily through his crooked mouth. A crash from somewhere overhead drove the women into each other's arms, to cling together.

'I'm going to make coffee,' Carrie said.

They drank it, sitting near the window, watching the lightning recede, leap into the mountains. Nora said, 'The rain's stopping. Look at the sky.'

The black clouds were streaming apart to show the dawn. A pale, tender sky, neither blue nor pink but halfway between, revealed itself as the banks of cumulus and the streaks of cirrus poured away over the mountain peak into the east. The rain lifted like a blind rolled up. One moment it was a cascade, the next it was gone, and the coming light showed gleaming pools of water and grass that glittered and sparkled.

'Try the phone again,' Nora said.

'It's dead,' said Carrie and, realising what she'd said, shivered.

'Do you think Lily's phone would be working? I could go down there and see. If her phone's down too, maybe she'd drive me into Hogan.'

'Please, Nora, would you? I can't leave him.'

The air was so fresh, it made her dizzy. It made her think how seldom most people ever breathe such air as this or know what it is, but that once the whole world's atmosphere was like this, as pure and as clean. The sun was rising, a red ball in a sea of pale lilac, and while on the jagged horizon black clouds still massed, the huge deep bowl of sky was scattered over with pink and golden cirrus feathers. Soon the sun would be hot and the land and air as dry as a desert.

She made her way down the hairpin bends of the mountain road, aware of how poor a walker she had become. An ache spread from her thighs into her hips, particularly on the right side, so that in order to make any progress she was forced to limp, shifting her weight on to the left. But she was near Lily Johansson's house now. Lily's two horses stood placidly by the gate into the field.

Then, suddenly, they wheeled round and cantered away down the meadow as if the sight of her had frightened them. She said aloud, 'What's wrong? What's happened?'

As if in answer, the animal came out of the flowery path on to the surface of the road. She was the size of an African lioness, so splendidly loose-limbed and in control of her long fluid body that she seemed to flow from the grass and the asters and the pink geraniums. On the road she stopped and turned her head. Nora could see her amber eyes and the faint quiver of her golden cheeks. She forgot about making herself tall, putting her hands high above her head, advancing menacingly. She was powerless, gripped by the beauty of this creature, this cougar she had longed for. And she was terribly afraid.

'Catamount, catamount,' she whispered, but no voice came.

The cougar dropped on to her belly, a quivering cat flexing her muscles, as she prepared to spring.

Walter's Leg

While he was telling the story about his mother taking him to the barber's, the pain in Walter's leg started again. A shooting pain – appropriate, that – and he knew very well what caused it. He shifted Andrew on to his other knee.

The story was about how his mother and he, on the way to get his hair cut, stopped on the corner of the High Street and Green Lanes to talk to a friend who had just come out of the fishmonger's. His mother was a talkative lady who enjoyed a gossip. The friend was like-minded. They took very little notice of Walter. He disengaged his hand from his mother's, walked off on his own down Green Lanes and into Church Road, found the barber's, produced sixpence from his pocket and had his hair cut. After that he walked back the way he had come. His mother and the friend were still talking. The five-year-old Walter slipped his little hand into his mother's and she looked down and smiled at him. His absence had gone unnoticed.

Emma and Andrew marvelled at this story. They had heard it before but they still marvelled. The world had changed so much, even they knew that at six and four. They were not even allowed to stand outside on the pavement on their own for two minutes, let alone go anywhere unaccompanied.

'Tell another,' said Emma.

As she spoke a sharp twinge ran up Walter's calf to the knee and pinched his thigh muscle. He reached down and rubbed his bony old leg.

'Shall I tell you how Haultrey shot me?'

'Shot you?' said Andrew. 'With a gun?'

'With an airgun. It was a long time ago.'

'Everything that's happened to you, Grandad,' said Emma, 'was a long time ago.'

'Very true, my sweetheart. This was sixty-five years ago. I was seven.'

'So it wasn't as long ago as when you had your hair cut,' said Emma, who already showed promise as an arithmetician.

Walter laughed. 'Haultrey was a boy I knew. He lived down our road. We used to play down by the river, a whole bunch of us. There were fish in the river then but I don't think any of us were fishing that day. We'd been climbing trees. You could get across the river by climbing willow trees, the branches stretched right across.

'And then one of us saw a kingfisher, a little tiny bright-blue bird it was, the colour of a peacock, and Haultrey said he was going to shoot it. I knew that would be wrong, even then I knew. Maybe we all did except Haultrey. He had an airgun, he showed it to us. I clapped my hands and the kingfisher flew away. All the birds went, we'd frightened them away with all the racket we were making. I had a friend called William Robbins, we called him Bill, he was my best friend, and he said to Haultrey that he'd bet he couldn't shoot anything, not aim at it and shoot it. Well, Haultrey wasn't having that and he said, yes, he could. He pointed to a stone sticking up out of the water and said he'd hit that. He didn't, though. He shot me.'

'Wow,' said Andrew.

'But he didn't mean to, Grandad,' said Emma. 'He didn't do it on purpose.'

'No, I don't suppose he did but it hurt all the same. The shot went into my leg, into the calf, just below my right knee. Bill Robbins went off to my house, he ran as fast as he could, he was a very good runner, the best in the school, and he fetched my dad and my dad took me to the doctor.'

'And did the doctor dig the bullet out?'

'A pellet, not a bullet. No, he didn't dig it out.' Walter rubbed his leg, just below the right knee. 'As a matter of fact, it's still there.'

'It's still *there?*'

Emma got off the arm of the chair and Andrew got off Walter's lap, and both children stood contemplating his right leg in its grey flannel trouser leg and grey-and-white Argyll pattern sock. Walter pulled up the trouser leg to the knee. There was nothing to be seen.

'If you like,' said Walter, 'I'll show you a photograph of the inside of my leg next time you come to my house.'

The suggestion was greeted with rapture. They wanted 'next time' to be now but were told by their mother that they would have to wait till Thursday. Walter was glad he'd come in the car. He wouldn't have fancied walking home, not with this pain. Perhaps he'd better go back to his GP, get a second opinion, ask to be sent to a – what would it be called? – an orthopaedic surgeon, presumably. Andrew, surely, had had the right idea when he asked if the doctor had dug the pellet out of his leg. Out of the mouths of babes and sucklings, thought old-fashioned Walter, hast thou ordained strength. It was hard to understand why the doctor hadn't dug it out sixty-five years ago, but in those days, so long as something wasn't life-threatening, they tended to leave well – or ill – alone. Ten years ago the specialist merely said he doubted if it was the pellet causing the pain, it was more likely arthritis. Walter must accept that he wasn't as young as he used to be.

Back home, searching through his desk drawers for the X-rays, Walter thought about something else Andrew had said. No, not Andrew, Emma. She'd said Haultrey hadn't done it on purpose and he'd said he didn't suppose he had. Now he wasn't so sure. For the first time in sixty-five years he recreated in his mind the expression on Haultrey's face that summer's evening when he boasted he could hit the stone.

Bill Robbins was sitting on the river bank, two other boys whose names he had forgotten were up the willow tree, while he, Walter, was down by the water's edge, looking up at the kingfisher, and Haultrey was higher up with his airgun. The sun had been low in a pale-blue July sky. Walter had clapped his hands then and when the kingfisher flew away, turned his head to look at Haultrey. And Haultrey's expression had been resentful and revengeful, too, because Walter had scared the bird away. That was when he started boasting about hitting the stone. So perhaps he had meant to shoot him, shot him in the leg because he'd been baulked of his desire. I didn't think of that at the time, though, Walter thought. I took it for an accident and so did everyone else.

'I'm imagining things,' he said aloud, and he laid the X-rays on top of the desk ready to show them to Emma and Andrew. Their mother brought the children along after school on Thursday. The pictures were admired and a repetition of the story demanded. In telling it, Walter said nothing about the look on Haultrey's face.

'You forgot the bit about Bill running to your house and being the best runner in the school,' said Emma.

'So I did but now you've put it in yourself.'

'What was his other name, Grandad? Haultrey what?'

'It must have been a case of what Haultrey,' said Walter and he thought, as he often did, of how times had changed. It would be incomprehensible to these children that one might have known someone only by his surname. 'I don't know what he was called. I can't remember.'

The children suggested names. In his childhood the ones they knew would have been unheard-of (Scott, Ross, Damian, Liam, Seth) or, strangely enough, too old-fashioned for popular use (Joshua, Simon, Jack, George). He put up some ideas himself, appropriate names for the time (Kenneth, Robert, Alan, Ronald) but none of them was right. He'd know Haultrey's name when he heard it.

His daughter Barbara was looking at the X-rays. 'You'll have to go back to the doctor with that leg, Dad.'

'It does give me jip.' Walter realised he'd used an expression that was out of date even when he was a boy. It was a favourite of his own father's. 'It does give me jip,' he said again.

'See if they can find you a different consultant. They must be able to do something.'

When Barbara and the children had gone he looked Haultrey up in the phone book. The chances were that Haultrey wouldn't be there, not in the same place after sixty-five years, and he wasn't. No Haultreys were in it. Walter's leg began to ache dreadfully. He tried massaging it with some stuff he'd bought when he'd pulled a muscle in his back. It heated the skin but did nothing for the pain. He tried to remember Haultrey's first name. It wasn't Henry, was it? No, Henry was old-fashioned in the twenties and not revived till the eighties. David? It was a possibility but Haultrey hadn't been called David.

Bill Robbins had known Haultrey a lot better than he had. The Haultreys and the Robbinses had lived next door but one to each other. Bill was dead, he'd died ten years before, but up until his death he and Walter had remained friends, played golf together, been fellow members of the Rotary Club, and Walter still kept in touch with Bill's son. He phoned John Robbins.

'How are you, Walter?'

'I'm fine but for a spot of arthritis in my leg.'

'We're none of us getting any younger.' This was generous from a man of forty-two.

'Tell me something. D'you remember those people called Haultrey who lived near your grandparents?'

'Vaguely. My gran would.'

'She's still alive?'

'She's only ninety-six, Walter. That's nothing in our family barring my poor dad.'

John Robbins said it would be nice to see him and to come over for a meal and Walter said thanks very much, he'd like to. Old Mrs Robbins was in the phone book, in the same house she'd lived in since she got married seventy-three years before. She answered the phone in a brisk, spry voice. Certainly she remembered the Haultreys, though they'd been gone since 1968, and she particularly remembered the boy with his airgun. He'd taken a pot-shot at her cat but he'd missed.

'Lucky for the cat.' Walter rubbed his leg.

'Lucky for Harold,' said Mrs Robbins grimly.

'That was his name, Harold,' said Walter.

'Of course it was. Harold Haultrey. He disappeared in the war.'

'Disappeared?'

'I mean he never came back here and I wasn't sorry. He was in the army, never saw active service, of course not. He was in a camp down in the West Country somewhere for the duration, took up with a farmer's daughter, married her and stopped there. I reckon he thought he'd come in for the farm and maybe he has. Why don't you ever come and see me, Walter? You come over for a meal and I'll cook you steak and chips, you were always partial to that.'

Walter said he would once he'd had his leg seen to. He got an appointment with an orthopaedic surgeon, a different one, who looked at the new X-rays and said Walter had arthritis. *Everyone* of Walter's age had arthritis somewhere. The children liked the new X-rays and Emma said they were an improvement on the old ones. Andrew asked for one of them to put on his bedroom wall along with a magazine cut-out of the Spice Girls and his *Lion King* poster.

'You ought to get a second opinion on that leg, Dad,' said Barbara.

'It would be a third opinion by now, wouldn't it?'

'Tell about Haultrey, Grandad,' said Andrew.

So Walter told it all over again, this time adding Haultrey's

Christian name. 'Harold Haultrey pointed at a stone in the water and said he'd shoot that, but he shot me.'

'And Bill Robbins, who was the fastest runner in the whole school, ran to your house and fetched your dad,' said Emma. 'But Harold didn't mean to do it, he didn't mean to hurt you, did he?'

'Who knows?' said Walter. 'It was a long time ago.'

They were all going away on holiday together, Barbara and her husband Ian and the children and Walter. It was a custom they'd established after Walter's wife died five years before. If he'd been completely honest, he'd have preferred not to go. He didn't much like the seaside or the food in the hotel and he was embarrassed about exposing his skinny old body in the swimming pool. And he suspected that if they were completely honest – perhaps they were, secretly, when alone together – Barbara and Ian would have preferred not to have him with them. The children liked him there, he was pretty sure of that, and that was why he went.

The night before they left he went round to old Mrs Robbins's. John was there and John's wife, and they all ate steak and chips and tiramisu, which Mrs Robbins had become addicted to in extreme old age. They all asked about Walter's leg and he had to tell them nothing could be done. A discussion followed on how different things would be these days if a child of seven had been shot in the leg by another child. It would have got into the papers and Walter would have had counselling. Haultrey would have had counselling too, probably.

Driving down to Sidmouth with Emma beside him, trying to keep in convoy with Ian and Barbara and Andrew in the car ahead, Walter asked himself if Haultrey had ever said he was sorry. He hadn't. There had been no opportunity, for Walter was sure he'd never seen Haultrey again. Suddenly he thought of something. Ever since the pain in his leg started he'd thought about Haultrey every single day. He was becoming obsessed with Haultrey.

'I'm bored, Grandad,' said Emma. 'Tell me a story.'

Not Haultrey. Not the visit to the barber, which for some reason reminded him of Haultrey. 'I'll tell you about our dog Pip who stole a string of sausages from the butcher's and once bit the postman's hand when he put it through the letter box.'

Another world, it was. Sausages no longer came in strings and supermarkets were more common than butchers. These days the postman would have had counselling and a tetanus injection, and Pip would have been threatened with destruction, only his parents would have fought the magistrates' decision and taken it to the High Court, and Pip's picture would have been in the papers. Walter was tired by the time they got to Sidmouth while Emma was as fresh as a daisy and raring to go. He had related the entire history of his childhood to her, or as much as he could recall, several times over.

His leg ached. He still thought exercise better for him than rest. While the others went down to the beach, he took a walk along the seafront and through streets of Georgian houses. He hardly knew what made him glance at the brass plate on one of the pillars flanking a front door, perhaps the brilliant polish on it caught the sun, but he did look and there he read: *Jenkins, Haultrey, Hall, Solicitors and Commissioners for Oaths*. It couldn't be his Haultrey, could it? Harold Haultrey as a solicitor was a laughable thought.

After dinner and a drink in the bar he went early to his room. Leave the young ones alone for a bit. He looked for a telephone directory and finally found one inside the wardrobe behind a spare blanket. Jenkins, Haultrey, Hall were there and so was Haultrey, A. P. at an address in the town. Under this appeared: Haultrey, H., Mingle Valley Farm, Harcombe. That was him all right. That was Harold Haultrey. The solicitor with the initials A. P. would be his son. Why don't I phone him, thought Walter, lying in bed, conjuring up pictures in the dark, why don't I phone him in the morning and ask him over for a drink? Meeting him will take him off my mind. I bet if I had counselling I'd be told to meet him. Confront him, that would be the word.

An answering machine was what he got. Of course, the voice wasn't recognisable. Not after all these years. It didn't say it was Harold Haultrey but that this was the Haultrey Jersey Herd and to leave a message after the tone. Walter tried again at midday and again at two. After that they all went to Lyme Regis and he had to leave it.

When he got back he expected the message light on his phone to be on but there was nothing. And nothing next day. Haultrey had chosen not to get in touch. Briefly, Walter thought of phoning the son, the solicitor, but dismissed the idea. If Haultrey didn't want to see him he certainly didn't want to see Haultrey. That evening Walter sat with the children while Ian and Barbara went out to dinner and on the following afternoon, because it was raining, they all went to the cinema and saw *The Hunchback of Notre-Dame*.

On these holidays Walter always behaved as tactfully as he could, doing his share of looking after the children and sometimes more than his share, but also taking care not to be intrusive. So it was his policy, on at least one occasion, to take himself off for the day. This time he had arranged to visit a cousin who lived in Honiton. Hearing he was coming to Sidmouth, the cousin had invited him to lunch.

On the way back, approaching Sidbury, he noticed a sign to Harcombe. Why did that ring a bell? Of course. Harcombe was where Haultrey lived, he and his Jersey herd. Walter had taken the Harcombe turning almost before he knew what he was doing. In the circumstances it would be ridiculous to be so near and not go to Mingle Valley Farm, an omission he might regret for the rest of his life.

Beautiful countryside, green woods, dark-red earth where the harvested fields had already been ploughed, a sparkling river that splashed over stones. He saw the cattle before he saw the house, cream-coloured elegant beasts, bony and mournful-eyed, hock-deep in the lush grass. Hundreds of them – well, scores. If he said 'scores' to Emma and Andrew they wouldn't know what he was talking about. On a gatepost, lettered in black on a white board, he read: *Mingle Valley Farm, the Haultrey Jersey Herd* and under that, *Trespassers Will Be Prosecuted*.

He left the car. Beyond the gate was only a path, winding away between flowery grass verges and tall trees. A pheasant made him jump, uttering its harsh, rattling cry and taking off on clumsy wings. The path took a turn to the left, the woodland ended abruptly, and there ahead of him stretched lawns and beyond them, the house. It was a sprawling half-timbered place, very picturesque, with diamond-paned windows. On the lawn rabbits cropped the grass.

He had counted fifteen rabbits when a man came out from behind the house. Even from this distance Walter could tell he was an old man. He could see, too, that this old man was carrying a gun. Six decades fell away and instead of a green Devon lawn, Walter saw a sluggish river on the outskirts of London, willow trees, a kingfisher. He did as he had done then and clapped his hands.

The rabbits scattered. Walter heard the sharp crack of the shotgun, expected to see a rabbit fall but fell himself instead. Rolled over as pain stabbed his leg. It was his left leg this time but the pain was much the same as it had been when he was seven. He sat up, groaning, blood all over his trousers. A man was standing over him with a mobile phone in one hand and the gun bent over in the middle – broken, did they call it? – in the other. Walter would have known that resentful glare anywhere, even after sixty-five years.

In the hospital they took the shot out and for good measure – 'might as well while you're in here' – extracted the pellet from his right leg. With luck, the doctor said, he'd be as good as new.

'Remember we're none of us getting any younger.'

'Really?' said Walter. 'I thought I was.'

Haultrey didn't come to see him in hospital. He told Barbara her father was lucky not to have been prosecuted for trespass.

The Professional

The girls had the best of it. Dressed in models from the Designer Room, they disposed themselves in one of the windows that fronted on to the High Street, one in a hammock from *House and Garden*, another in an armchair from *Beautiful Interiors*, holding best-sellers from the book department and pretending to read them. Small crowds gathered and stared at them, as if they were caged exotic animals.

The boys had seats inside, between Men's Leisurewear and Perfumery, facing the escalators. Anyone coming down the escalators was obliged to look straight at them. They sat surrounded by the materials of their craft, ten pairs of brushes each, thirty different kinds of polishes and creams and sprays, innumerable soft cloths, all of different colours, all used just the once, then discarded. Customers had comfortable leather chairs to sit in and padded leather footrests for their feet. A big notice said: *Let our professionals clean your shoes to an unrivalled high standard. £2.50.*

It was a lot harder work than what the girls did. Nigel resented the girls, lounging about doing bugger all, getting to wear the sort of kit they'd never afford in their wildest dreams. But Ross pointed out to him that the boys would do better out of it in the long run. After all, it was a load of rubbish Karen and Fiona thinking this was the first step to a modelling career. As if it was

Paris (or even London), as if they were on the catwalk instead of in a department store window in a city that had one of the highest rates of unemployment in the country.

Besides, he and Nigel were trained. They'd both had two weeks' intensive training. When he had been at his pitch at the foot of the escalator a week, Ross's parents came in to see how he was getting on. Ross hadn't much liked that, it was embarrassing, especially as his father thought he could get his shoes cleaned for free. But his mother understood.

'Professional,' she said, nudging his father, 'you see that. That's what it says, "our professionals". You always wanted him to get some real training and now he's got it. For a profession.'

The W. S. Marsh Partnership got a subsidy for taking them on. Sixty pounds a week per head, someone had told him. And a lot of praise and a framed certificate from the Chamber of Commerce for their 'distinguished contribution to alleviating youth unemployment'. The certificate hung up on the wall at the entrance to Men's Leisurewear, which Ross privately thought rather too close for comfort. Still, it was a job and a job for which he was trained. He was twenty and it was the first employment he'd had since he left school four years before.

At school, when he was young and didn't know any better, he was ambitious. He thought he could be an airline pilot or something in the media.

'Yeah, or a brain surgeon,' said Nigel.

But of course it turned out that any one of those was as unlikely as the others. His aims were lower now, but at least he could have aims. The job with the W. S. Marsh Partnership had made that possible. He'd set his sights on the footwear trade. Manager of a shoe shop. How to get there he didn't know because he didn't know how managers of shoe shops got started but still he thought he had set his foot on to the lowest rung of the ladder. While he cleaned shoes he imagined himself fitting on shoes, or better still, calling to an assistant to serve this customer or that. In these daydreams of his the assistant was always Karen, obliged to do his bidding, no longer favouring him with disdainful glances as he walked by her window on his way to lunch. Karen, though, not Fiona. Fiona sometimes lifted her head and smiled.

The customers – Nigel called them 'punters' – mostly treated him as if he didn't exist. Once they'd paid, that is, and said what they wanted done. But no, that wasn't quite right. Not as if he didn't exist, more as if he was a machine. They sat down, put their feet on the footrest and nodded at him. They kept their shoes on. Women always took their shoes off, passed him the shoes and left their slender and delicate stockinged feet dangling. They talked to him, mostly about shoes, but they talked. The women were nicer than the men.

'Yeah, well, you know what they're after, don't you?' said Nigel.

It was a good idea, but Ross didn't think it was true. If he had asked any of those pretty women who showed off their legs in front of him what they were doing that evening or did they fancy a movie, he'd have expected to get his face smacked. Or be reported. Be reported and probably sacked. The floor manager disliked them anyway. He was known to disapprove of anything that seemed designed to waylay or entrap customers. No assistants stood about in Perfumery spraying passing customers with scent. Mr Costello wouldn't allow it. He even discouraged assistants from asking customers if they might help them. He believed in the total freedom of everyone who entered W. S. Marsh's doors. Short of shoplifting, that is.

Every morning, when Ross and Nigel took up their position facing the escalators ten minutes before the store opened at nine, Mr Costello arrived to move them back against the wall, to try to reduce their allotted space and to examine both of them closely, checking that they were properly dressed, that their hair was short enough and their hands clean. Mr Costello himself was a model of elegance, six feet tall, slender, strongly resembling Linford Christie, if you could imagine Linford Christie dressed in a black suit, ice-white shirt and satin tie. When he spoke he usually extended one long – preternaturally long – well-manicured sepia forefinger in either Nigel's direction or Ross's and wagged it as if beating time to music.

'You do not speak to the customers until they speak to you. You do not say "hi", you do not say "cheers".' Here the unsmiling glance was turned on Nigel and the finger wagged. ' "Cheers" is no substitute for "thank you". You do not attract attention to yourselves. Above all, you do not catch customers' eyes or seem to be trying to attract their attention. Customers of the W. S. Marsh Partnership must be free to pay *untrammelled* visits to this store.'

Mr Costello had a degree in business studies and 'untrammelled' was one of his favourite words. Neither Ross nor Nigel knew what it meant. But they both understood that Mr Costello would prefer them not to be there. He would have liked an excuse to be rid of them. Once or twice he had been heard to say that no one paid an employer to take him on when he was twenty, he had been obliged to take an evening job to make ends meet at college. Any little thing would be an excuse, Ross sometimes thought, any stepping out of line in the presence of a customer.

But they had few customers. After those early days when he and Nigel had been a novelty, business ceased to boom. Having your shoes cleaned at W. S. Marsh was expensive. Out in the High Street you could get it done for a pound and guests in the hotels used the electric shoe polisher for nothing. Mostly it was the regulars who came to them, businessmen from the big office blocks, women who had nothing to do but go shopping and had time on their hands. This worried Ross, especially as in Mr Costello's opinion, sixty pounds a week or no sixty pounds, no commercial concern was going to keep them on in idleness.

'It's not as if you are an ornament to the place,' he said with an unpleasant smile.

And they were often idle. After the half-dozen who came first thing in the morning would come a lull until, one by one and infrequently, the women appeared. It was typical of the women to stand and look at them, to consider, maybe discuss the matter with a companion, smile at them and pass on into Perfumery.

Ross sat on his stool, gazing up the escalator. If you did what Nigel did and stared at the customers at ground level, if you happened to eye the girls' legs, you got a reprimand. Mr Costello walked round the ground floor all day, passing the foot of the escalators once an hour, observing everything with his Black and Decker drill eyes. When there was nothing to do Ross watched the people going up the escalator on the right-hand side and coming down the escalator on the left. And he watched them with his face fixed into a polite expression, careful to catch no eyes.

Karen and Fiona seldom came to get their shoes cleaned. After all, they only wore their own shoes to come in and go home in. But sometimes, on wet days, at lunchtime, one or other of them would present herself to Ross to have a pair of damp or muddy loafers polished. They didn't like the way Nigel looked at them and both preferred Ross.

Karen didn't open her mouth while he cleaned her suede boots. Her eyes roved round the store as if she was expecting to see someone she knew. Fiona talked, but still he couldn't believe his luck when, extending a slim foot and handing him a green leather brogue, she asked him if he'd like to go for a drink on the way home. He nodded, he couldn't speak, but looked deep into her large turquoise eyes. Then she went, her shoes sparkling, turning once to flash him a smile. Nigel pretended he hadn't heard but a flush turned his face a mottled red. Ross, his heart thudding, gazed away to where he always gazed, the ascending and descending escalators.

He was getting somewhere. He was trained, a professional. It could only lead onwards and to better things. Fiona, of the kingfisher eyes and the cobweb-fine feet, was going to have a drink with him. He gazed upwards, dreaming, seeing his future as the escalator that ceaselessly and endlessly climbed. Then he saw something else.

At the top of the escalator stood a woman. She was holding on to the rail and looking back over one shoulder towards the man who came up behind her. Ross recognised the man, he had once or twice cleaned his shoes and actually been talked to and smiled at and thanked. And once he had seen him outside, giving a passing glance at Fiona's and Karen's window. He was about forty but the woman was older, a thin, frail woman in a very short skirt that showed most of her long bony legs. She had bright hair, the colour of the yellow hammock Fiona reclined in. As she turned her head to look down the escalator, as she stepped on to it, Ross saw the man put out one hand and give her a hard push in the middle of her back.

Everything happened very fast. The woman fell with a loud protracted scream. She fell forward, just like someone diving into deep water, but it wasn't water, it was moving metal, and halfway down as her head caught against one of the steps she rolled over in a perfect somersault. All the time she was screaming.

The man behind her was shouting as he ran down. People at the top of the escalator shrank back from it as the man went down alone. Ross and Nigel had sprung to their feet. The screaming had fetched assistants and customers running from Perfumery and Men's Leisurewear but it had stopped. It had split the air as an earthquake splits rock but now it had stopped and for a moment there was utter silence.

In that moment Ross saw her, lying spread at the foot of the escalator. A funny thought came to him, that he'd never seen anyone look so relaxed. Then he understood she looked relaxed because she was dead. He made a sound, a kind of whimper. He could no longer see her, she was surrounded by people, but he could see the man who had pushed her, he was so tall, he towered above everyone, even above Mr Costello.

Nigel said, 'Did you see her shoes? Five-inch heels, at least five-inch. She must have caught her heel.'

'She didn't catch her heel,' Ross said.

A doctor had appeared. There was always a doctor out shopping, which was the reason the National Health Service was in such a mess, Ross's mother said. The main doors burst open and an ambulance crew came running in. Mr Costello cleared a path among the onlookers to let them through and then he tried to get people back to work or shopping or whatever they'd been doing. But before he had got very far a voice came over the public address system telling customers the south escalators would be out of service for the day and Perfumery and Men's Leisurewear closed.

'What d'you mean, she didn't catch her heel?' said Nigel.

Ross ought to have said then. This was his first chance to tell. He nearly did. He nearly told Nigel what he'd seen. But then he got separated from Nigel by the ambulance men carrying the woman out on a stretcher, pushing Nigel to one side and him to the other, the tall man walking behind them, his face white, his head bowed.

Mr Costello came up to them. 'I suppose you thought you could skive off for the rest of the day,' he said. 'Sorry to disappoint you. We're making you a new pitch upstairs in Ladies' Shoes.'

This was his second chance. Mr Costello stood there while they packed their materials into the cases. Nigel carried the notice board that said *Let our professionals clean your shoes to an unrivalled high standard. £2.50.* The escalators had stopped running, so they followed Mr Costello to the lifts, and Ross pressed the button and they waited. Now was the time to tell Mr Costello what he had seen. He should tell Mr Costello and through Mr Costello the top management and through them, or maybe before they were brought into it, the police.

'I saw the man that was with her push her down the escalator.'

He didn't say it. The lift came and took them up to the second floor. The departmental manager, a woman, showed them their new pitch and they laid out their things. No one had their shoes cleaned but a girl Nigel knew who worked in the stockroom came over and told them that the woman who fell down the escalator was a Mrs Russell, the tall man with her was her husband and they had a big house up on The Mount, which was the best part where all the nobs lived. They were good customers of the Marsh Partnership, they were often in the store, Mrs Russell had an account there and a Marsh Partnership Customer Card. Ross went off for his lunch and when he returned Nigel went off for his, coming back to add more details that he had picked up in the cafeteria. Mr and Mrs Russell had only been married a year, they were devoted to each other.

'Mr Russell is devastated,' said Nigel. 'They're keeping him under sedation.'

When the departmental manager came along to see how they were getting on, Ross knew that this was his third chance and perhaps his last. She told them everything would be back to normal next day, they'd be back at the foot of the escalator between Perfumery and Men's Leisurewear, and now he should tell her what he had seen. But he didn't and he wouldn't. He knew that now because he saw very clearly what would happen if he told.

He would attract attention to himself. In fact, it was hard to think of any way to attract *more* attention to himself. He would have to describe what he had seen, identify Mr Russell – a customer, a good customer! – say he had seen Mr Russell put his hand in the middle of his wife's back and push her down the escalator. He alone had seen it. Not Nigel, not the other customers, but himself alone. They wouldn't believe him, he'd get the sack. He had had this job just six weeks and he would get the sack.

So he wouldn't tell. At least, he wouldn't tell Mr Costello. There was only one person he really wanted to tell and that was Fiona, but when they met and had their drink and talked and had another drink and she said she'd see him again the next night, he didn't say anything about Mr Russell. He didn't want to spoil things, have her think he was a nut or maybe a liar. Once he was at home he thought about telling his mother. Not his father, his father would just get on to the police, but his mother who sometimes had glimmerings of understanding. But she had gone to bed and next morning he wasn't in the mood for talking about it.

Something strange had happened in the night. He was no longer quite sure of his facts. He had begun to doubt. Had he really seen that rich and powerful man, that tall middle-aged man, one of the few men who had ever talked to him while he had his shoes cleaned, had he really seen that man push his wife down the escalator? Was it reasonable? Was it *possible*? What motive could he have had? He was rich, he had only recently married, he was known for being devoted to his wife.

Ross tried to re-create the sight in his mind, to rewind the film, so to speak, and run it through once more. To stop it at that point and freeze the frame. With his eyes closed he attempted it. He could get Mrs Russell to the top of the escalator, he could turn her head round to look back at her approaching husband, he could turn her head once more towards the escalator, but then came a moment of darkness, of a blank screen, as had happened once or twice to their TV set when there was a power cut. His power cut lasted only ten seconds but when the electricity came on again it was to show Mrs Russell plunging forward and to transmit the terrible sound of her scream. The bit where Mr Russell had put his hand on her back and pushed her had vanished.

They were back that morning at the foot of the escalator. Things were normal, as if it had never happened. Ross could hardly believe his ears when Mr Costello came by and said he wanted to congratulate them, him and Nigel, for keeping their heads the day before, behaving politely, not attracting unnecessary attention to themselves. Nigel blushed at that but Ross smiled with pleasure and thanked Mr Costello.

Business picked up wonderfully from that day onwards. One memorable Wednesday afternoon there was actually a queue of customers waiting to have their shoes cleaned. The accident had been in all the papers and someone had got a photograph. Just as there is always a doctor on hand, so is there always someone with a camera. People wanted to have their shoes cleaned by the two professionals who had seen Mrs Russell fall down the stairs, who had been there when it was all happening.

Fall down the stairs, not get pushed down. The more Ross heard the term 'fall down' the more 'pushed down' faded from his consciousness. He hadn't seen anything, of course he hadn't, it had been a dream, a fantasy, a craving for excitement. He was very polite to the customers, he called them sir and madam with every breath, but he never talked about the accident beyond saying how unfortunate it was and what a tragedy. When they asked him directly he always said, 'I'm afraid I wasn't looking, madam, I was attending to a customer.'

Mr Costello overheard approvingly. Three months later, when there was a vacancy in Men's Shoes, he offered Ross the job. By that time Ross and Fiona were going steady, she had given up all ideas of modelling for hairdresser training and they had moved together into a studio flatlet. Karen had disappeared. Fiona had never known her well, she was a deep one, never talked about her personal life, and now she was gone and the window where they had both sat and pretended to read best-sellers from the book department had been given over to Armani for Men.

While in Men's Shoes, Ross managed to get into a day release scheme and took a business studies course at the metropolitan college. His mother was disappointed because he wasn't a professional any more but everyone else saw all this as a great step forward. And so it was, for two weeks before he and Fiona got engaged he was taken on as assistant manager at a shop in the precinct called The Great Boot Sale at twice the salary he was getting from the Marsh Partnership.

In all that time he had heard very little of Mr Russell beyond that he had let the house on The Mount and moved away. It was his mother who told Ross he was back and having his house done up, before moving into it with his new wife. 'It's a funny thing,' she said, 'but I've noticed it time and time again. A man who's been married to a woman a lot older than him will always marry a woman a lot younger than him the second time round. Now why is that?'

No one knew. Ross thought very little of it. He had long ago convinced himself that the whole escalator incident had been in his imagination, a kind of daydream, probably the result of the kind of videos he had been watching. And when he encountered Mr Russell in the High Street he wasn't surprised the man didn't recognise him. After all, it was a year ago.

But to see Karen walk past with her nose in the air did surprise him. She tucked her hand into Mr Russell's arm – the hand with the diamond ring on it and the wedding ring – and turned him round to look where she was looking, into the jeweller's window. Ross looked at their reflections in the glass and shivered.

The Beach Butler

The woman was thin and stringy, burnt dark brown, in a white bikini that was too brief. Her hair, which had stopped looking like hair long ago, was a pale dry fluff. She came out of the sea, out of the latest crashing breaker, waving her arms and crying, screaming of some kind of loss. Alison, in her solitary recliner, under her striped hood (hired at $6 a morning or $10 a whole day) watched her emerge, watched people crowd about her, heard complaints made in angry voices, but not what was said.

As always, the sky was a cloudless blue, the sea a deeper colour. The Pacific but not peaceable. It only looked calm. Not far from the shore a great swell would bulge out of the sea, rise to a crest and crash on whoever happened to be there at the time, in a cascade of overwhelming, stunning, irresistible water, so that you fell over before you knew what was happening. Just such a wave had crashed on the woman in the white bikini. When she had struggled to her feet she had found herself somehow damaged or bereft.

Alone, knowing nobody, Alison could see no one to ask. She put her head back on the pillow, adjusted her sunglasses, returned to her book. She had read no more than a paragraph when she heard his gentle voice asking her if there was anything she required. Could he get her anything?

When first she heard his – well, what? His title? – when first she heard he was called the beach butler it had made her laugh, she could hardly believe it. She thought of telling people at home and watching their faces. The beach butler. It conjured up a picture of an elderly man with a paunch wearing a white dinner jacket with striped trousers and pointed patent shoes like Hercule Poirot. Agustin wasn't like that. He was young, handsome, he was wary and polite, and he wore shorts and the white trainers. His T-shirts were always snow-white and immaculate, he must get through several a day. She wondered who washed them. A mother? A wife?

He stood there, smiling, holding the pad on which he wrote down orders. She couldn't really afford to order anything, she hadn't known the package didn't include drinks and midday meals and extras like this recliner and hood. On the other hand, she could hardly keep pretending she never wanted a drink. 'A Diet Coke then,' she said.

'Something to eat, ma'am?'

It must be close on lunchtime. 'Maybe some crisps.' She corrected herself. 'I mean, chips.'

Agustin wrote something on his pad. He spoke fairly good English but only, she suspected, when food was the subject. Still, she would try. 'What was wrong with the lady?'

'The lady?'

'The one who was screaming.'

'Ah. She lose her . . .' He resorted to miming, holding up his hands, making a ring with his fingers round his wrist. 'The ocean take her – these things.'

'Bracelet, do you mean? Rings?'

'All those. The ocean take. Bracelet, rings, these . . .' He put his hands to the lobes of his ears.

Alison shook her head, smiling. She had seen someone go into the sea wearing sunglasses and come out, having lost them to the tide. But jewellery . . . !

'One Diet Coke, one chips,' he said. 'Suite number, please?'

'Six-o-seven – I mean, six-zero-seven.'

She signed the chit. He passed on to the couple sitting in chairs under a striped umbrella. It was all couples here, couples or families. When they decided to come, she and Liz, they hadn't expected that. They'd expected young unattached people. Then Liz had got appendicitis and had to cancel and Alison had come alone, she'd paid, she couldn't afford not to come, and she'd even been excited at the prospect. Mostly Americans, the travel agent had said and she had imagined Tom Cruise lookalikes. American men were all tall and in the movies they were all handsome. On the long flight over she had speculated about meeting them. Well, about meeting one.

But there were no men. Or, rather, there were plenty of men of all ages, and they were tall enough and good-looking enough, but they were all married or with partners or girlfriends and most of them were fathers of families. Alison had never seen so many children all at once. The evenings were quiet, the place gradually becoming deserted, as all these parents disappeared into their suites – there were no rooms here, only suites – to be with their sleeping children. By ten the band stopped playing, for the children must be allowed to sleep, the restaurant staff brought the tables indoors, the bar closed.

She had walked down to the beach that first evening, expecting lights, people strolling, even a barbecue. It had been dark and silent, no one about but the beach butler, cleaning from the sand the day's litter, the drinks cans, the crisp bags and the cigarette butts.

He brought her Diet Coke and her crisps. He smiled at her, his teeth as white as his T-shirt. She had a sudden urge to engage him in conversation, to get him to sit in a chair beside her and talk to her, so as not to be alone. She thought of asking him if he had had his lunch, if he'd have a drink with her, but by the time the words were formulated he had passed on. He had gone up to the group where sat the woman who had screamed.

Alison had been taught by her mother and father and her swimming teacher at school that you must never go into sea or pool until two hours have elapsed after eating. But last week she had read in a magazine that this theory is now old hat, you may go swimming as soon as you like after eating. Besides, a packet of crisps was hardly a meal. She was very hot, it was the hottest time of the day.

Looking at herself in one of the many mirrors in her suite, she thought she looked as good in her black bikini as any woman there. Better than most. Certainly thinner, and she would get even thinner because she couldn't afford to eat much. It was just that so many on the beach were younger than she, even the ones with two or three children. Or they looked younger. When she thought like that panic rushed upon her, a seizure of panic that gripped her like physical pain. And the words which came with it were 'old' and 'poor'. She walked down to the water's edge. Showing herself off, hoping they were watching her. Then she walked quickly into the clear warm water.

The incoming wave broke at her feet. By the time the next one had swollen, reared up and collapsed in a roar of spray, she was out beyond its range. There were sharks but they didn't come within a thousand yards of the beach and she wasn't afraid. She swam, floated on the water, swam again. A man and a woman, both wearing sunglasses, swam out together, embraced, began a passionate kissing while they trod water. Alison looked away and up towards the hotel, anywhere but at them.

In the travel brochure the hotel had looked very different, more golden than red and the mountains behind it less stark. It hadn't looked like what it was, a brick-red building in a brick-red desert. The lawns around it weren't exactly artificial but they were composed of the kind of grass that never grew and so never had to be cut. Watering took place at night. No one knew where the water came from because there were no rivers or reservoirs and it never rained. Brilliantly coloured flowers, red, pink, purple, orange, hung from every balcony and the huge tubs were filled with hibiscus and bird of paradise. But outside the grounds the only thing that grew was cactus, some like swords and some like plates covered with prickles. And through the desert went the white road that came from the airport and must go on to somewhere else.

Alison let the swell carry her in, judged the pace of the waves, let one break ahead of her, then ran ahead through the shallows, just in time before the next one came. The couple who had been kissing had both lost their sunglasses. She saw them complaining and gesticulating to Agustin as if he were responsible for the strength of the sea.

The tide was going out. Four little boys and three girls began building a sandcastle where the sand was damp and firm. She didn't like them, they were a nuisance, the last thing she wanted was for them to talk to her or like her, but they made her think that if she didn't hurry up she would never have children. It would be too late, it was getting later every minute. She dried herself and took the used towel to drop it into the bin by the beach butler's pavilion. Agustin was handing out snorkelling equipment to the best-looking man on the beach and his beautiful girlfriend. Well, the best-looking man after Agustin.

He waved to her, said, 'Have a nice day, ma'am.'

The hours passed slowly. With Liz there it would have been very different, despite the lack of available men. When you have someone to talk to you can't think so much. Alison would have preferred not to keep thinking all the time but she couldn't help herself. She thought about being alone and about apparently being the only person in the hotel who was alone. She thought about what this holiday was costing, some of it already paid for, but not all.

When she had arrived they had asked for an imprint of her credit card and she had given it, she didn't know how to refuse. She imagined a picture of her pale-blue and grey credit card filling a computer screen and every drink she had and slice of pizza she ate and every towel she used and recliner she sat in and video she watched depositing a red spot on its pastel surface, until the whole card was filled up with scarlet. Until it burst or rang bells and the computer printed 'no, no, no' across the screen.

She lay down on the enormous bed and slept. The air-conditioning kept the temperature at the level of an average January day in England and she had to cover herself up with the thick quilt they called a comforter. It wasn't much comfort but was slippery and cold to the touch. Outside the sun blazed on to the balcony and flamed on the glass so that looking at the windows was impossible. Sleeping like this kept Alison from sleeping at night but there was nothing else to do. She woke in time to see the sunset. The sun seemed to sink into the sea or be swallowed up by it, like a red-hot iron plunged in water. She could almost hear it fizz. A little wind swayed the thin palm trees.

After dinner, pasta and salad and fruit salad and a glass of house wine, the cheapest things on the menu, after sitting by the pool with the coffee that was free – they endlessly refilled one's cup – she went down to the beach. She hardly knew why. Perhaps it was because at this time of the day the hotel became unbearable with everyone departing to their rooms, carrying exhausted children or hand in hand or arms round each other's waists, so surely off to make love it was indecent.

She made her way along the pale paths, under the palms, between the tubs of ghost-pale flowers, now drained of colour. Down the steps to the newly cleaned sand, the newly swept red rocks. Recliners and chairs were all stacked away, umbrellas furled, hoods folded up. It was warm and still, the air smelling of nothing, not even of salt. Down at the water's edge, in the pale moonlight, the beach butler was walking slowly along, pushing ahead of him something that looked from where she stood like a small vacuum cleaner.

She walked towards him. Not a vacuum cleaner, a metal detector. 'You're looking for the jewellery people lose,' she said.

He looked at her, smiled. 'We never find.' He put his hand into the pocket of his shorts. 'Find this only.'

Small change, most of it American, a handful of sandy nickels, dimes and quarters.

'Do you get to keep it?'

'This money? Of course. Who can say who has lost this money?'

'But jewellery, if you found that, would it be yours?'

He twitched off the detector. 'I finish now.' He seemed to consider, began to laugh.

From that laughter she suddenly understood so much, she was amazed at her own intuitive powers. His laughter, the tone of it, the incredulous note in it, told her his whole life; his poverty, the wonder of having this job, the value to him of five dollars in small change, his greed, his fear, his continuing amazement at the attitudes of these rich people. A lot to read into a laugh but she knew she had got it right. And at the same time she was overcome by a need for him that included pity and empathy and desire. She forgot about having to be careful, forgot that credit card. 'Is there any drink in the pavilion?'

The laughter had stopped. His head a little on one side, he was smiling at her. 'There is wine, yes. There is rum.'

'I'd like to buy you a drink. Can we do that?'

He nodded. She had supposed the pavilion was closed and he would have to unlock a door and roll up a shutter, but it was still open. It was open for the families who never came after six o'clock. He took two glasses down from a shelf.

'I don't want wine,' she said. 'I want a real drink.'

He poured tequila into their glasses and soda into hers. His he drank down at one gulp and poured himself a refill. 'Suite number, please,' he said.

It gave her a small unpleasant shock to be asked. 'Six-zero-seven,' she said, not daring to read what it cost, and signed the chit. He took it from her, touching her fingers with his fingers. She asked him where he lived.

'In the village. It is five minutes.'

'You have a car?'

He started laughing again. He came out of the pavilion carrying the tequila bottle. When he had pulled down the shutters and locked them and locked the door, he took her hand and said, 'Come.' She noticed he had stopped calling her ma'am. The hand that held hers went round her waist and pulled her closer to him. The path led up among the red rocks, under pine trees that looked black by night. Underfoot was pale dry sand. She had thought he would take her to the village but instead he pulled her down on to the sand in the deep shadows.

His kisses were perfunctory. He threw up her long skirt and pulled down her tights. It was all over in a few minutes. She put up her arms to hold him, expecting a real kiss now and perhaps a flattering word or two. He sat up and lit a cigarette. Although it was two years since she had smoked she would have liked one too, but she was afraid to ask him; he was so poor, he probably rationed his cigarettes.

'I go home now,' he said and he stubbed out the cigarette into the sand he had cleaned of other people's butts.

'Do you walk?'

He surprised her. 'I take the bus. In poor countries are always many buses.' He had learned that. She had a feeling he had said it many times before.

Why did she have to ask? She was half afraid of him now but his attraction for her was returning. 'Shall I see you again?'

'Of course. On the beach. Diet Coke and chips, right?' Again he began laughing. His sense of humour was not of a kind she had come across before. He turned to her and gave her a quick kiss on the cheek. 'Tomorrow night, sure. Here. Same time, same place.'

Not a very satisfactory encounter, she thought as she went back to the hotel. But it had been sex, the first for a long time, and he was handsome and sweet and funny. She was sure he would never do anything to hurt her and that night she slept better than she had since her arrival.

All mornings were the same here, all bright sunshine and mounting heat and cloudless sky. First she went to the pool. He shouldn't think she was running after him. But she had put on her new white swimming costume, the one that was no longer too tight, and after a while, with a towel tied round her sarong-fashion, she went down to the beach.

For a long time she didn't see him. The American girl and the Caribbean man were serving the food and drink. Alison was so late getting there that all the recliners and hoods had gone. She was provided with a chair and an umbrella, inadequate protection against the sun. Then she saw him, leaning out of the pavilion to hand someone a towel. He waved to her and smiled. At once she was elated and, leaving her towel on the chair, she ran down the beach and plunged into the sea.

Because she wasn't being careful, because she had forgotten everything but him and the hope that he would come and sit with her and have a drink with her, she came out without thinking of the mountain of water that pursued her, without any awareness that it was behind her. The great wave broke, felled her and roared on, knocking out her breath, drenching her hair. She tried to get a purchase with her hands, to dig into the sand and pull herself up before the next breaker came. Her eyes and mouth and ears were full of salt water. She pushed her fingers into the wet slippery sand and encountered something she thought at first was a shell. Clutching it, whatever it was, she managed to crawl out of the sea while the wave broke behind her and came rippling in, a harmless trickle.

By now she knew that what she held was no shell. Without looking at it she thrust it into the top of her swimming costume, between her breasts. She dried herself, dried her eyes that stung with salt, felt a raging thirst from the brine she had swallowed. No one had come to her aid, no one had walked down to the water's edge to ask if she was all right. Not even the beach butler. But he was here now beside her, smiling, carrying her Diet Coke and packet of crisps as if she had ordered them.

'Ocean smack you down? Too bad. I don't think you lose no jewels?'

She shook her head, nearly said, 'No, but I found some.' But now wasn't the time, not until she had had a good look. She drank her Diet Coke, took the crisps upstairs with her. In her bathroom, under the cold tap, she washed her find. The sight came back to her of Agustin encircling his wrist with his fingers when he told her of the white bikini woman's loss. This was surely her bracelet or some other rich woman's bracelet.

It was a good two inches wide, gold set with broad bands of diamonds. They flashed blindingly when the sun struck them. Alison examined its underside, found the assay mark, the proof the gold was 18 carat. The sea, the sand, the rocks, the salt, had damaged it not at all. It sparkled and gleamed as it must have done when first it lay on blue velvet in some Madison Avenue or Beverly Hills jeweller's shop.

She took a shower, washed her hair and blew it dry, put on a sundress. The bracelet lay on the coffee table in the living area of the suite, its diamonds blazing in the sun. She had better take it downstairs and hand it over to the management. The white bikini woman would be glad to have it back. No doubt, though, it was insured. Her husband would already have driven her to the city where the airport was (Ciudad something) and bought her another.

What was it worth? If those diamonds were real, an enormous sum. And surely no jeweller would set any but real diamonds in 18-carat gold? Alison was afraid to leave it in her suite. A safe was inside one of the cupboards. But suppose she put the bracelet into the safe and couldn't open it again? She put it into her white shoulder bag. The time was only just after three. She looked at the list of available videos, then, feeling reckless, at the room service menu. Having the bracelet – though of course she meant to hand it in – made her feel differently about that credit card. She picked up the phone, ordered a pina colada, a half bottle of wine, seafood salad, a double burger and french fries, and a video of *Shine*.

Eating so much didn't keep her from a big dinner four hours

later. She went to the most expensive of the hotel's three restaurants, drank more wine, ate smoked salmon, lobster thermidor, raspberry Pavlova. She wrote her suite number on the bill and signed it without even glancing at the amount. Under the tablecloth she opened her bag and looked at the gold and diamond bracelet. Taking it to the management now would be very awkward. They might be aware that she hadn't been to the beach since not long after lunchtime, they might want to know what she had been doing with the bracelet in the meantime. She made a decision. She wouldn't take it to the management, she would take it to Agustin.

The moon was bigger and brighter this evening, waxing from a sliver to a crescent. Not quite sober, for she had had a lot to drink, she walked down the winding path under the palms to the beach. This time he wasn't plying his metal detector but sitting on a pile of folded beach chairs, smoking a cigarette and staring at the sea. It was the first time she had seen the sea so calm, so flat and shining, without waves, without even the customary swell.

Agustin would know what to do. There might be a reward for the finder, almost sure to be. She would share it with him, she wouldn't mind that, so long as she had enough to pay for those extras. He turned round, smiled, extended one hand. She expected to be kissed but he didn't kiss her, only patted the seat beside him.

She opened her bag, said, 'Look.'

His face seemed to close up, grow tight, grow instantly older. 'Where you find this?'

'In the sea.'

'You tell?'

'You mean, have I told anyone? No, I haven't. I wanted to show it to you and ask your advice.'

'It is worth a lot. A lot. Look, this is gold. This is diamond. Worth maybe fifty thousand, hundred thousand dollar.'

'Oh, no, Agustin!'

'Oh, yes, yes.'

He began to laugh. He crowed with laughter. Then he took her in his arms, covered her face and neck with kisses. Things were quite different from the night before. In the shadows, under the pines, where the rocks were smooth and the sand soft, his love-making was slow and sweet. He held her close and kissed her gently, murmuring to her in his own language.

The sea made a soft lapping sound. A faint strain of music, the last of the evening, reached them from somewhere. He was telling her he loved her. I love you, I love. He spoke with the accents of California and she knew he had learned it from films. I love you.

'Listen,' he said. 'Tomorrow we take the bus. We go to the city . . .' Ciudad Something was what he said but she didn't catch the name. '. . . We sell this jewel, I know where, and we are rich. We go to Mexico City, maybe Miami, maybe Rio. You like Rio?'

'I don't know. I've never been there.'

'Nor me. But we go. Kiss me. I love you.'

She kissed him. She put her clothes on, picked up her handbag. He watched her, said, 'What are you doing?' and when she began to walk down the beach, called after her, 'Where are you going?'

She stood at the water's edge. The sea was swelling into waves now, it hadn't stayed calm for long, its gleaming ruffled surface black and silver. She opened her bag, took out the bracelet and threw it as far as she could into the sea.

His yell was a thwarted child's. He plunged into the water. She turned and began to walk away up the beach towards the steps. When she was under the palm trees she turned to look back and saw him splashing wildly, on all fours scrabbling in the sand, seeking what could never be found. As she entered the hotel the thought came to her that she had never told him her name and he had never asked.

The Astronomical Scarf

It was a very large square, silk in the shade of blue called midnight which is darker than royal and lighter than navy, and the design on it was a map of the heavens. The Milky Way was there and Charles's Wain, Orion, Cassiopeia and the Seven Daughters of Atlas. A young woman who was James Mullen's secretary saw it in a shop window in Bond Street, draped across the seat of a (reproduction) Louis Quinze chair with a silver chain necklace lying on it and a black picture hat with a dark-blue ribbon covering one of its corners.

Cressida Chilton had been working for James Mullen for just three months when he sent her out to buy a birthday present for his wife. Not jewellery, he had said. Use your own judgement, I can see you've got good taste, but not jewellery. Cressida could see which way the wind was blowing there.

'Not jewellery' were the fateful words. Elaine Mullen was his second wife and had held that position for five years. Office gossip had it that he was seeing one of the manangement trainees in Foreign Securities. I wish it were me, thought Cressida, and she went into the shop and bought the scarf – appropriately enough, for an astronomical price – and then, because no shops gift-wrapped in those days, into a stationer's round the corner for a sheet of pink and silver paper and a twist of silver string.

Elaine knew the meaning of the astronomical scarf. She knew

who had wrapped it up too and it wasn't James. She had expected a gold bracelet and she could see the writing on the wall as clearly as if James had turned graffitist and chalked up something to the effect of all good things coming to an end. As for the scarf, didn't he know she never wore blue? Hadn't he noticed that her eyes were hazel and her hair light-brown? That secretary, the one who was in love with him, had probably bought it out of spite. Elaine gave it to her blue-eyed sister who happened to come round and saw it lying on the dressing table. It was the very day she was served with her divorce papers under the new law, Matrimonial Causes Act, 1973.

Elaine's sister wore the scarf to a lecture at the Royal Society of Lepidopterists, of which she was a fellow. Cloakroom arrangements in the premises of learned societies are often somewhat slapdash and here, in a Georgian house in Bloomsbury Square, fellows, members and their guests were expected to hang up their coats themselves on a row of hooks in a dark corner of the hall. When all the hooks were in use coats had either to be placed over those already there or laid on the floor. Elaine's sister, arriving rather late, took off her coat, threaded the astronomical scarf through one sleeve, in at the shoulder and out at the cuff, and draped the coat over someone's very old ocelot.

Sadie Williamson was a world authority on the genus *Argynnis*, its global distribution and habitats. She was also a thief. She stole something nearly every day. The coat she was wearing she had stolen from Harrods and the shoes on her feet from a friend's clothes cupboard after a party. She was proud too (to herself) that she had never given anyone a present she had had to pay for. Now, in the dim and deserted hall, on the walls of which a few eighteenth-century prints of British butterflies were just visible, Sadie searched among the garments for some trifle worth picking up.

An unpleasant smell arose from the clothes, compounded of dirty cloth, old sweat, mothballs, cleaning fluid and something in the nature of wet sheep. Sadie curled up her nose distastefully.

She would have liked to wash her hands but someone had hung an *Out of Order* sign on the washroom door. Not much worth bothering about here, she was thinking, when she saw the hand-rolled and hemstitched corner of a blue scarf protruding from a coat sleeve. She gave it a tug. Rather nice, she was thinking, and quickly tucked it into her coat pocket because she could hear footsteps coming from the lecture room.

Next day she took it round to the cleaners. Most things she stole she had dry-cleaned, even if they were fresh off a hanger in a shop. You never knew who might have tried them on.

'The Zodiac,' said the woman behind the counter. 'Which sign are you?'

'I don't believe in it but I'm Cancer.'

'Oh, dear,' said the woman, 'I never think that sounds very nice, do you?'

Sadie put the scarf into a box that had contained a pair of tights she had stolen from Selfridges, wrapped it up in a piece of paper that had wrapped a present given to *her* and sent it to her godchild for Christmas. The parcel never got there. It was one of those lost in the robbery of a mail train travelling between Norwich and London.

Of the two young men who snatched the mailbags, it was the elder who helped himself to the scarf. He thought it was new, it looked new. He gave it to his girlfriend. She took one look and asked him who he thought she was, her own mother? What was she supposed to do with it, tie it round her head when she went to the races?

She meant to give it to her mother but accidentally left it in the taxi in which she was travelling from Kilburn to Acton. It was found, along with a pack of two hundred cigarettes, two cans of Diet Coke and a copy of *Playboy*, the lot in a rather worn Harrods carrier, by the taxi driver's next fare. She happened to be Cressida Chilton, who was still James Mullen's secretary, but who failed to recognise the scarf because it was enclosed in the paper wrapped round it by Sadie Williamson. Besides, she was still in a state of shock from what she had read in the paper that morning, the announcement of James's imminent marriage, his third.

'This was on the floor,' she said, handing the bag over with the taxi driver's tip.

'They go about in a dream,' he said. 'You wouldn't believe the stuff they leave behind. I had a full set of Masonic regalia left in my cab last week and the week before that it was a baby's pot, no kidding, and a pair of wellies. How am I supposed to know who the stuff belongs to? They'd leave themselves behind only they have to get out when they pay, thank God. I mean, what is it this time? Packets of fags and a dirty book . . .'

'I hope you find the owner,' said Cressida, and she rushed off through the swing door and up in the lift to be sure of getting there before James did, to be ready with her congratulations, all smiles.

'Find the owner, my arse,' said the taxi driver to himself.

He drew up at the red light next to another taxi whose driver he knew and, having already seen this copy, passed him *Playboy* through their open windows. The cigarettes he smoked himself. He gave the Diet Coke and the scarf to his wife. She said it was the most beautiful scarf she had ever seen and she wore it every time she went anywhere that required dressing up.

Eleven years later her daughter Maureen borrowed it. Repeatedly the taxi driver's wife asked for it back and Maureen meant to give it back, but she always forgot. Until one day when she was about to go to her mother's and the scarf came into her head, a vision inspired by a picture in the *Radio Times* of the night sky in September. Her flat was always untidy, a welter of clothes and magazines and tape cassettes and full ashtrays. But once she had started looking she really wanted to find the scarf. She looked everywhere, grubbed about in cupboards and drawers, threw stuff on the floor and fumbled through half-unpacked suitcases. The result was that she was very late in getting to her mother's but she had not found the astronomical scarf.

This was because it had been taken the previous week –

borrowed, she too would have said – by a boyfriend who was in love with her but whose love was unrequited. Or not as fully requited as he wished. The scarf was not merely intended as a sentimental keepsake but to be taken to a clairvoyant in Shepherd's Bush who had promised him dramatic results if she could only hold in her hands 'something of the beloved's'. In the event, the spell or charm failed to work, possibly because the scarf belonged not to Maureen but to her mother. Or did it? It would have been hard to say who its owner was by this time.

The clairvoyant meant to return the scarf to Maureen's boyfriend at his next visit but that was not due for two weeks. In the meantime she wore it herself. She was only the second person into whose possession it had come to look on it with love and admiration. Elaine Mullen's sister had worn it because it was obviously of good quality and because it was *there*; Sadie Williamson had recognised it as expensive; Maureen had borrowed it because the night had turned cold and she had a sore throat. But only her mother and now the clairvoyant had truly appreciated it.

This woman's real name was not known until after she was dead. She called herself Thalia Essene. The scarf delighted her, not because of the quality of the silk, nor its hand-rolled hem, nor its colour, but because of the constellations scattered across its midnight-blue. Such a map was to her what a chart of the Atlantic Ocean might have been to some early navigator, essential, enrapturing, mysterious, indispensable, life-saving. Its stars were the encyclopaedia of her trade, the impenetrable spaces between them the source of her predictions. She sat for many hours in meditative contemplation of the scarf, which she spread on her lap, stroking it gently and sometimes murmuring incantations. When she went out she wore it along with her layers of trailing garments, black cloak and pomander of asafoetida grass.

Roderick Thomas had never been among her clients. He was a neighbour, having just moved into one of the rooms below her flat in the Uxbridge Road. Years had passed since he had done any work or anyone had shown the slightest interest in him, wished for his company or paid attention to what he said, let alone cared about him. Thalia Essene was one of the few people who actually spoke to him and all she said when she saw him was 'Hi', or 'Rain again'.

One day, though, she made the mistake of saying a little more. The sun was shining out of a cloudless sky. 'The goddess loves us this morning.'

Roderick Thomas looked at her with his mouth open. 'You what?'

'I said, the goddess loves us today. She's shedding her glorious sunshine on to the face of the earth.'

Thalia smiled at him and walked on. She was on her way to the shops in King Street. Roderick Thomas started shambling after her. For some years he had been on the lookout for the Antichrist, who he knew would come in female form. He followed Thalia into Marks and Spencer's and the cassette shop where she was in the habit of buying music as background for her fortune-telling sessions. She was well aware of his presence and, growing increasingly angry, then nervous, went home in a taxi.

Next day he hammered on her door. She told him to go away.

'Say that about the sunshine again,' he said.

'It's not sunny today.'

'You could pretend. Say about the goddess.'

'You're mad,' said Thalia.

A client who had been having his palm read and had heard it all, gave her a funny look. She told him his lifeline was the longest she had ever seen and he would probably make it to a hundred. When she went downstairs Roderick Thomas was waiting for her in the hall. He looked at the scarf.

'Clothed in the sun,' he said, 'and upon her head a crown of twelve stars.'

Thalia said something so alien to her philosophy of life, so contrary to all her principles, that she could hardly believe she'd uttered it. 'If you don't leave me alone I'll call the police.'

He followed her just the same. She walked up to Shepherd's Bush Green. Her threats gave her a dark aura and he saw the stars encircling her. She fascinated him, though he was beginning to see her as a source of danger. In Newcastle, where he had been living until two years before, he had killed a woman he had mistakenly thought was the Antichrist because she told him to go to hell when he spoke to her. For a long time he expected to be sent to hell and although the fear had somewhat abated, it came back when he was confronted by manifestly evil women.

A man was standing on one of the benches on the green, preaching to the multitude. Well, to four or five people. Roderick Thomas had followed Thalia to the tube station but there he had to abandon pursuit for lack of money to buy a ticket. He wandered on to the green. The man on the bench stared straight at him and said, 'Thou shalt have no other gods but me!'

Roderick took that for a sign, you'd have to be daft not to get the message, but he asked his question just the same. 'What about the goddess?'

'For Solomon went after Ashtaroth,' said the man on the bench, 'and after Milcom the abomination of the Ammonites. Wherefore the Lord said unto Solomon, I will surely rend the kingdom from thee and will give it to thy servant.'

That was fair enough. Roderick went home and bided his time, listening to the voice of the preacher which had taken over from the usual voice he heard during his waking hours. It told him of a woman in purple sitting on a scarlet-coloured beast, full of names of blasphemy, having seven heads and ten horns. He watched from his window until he saw Thalia Essene come in, carrying a large recycled paper bag in a dull purple with *Celestial Seconds* printed on its side.

Thalia was feeling happy because she hadn't seen Roderick for several hours and believed she had shaken him off. She was going out that evening to see a play at the Lyric, Hammersmith, in the company of a friend who was a famous water diviner. To this end she had bought herself a new dress or, rather, a 'nearly new' dress, purple Indian cotton with mirror work and black embroidery. The blue starry scarf, which she had taken to calling the *astrological* scarf, went well with it. She draped it round her neck, lamenting the coldness of the night. A shawl would be inadequate and all this would have to be covered by her old black coat.

A quick glance at her engagement book showed her that Maureen's boyfriend was due for a consultation next morning. The scarf must be returned to him. She would wear it for the last time. As it happened, Thalia was wearing all these clothes for the last time, doing everything she did for the last time but, clairvoyant though she was, of her imminent fate she had no prevision.

She walked along, looking for a taxi. None came. She had plenty of time and decided to walk to Hammersmith. Roderick Thomas was behind her but she had forgotten about him and she didn't look round. She was thinking about the water diviner whom she hadn't seen for eighteen months but who was reputed to have split up from his girlfriend.

Roderick Thomas caught up with her in one of the darker spots of Hammersmith Grove. It wasn't dark to him but illuminated by the seven times seventy stars on the clothing of her neck and the sea of glass like unto crystal on the hem of her garment. He spoke not a word but took the two ends of the starry cloth in his hands and strangled her.

After they had found the body her killer was not hard to find. There was little point in charging Roderick Thomas with anything or bringing him up in court but they did. The astronomical scarf was Exhibit A at the trial. Roderick Thomas was found guilty of the murder of Noreen Blake, for such was Thalia's real name, and committed to a prison for the criminally insane.

The exhibits would normally have ended up in the Black Museum but a young police officer called Karen Duncan, whose job it was to collect together such memorabilia, thought it all so sad and distasteful – the poor devil should never have been allowed out into the community in the first place – that she put Thalia's carrier bag and theatre ticket in the shredder and took the scarf home with her. Although it had been dry-cleaned, the scarf had never been washed. Karen washed it in cold water gel for delicates and ironed it with a cool iron. Nobody would have guessed it had been used for such a macabre purpose, there wasn't a mark on it.

But an unforeseen problem arose. Karen couldn't bring herself to wear it. It wasn't the scarf's history that stopped her so much as her fear other people might recognise it. There had been some publicity for the Crown Court proceedings and much had been made of the midnight-blue scarf patterned with stars. Cressida Chilton had read about it and wondered why it reminded her of James Mullen's second wife, the one before the one before his present one. She didn't think she could face a fourth divorce and fifth marriage, she'd have to change her job. Sadie Williamson read about the scarf and for some reason there came into her head a picture of butterflies and a dark house in Bloomsbury.

After some inner argument, reassurance countered by denial and self-rebuke, Karen Duncan took the scarf round to the charity shop where they let her exchange it for a black velvet hat. Three weeks later it was bought by a woman who didn't recognise it, though the man who ran the charity shop did and had been in a dilemma about it ever since Karen brought it in. Its new owner wore it for a couple of years. At the end of that time she got married to an astronomer. The scarf shocked and enraged him. He explained to her what an inaccurate representation of the heavens it was, how it was quite impossible for these constellations to be adjacent to each other or even visible at the same time, and if he didn't forbid her to wear it that was because he wasn't that kind of man.

The astronomer's wife gave the scarf to the woman who did the cleaning three times a week. Mrs Vernon never wore the scarf, she didn't like scarves, could never keep them from slipping off, but it wouldn't have occurred to her to say no to something that was offered to her. When she died, three years later, her daughter came upon it among her effects.

Bridget Vernon was a silversmith and member of a celebrated craft society. One of her fellow members made quilts and was always on the lookout for likely fabrics to use in patchwork. The quiltmaker, Fenella Carbury, needed samples of blue, cream and ivory silks for a quilt which had been commissioned by a millionaire businessman, well known for his patronage of arts and crafts, and for his charitable donations. No charity was involved here. Fenella worked hard and she worked long hours. The quilt would be worth every penny of the £2000 she would be asking for it.

For the second time in its life the scarf was washed. The silk was as good as new, its dark blue unfaded, its stars as bright as they had been twenty years before. From it Fenella was able to cut forty hexagons which, interspersed with forty ivory damask diamond shapes and forty sky-blue silk lozenge shapes from a fabric shop cut-off, formed the central motif of the quilt. When finished it was large enough to cover a king-size bed.

James Mullen allowed it to hang on exhibition in Chelsea at the Chenil Gallery for precisely two weeks. Then he collected it and gave it to his new bride for a wedding present along with a diamond bracelet, a cottage in Derbyshire and a Queen Anne four-poster to put the quilt on.

Cressida Chilton had waited through four marriages and twenty-one years. Men, as Oscar Wilde said, marry because they are tired. Men, as Cressida Mullen said, always marry their secretaries in the end. It's dogged as does it and she had been dogged, she had persevered and she had her reward.

Before getting into bed on her wedding night, she contemplated the £2000 quilt and told James it was the loveliest thing she had ever seen.

'The middle bit reminds me of you when you first came to work for me,' said James. 'I should have had the sense to marry you then. I can't think why it reminds me, can you?'

Cressida smiled. 'I suppose I had stars in my eyes.'

High Mysterious Union

Before Ben, I'd never lent the house to anyone. No one had ever asked. By the time Ben asked I had doubts about it being the kind of place to inflict on a friend, but I said yes because if I'd said no I couldn't have explained why. I said nothing about the odd and disquieting things, only that I hadn't been there myself for months.

I'm not talking about the house. The house was all right. Or it would have been if it hadn't been where it was. A small grey Gothic house with a turret would have been fine by a Scottish loch or in some provincial town, only this one, mine, was in a forest. To put it precisely, on the edge of the great forest that lies on the western borders of – well, I won't say where. Somewhere in England, a long drive from London. It was for its position that I bought it. This beautiful place, the village, the woods, the wetlands, had changed very little while everything else all around was changing. My house was about a mile outside the village, at the head of a large man-made lake. And the western tip of the forest enclosed house and lake in a curved sweep with two embracing arms, the shape of a horseshoe.

It was the village that was wrong; right for the people and

wrong for the others, a place to be born in, to live and die in, not for strangers.

Ben had been there once to stay with me. Just for the weekend. His wife was to have come too but cried off at the last moment. Ben said later she took her chance to spend a night with the man she's with now. It was July and very hot. We went for a walk but the heat was too much for us and we were glad to reach the shade of the trees on the lake's eastern side. Then we saw the bathers. They must have gone into the water after we'd started our walk, for they were up near the house, had gone in from the little strip of gravel I called 'my beach'.

The sky was cloudless and the sun hot in the way it only is in the east of England, brilliant white, dazzling, the clean hard light falling on a greenness that is so bright because it's well watered. The lake water, absolutely calm, looked phosphorescent, as if a white fire burned on the flat surface. And out of that blinding fiery water we saw the bathers rise and extend their arms, stand up and with uplifted faces, slowly rotate their bodies to and away from the sun.

It hurt the eyes but we could see. They wanted us to see, or one of them did.

'They're children,' I said.

'She's not a child.'

She wasn't, but I knew that. We're all inhibited about nudity, especially when we come upon it by chance and in company, when we're unprepared. It's all right if we can see it when alone and ourselves unseen. Ben wasn't especially prudish but he was rather shy and he looked away.

The girl in the burning water, entirely naked, became more and more clearly visible to us, for we continued to walk towards her, though rather slowly now. We could have stopped and at once become voyeurs. Or turned back and provoked – I knew –

laughter from her and her companions. And from God knows who else hidden, for all I could tell, among the trees.

They were undoubtedly children, her companions, a boy and a girl. The three of them stretched upwards and gazed at the dazzling blueness while the sun struck their wet bodies. That was another thing that troubled me, *that* sun, inflicting surely a fierce burning on white skin. For they were all white, white as milk, as white lilies, and the girl's uplifted breasts, raised by her extended arms, were like plump white buds, tipped with rosy pink.

What Ben thought of it I didn't quite know. He said nothing about it till much later. But his face flushed darkly, reddening as if with the sun, as those bodies should have reddened but somehow, I knew, would not, would stay, by the not always happy magic of this place, inviolable and unstained. He had taken his hands from his eyes and was feeling with his fingertips the hot red of his cheeks.

He didn't look at the bathers again. He kept his head averted, staring into the wood as if spotting there an array of interesting wildlife. They waded out of the water as we approached, the children running off to the shelter of the trees. But the girl stood for a moment on the little beach, no longer exposing herself to us but rather as if – there is only one word I can use, only one that gives the real sense of how she was – as if *ashamed*. Her stance was that of Aphrodite on her shell in the painting, one hand covering the pale fleece of hair between her thighs, the other, and the white arm glittering with water drops, across her breasts. But Aphrodite gazes innocently at the onlooker. This girl stood with hanging head, her long white-blonde hair dripping, and though there was nothing to detain her there, remained in her attitude of shame as might a slave exhibited in a market place.

Yet she was enjoying herself. She was acting a part and enjoying what she acted. You could tell. I thought even then, before I knew much, that she might equally have chosen to be the bold visitor to the nude beach or the flaunting stripper or the shopper surprised

145

in the changing room, but she had chosen the slave. It was a game, yet it was part of her nature.

When we were some twenty yards from her, she lifted her head and behaved as if she had only just seen us. We were to think, for it can't have been sincere, that until that moment she had been unconscious of our approach, of our being there at all. She gave a little artificial shriek, then a laugh of shocked merriment, waving her arms in a mime of someone grasping at clothes, seizing invisible garments out of the air and wrapping them round her, as she ran into the long grass, the low bushes and at last into the tall, concealing trees.

'I don't know who that was,' I said to him as we went into the house. 'One of the village people perhaps.'

'Why not a visitor?' he said.

'No, I'm sure. One of the village people.'

I was sure. There were ways of telling, though I hardly ever went near the village. Not by that time. Not to the church or the pub or the shop. And I didn't take Ben there. The place was gradually becoming less and less attractive to me, Gothic House somewhere I thought I ought occasionally to go to but put off visiting. You could only reach it with ease by driving through the village and I avoided that village as much as I could. By the time he asked me if he could borrow it I had already decided to sell the house.

His wife had left him. Or made it plain to him she expected him to leave *her*, leave her, that is, the house they lived in. He'd bought a flat in London but before he ever lived in it he'd had a kind of breakdown from an accumulation of causes but mainly Margaret's departure. He wanted to get away somewhere, to get away from everyone and everything he knew, the people and places and things that reminded him. And he wanted to be somewhere he could work in peace.

Ben is a translator. He translates from French and Italian,

fiction and non-fiction, and was about to embark on the biggest and most complex work he'd ever undertaken, a book called *The Golden Apple* by a French psychoanalyst that examined from a Jungian viewpoint the myths attendant on the Trojan War, Helen of Troy and Paris, Priam and Hecabe and the human mind. He took his word processor with him, his Collins–Robert French dictionary and his Liddell and Scott Greek dictionary, and Graves's *The Greek Myths*.

I gave him a key to Gothic House. 'There are only two in existence. Sandy has the other.'

'Who's Sandy?'

'A sort of odd-job man. Someone has to be able to get in in case of fire or, more likely, flood.'

Perhaps I said it unhappily, for he gave me an enquiring look, but I didn't enlighten him. What was there to say without saying it all?

There was nothing sinister about the village and its surroundings. It is important that you understand that. It was the most beautiful place and in spite of all the trees, the crowding forest that stretched to the horizon, it wasn't dark. The light even seemed to have a special quality there, the sky to be larger and the sun out for longer than elsewhere. I am sure there were more unclouded skies than to the north and south of us. Mostly, if you saw clouds, you saw them rolling away towards that bluish wooded horizon. Sunsets were pink, the colour of a bullfinch's breast.

I don't know how it happened that the place was so unspoilt. Trunk roads passed within ten miles on either side but the two roads into the village and the three out were narrow and winding. New building had taken place but not much and what there was by some lucky chance was tasteful and plain. The old school still stood, no industry had come there and no row of pylons marched across the fields of wheat and the fields of grazing beasts. Nothing interrupted the view everyone in the village had of the green forest of oak and ash, and the black forest of fir and pine. The church had a round tower like a castle, but its surface was of cut flints.

That is not to say there were no strangenesses. I am sure there was much that was unique in the village and much of what happened there happened nowhere else in England. Well, I know it now, of course, but even then, when I first came and in those first years . . .

I told Ben some of it before he left. I thought I owed him that.

'I shan't want to socialise with a lot of middle-class people,' he said.

'You won't be able to. There aren't any.'

His lack of surprise was due, I think, to his ignorance of country life. I had told him that the usual mix of the working people whose families had been there for generations with commuters, doctors, solicitors, retired bank managers, university and school-teachers and businessmen wasn't to be found. A parson had once been in the rectory but for a couple of years the church had been served by the vicar of a parish some five miles away who held a service once a week.

'I'd never thought of you as a snob,' said Ben.

'It isn't snobbery,' I said, 'it's fact.'

There were no county people, no 'squire', no master of foxhounds or titled lady. No houses existed to put them in. A farmer from Lynn had bought the rectory. The hall, a pretty Georgian manor house of which a print hung in my house, had burned down in the fifties.

'It belongs to the people,' I said. 'You'll see.'

'A sort of ideal communism,' he said, 'the kind we're told never works.'

'It works. For them.'

Did it? I wondered, after I'd said it, what I'd meant. Did it really belong to the people? How could it? The people there were as poor and hard-pressed as anywhere else, there was the same unemployment, the same number living on benefit, the same lack of work for the agricultural labourer, driven from the land by mechanisation. Yet another strange thing was that the young people didn't leave. There was no exodus of school leavers and the newly married. They stayed and somehow there were enough houses to accommodate them. The old people, when they became infirm, were received, apparently with joy, into the homes of their children.

Ben went down there one afternoon in May and he phoned that night to tell me he'd arrived and all was well. That was all he said, then. Nothing about Sandy and the girl. For all I knew he had simply let himself into the house without seeing a soul.

'I can hear birds singing,' he said. 'It's dark and I can hear birds. How can that be?'

'Nightingales,' I said.

'I didn't know there were such things any more.'

And though he didn't say, I had the impression he put the phone down quickly so that he could go outside and listen to the nightingales.

The front door was opened to him before he had a chance to use his key. They had heard the car or seen him coming from a window, having plenty of opportunity to do that, for he had stopped for a while at the point where the road comes closest to the lake. He wanted to look at the view.

He'd left London much later than I thought he would, not till after six, and the sun was setting. The lake was glazed with pink and purple, reflecting the sky, and it was perfectly calm, its smooth and glassy surface broken only by the dark-green pallets of water lily pads. Beyond the further shore the forest grew black and mysterious as the light withdrew into that darkening sky.

He'd been depressed, 'feeling low', as he put it, and the sight of the lake and the woodland, the calmness and the colours, if they hardly made him happy, comforted him and steadied him into a kind of acceptance of things. He must have stood there gazing, watching the light fade, for some minutes, perhaps ten, and they must have watched him and wondered how long it would be before he got back into the car.

The front door came open as he was feeling in his pocket for the key. A girl stood there, holding the door, not saying anything, not smiling, just holding the door and stepping back to let him come in. The absurd idea came to him that this was the *same* girl, the one he had seen bathing, and for a few minutes he was sure it was, it didn't seem absurd to him.

He even gave some sort of utterance to that thought. 'You,' he said. 'What are you . . . ?'

'Just here to see everything's all right, sir.' She spoke deferentially but in a practical way, a sensible way. 'Making sure you're comfortable.'

'But haven't I – no. No, I'm sorry.' He saw his mistake in the light of the hallway. 'I thought we'd –' 'met' was not quite the word he wanted '– seen each other before.'

'Oh, no.' She looked at him gravely. 'I'd remember if I'd seen you before.'

She spoke with the broad up-and-down intonation they have in this part of the country, a woodland sing-song burr. He saw now in the lamplight that she was much younger than the woman he had seen bathing, though as tall. Her height had deceived him, that and her fairness and her pallor. He thought then that he had never seen anyone who was not ill look so delicate and so fragile.

'Like a drawing of a fairy,' he said to me, 'in a children's book. Does that give you an idea? Like a mythological creature from this book I'm translating, Oenone, the fountain-nymph, perhaps. Tall but so slight and frail that you wonder she could have a physical existence.'

She offered to carry his luggage upstairs for him. It seemed to him the most preposterous suggestion he had ever heard, that this fey-like being, a flower on a stalk, should be able to lift even his laptop. He fetched the cases himself and she watched him, smiling. Her smile was intimate, almost conspiratorial, as if they shared some past unforgettable experience. He was halfway up the stairs when the man spoke. It froze him and he turned round.

'What were you thinking of, Lavinia, to let Mr Powell carry his own bags?'

Hearing his own name spoken like that, so casually, as if it was daily on the speaker's lips, gave him a shock. Come to that, to hear it at all . . . How did the man know? Already he knew there would be no explanation. He would never be able to fetch out an explanation, now or at any time – not, that is, a true one – a real, factual, honest account of why anything was or how. Somehow he knew that.

'Alexander Clements, Mr Powell. Commonly known as Sandy.'

The girl followed him upstairs and showed him his bedroom. I'd told him to sleep where he liked, he had the choice of four rooms, but the girl showed him to the big one in the front with the view of the lake. That was his room, she said. Would he like her to unpack for him? No one had ever asked him that before. He had never stayed in the kind of hotel where they did ask. He shook his head, bemused. She drew the curtains and turned down the bedcovers.

'It's a nice big bed, sir. I put the clean sheets on for you myself.'

The smile returned and then came a look of a kind he had never seen before – well, he had but in films, in comedy Westerns and a movie version of a Feydeau farce. At any rate, he recognised it for what it was. She looked over her shoulder at him. Her expression was one of sweet naughty coyness, her head dipped to one side. Her eyebrows went up and her eyes slanted towards him and away. 'You'll be lonely in that big bed, won't you?'

He wanted to laugh. He said in a stifled voice, 'I'll manage.'

'I'm sure you'll *manage*, sir. It's just Sandy I'm thinking of, I wouldn't want to get on the wrong side of Sandy.'

He had no idea what she meant but he got out of that bedroom quickly.

Sandy was waiting for him downstairs and the table was laid for one, cold food on it and a bottle of wine. 'I hope everything's to your liking, Mr Powell?'

He said it was, thank you, but he hadn't expected it, he hadn't expected anyone to be there.

'Arrangements were made, sir. It's my job to see things are done properly and I hope they have been. Lavinia will be in to keep things shipshape for you and see to any necessary cookery. I'll be on hand for the more masculine tasks, if you take my meaning, your motor and the electricals et cetera. Never underrate the importance of organisation.'

'What organisation?' I said when he told me. 'I didn't arrange anything. I knew Sandy Clements still had a key and I've been meaning to ask for it back. Still, as for asking him to organise anything, to make "arrangements" . . .'

'I thought you'd got them in, Sandy and the girl. I thought she came in to clean for you and you'd arranged she'd do the same for me. I didn't want her but I hardly liked to interfere with your arrangement.'

'No,' I said, 'no, I see that.'

They stood there until he was seated at the table and unfolding the white napkin Lavinia had presumably provided. I don't know where it came from, I haven't any white table linen. Sandy opened the bottle of wine, which Ben saw to his dismay was a supermarket Riesling. The horror was compounded by Sandy's pouring an inch of it into Ben's wineglass and watching while Ben tasted it.

He said he was almost paralysed by this time, though seeing what he thought then was 'the funny side'. After a while he didn't find anything particularly funny but he did that evening. They had cheered him up. He saw the girl as a sort of stage parlourmaid. She was even dressed somewhat like that, a white apron with its sash tied tightly round her tiny waist, a white bow on her pale-blonde hair. He thought they were trying to please him. These unsophisticated rustics were doing their best, relying on an experience of magazines and television, to entertain the visitor from London in the style to which he was accustomed.

Once he'd started eating they left. It was quite strange, the manner in which they left. Lavinia opened the door and let Sandy pass through ahead of her, looking back to give him another of those conspiratorial naughty looks. She delayed for longer than was necessary, her eyes meeting his until his turned away. A fleeting smile and then she was gone, the door and the front door closing behind her.

Only a few seconds passed before he heard the engine of Sandy's van. He got up to draw the curtains and saw the van moving off down the road towards the village, its red tail lights growing small and dimmer until they were altogether swallowed up in the dark. A bronze-coloured light that seemed to be slowly ascending showed through the treetops. It took him a little while before he realised it was the moon he was looking at, the coppery golden disc of the moon.

He ate some of the ham and cheese they had left him and managed to drink a glass of the wine. The deep silence that prevailed after Sandy and the girl had gone was now broken by birdsong, unearthly trills of sound he could hardly at first believe in, and he went outside to try to confirm that he had really heard birds singing in the dark.

The rich yet cold singing came from the nearest trees of the wood, was clear and unmistakable, but it seemed unreal to him, on a par, somehow, with the behaviour he had just witnessed, with the use of his name, with the fountain-nymph's coy glances and come-hither smiles. Yet when he came inside and phoned me it was the nightingales' song he talked about. He said nothing of the man and the girl, the food, the bed, the 'arrangements'.

'Why didn't you?' I asked him when I came down for a weekend in June. 'Why didn't you say?'

'I don't know. I consciously made up my mind I wouldn't. You see, I thought they were ridiculous but at the same time I thought they were your – well, "help", your cleaner, your handyman. I felt I couldn't thank you for making the arrangement with Lavinia without laughing about the way she dressed and the way Sandy talked. Surely you can see that?'

'But you never mentioned it. Not ever till now.'

'I know,' he said. 'You can understand why, can't you?'

2

When I first came to Gothic House Sandy was about twenty-five, so by the time Ben went there he would have been seven years older than that, a tall fair man with very regular features who still escaped being quite handsome. His eyes were too pale and the white skin of his face had reddened, as it does with some of the locals after thirty.

He came to me soon after I bought Gothic House and offered his services. I told him I couldn't afford a gardener or a handyman and I didn't need anyone to wash my car. He held his head a little on one side. It's an attitude that implies total understanding of the other person's mind, indulgence, even patience. 'I wouldn't want paying.'

'And I wouldn't consider employing you without paying you.'

He nodded. 'We'll see how things go then, shall we? We'll leave things as they are for now.'

'For now' must have meant a couple of weeks. The next time I went to Gothic House for the weekend the lawn in front of the house that slopes down to the wall above the lake shore had been mown. A strip of blocked guttering on the back that I had planned to see to had been cleared. If Sandy had presented himself while I was there I would have repeated my refusal of his services, and done so in definite terms, for I was angry. But he didn't present himself and at that time I had no idea where he lived.

On my next visit I found part of the garden weeded. Next time the windows had been cleaned. But when I came down and found a window catch mended, a repair that could only have been done after entry to the house, I went down into the village to try to find Sandy.

That was my first real exploration of the village, the first time I noticed how beautiful it was and how unspoilt. Its centre, the green, was a triangle of lawn on which the trees were the kind generally seen on parkland, cedars and unusual oaks and a swamp cypress. The houses and cottages either had rendered walls or were faced with flints, roofs of slate or thatch. It was high summer and the gardens, the tubs, the window boxes were full of flowers. Fuchsia hedges had leaves of a deep soft green spangled with sharp red blossoms. The whole place smelt of roses. It was the sort of village television production companies dream of finding when they film Jane Austen serials. The cars would have to be hidden, but otherwise it looked unchanged from an earlier century.

A woman in the shop identified Sandy for me and told me where he lived. She smiled and spoke about him with a kind of affectionate admiration. Sandy, yes, of course, Sandy was much in demand. But he wouldn't be at home that morning, he'd be up at Marion Kirkman's. This was a cottage facing the pretty green and easily found. I recognised Sandy's van parked outside, opened the gate and went into the garden.

By this time my anger had cooled – the shop woman's obvious liking for and trust of Sandy had cooled it – and I asked myself if I could legitimately go up to someone's front door, demand to see her gardener and harangue him in front of her. In the event I didn't have to do that. I walked round to the back, hoping to find him alone there and I found him – with her.

They had their backs to me, a tall fair man and a tall fair woman, his arm round her shoulders, hers round his waist. They were looking at something, a flower on a climber or an alighted butterfly perhaps, and then they turned to face each other and kissed. A light, gentle, loving kiss such as lovers give each other after desire has been satisfied, after desire has been satisfied many times over months or even years, a kiss of acceptance and trust, and deep mutual knowledge.

It was not so much the kiss as their reaction to my presence that decided me. They turned round. They were not in the least taken aback and they were quite without guilt. For a few moments they left their arms where they were while smiling at me in innocent friendliness. And I could see at once what I'd stumbled upon, a long-standing loving relationship and one that, in spite of Marion Kirkman's evident seniority, would likely result in marriage.

Two women, then, in the space of twenty minutes, had given their accolade to Sandy. I asked him only how he had got into my house.

'Oh, I've keys to a good many houses round here,' he said.

'Sandy makes it his business to have keys,' Marion Kirkman said. 'For the security, isn't it, Sandy?'

'Like a neighbourhood watch, you might say.'

I couldn't quite see where security came into it, understanding as I always had that the fewer keys around the safer. But the two of them, so relaxed, so smiling, so firm in their acceptance of Sandy's perfect right of access to anyone's house, seemed pillars of society, earnest upholders of social order. I accepted Marion's invitation to a cup of coffee. We sat in a bright kitchen, all its cupboards refitted by Sandy, I was told, the previous year. It was then that I said I supposed it would be all right, of course he must come and do these jobs for me.

'You'll be alone in this village otherwise,' said Marion, laughing, and Sandy gave her another kiss, this time planted in the centre of her smooth pink cheek.

'But I'm going to insist on paying you.'

'I won't say no,' said Sandy. 'I'm not an arguing man.'

And after that he performed all these necessary tasks for me, regularly, unobtrusively, efficiently, winning my trust, until one day things (as he might have put it) changed. Or they would have changed, had Sandy had his way. Of course, they changed anyway, life can never be the same between two people after such a happening, but though Sandy kept my key he was no longer my handyman and I ceased paying him. I believed that I was in control.

So why did I say nothing of this to Ben before he went to Gothic House? Because I was sure, for reasons obvious to me, that the same sort of thing couldn't happen to him.

The therapist Ben had been seeing since his divorce advised him to keep a diary. He was to set down his thoughts and feelings rather than the actual events of each day, his emotions and his dreams. Now Ben had never done this, he had never 'got around to it', until he came to Gothic House. There, perhaps because – at first – he had few distractions and there wasn't much to do once he'd worked on his translation and been out for a walk, he began a daily noting down of what passed through his mind.

This was the diary he later allowed me to see part of, other entries he read aloud to me and he had it by him to refer to when he recounted the events of that summer. It had its sensational parts but to me much of it was almost painfully familiar. At first, though, he confined himself to descriptions of his state of mind, his all-pervading sadness, a feeling that his life was over, the beauties of the place, the lake, the woodland, the sunshine, the huge blue cirrus-patterned sky, somehow remote from him, belonging to other people.

He walked daily: around the lake, along a footpath high above damp meadows crossed by ditches full of watercress; down the lane to a hamlet where there was a green and a crossroads and a pub, though he never at that time ventured into the forest. Once he went to the village and back, but saw no one. Though it was warm and dry, nobody was about. He knew he was watched, he saw eyes looking at him from windows, but that was natural and to be expected. Villagers were always inquisitive about and even antagonistic to newcomers, that was a cliché that even he, as a townee, had grown up with. Not that he met with antagonism. The postman, collecting from the pillar box, hailed him and wished him good morning. Anne Whiteson, the shop woman, was friendly and pleasant when he went into the shop for teabags and a loaf. He supposed he couldn't have a newspaper delivered? He could. Indeed he could. He had only to say what he wanted and 'someone' would bring it up every morning.

The 'someone' turned out to be Sandy, arriving at eight thirty with his *Independent*. Lavinia Fowler had already been twice but this was the first time he had seen Sandy since that first evening. Though unasked, Lavinia brought tea for both of them, so Ben was obliged to put up with Sandy's company in the kitchen while he drank it. How was he getting on with Lavinia? Was she giving satisfaction?

Ben thought this a strange, almost archaic, term. Or should another construction be put on it? Apparently it should, for Sandy followed up his enquiry by asking if Ben didn't think Lavinia a most attractive girl. The last thing Ben intended to do, he said, was enter into this sort of conversation with the handyman. He was rather short with Sandy after that, saying he had work to do and to excuse him.

But he found it hard to settle to *The Golden Apple*. He had come to a description of the contest between the three goddesses when Paris asks Aphrodite to remove her clothes and let fall her magic girdle, but he could hear sounds from the kitchen, once or twice a giggle, the soft murmur of voices. Too soft, he said, too languorous and cajoling, so that, in spite of himself, he got up and went to listen at the door.

He heard no more and shortly afterwards saw Sandy's van departing along the lake shore. But, as a result of what Sandy had said, he found himself looking at Lavinia with new eyes. Principally, she had ceased to be a joke to him and when she came in with his mid-morning coffee he was powerfully aware of her femininity, that fragile quality of hers, her vulnerability. She was so slender, so pale and her white thin skin looked – these were his words, the words he put in his diary – as if waiting to be bruised.

Her fair hair was as fine and soft as a baby's but longer than any baby ever had, a gauzy veil, almost waist-length, very clean and smelling faintly of some herb. Thyme, perhaps, or oregano. As she bent over his desk to put the cup down her hair just brushed his cheek and he felt that touch with a kind of inner shiver just as he felt the touch of her finger. For he put out his hand to take the coffee mug while she still held it. Instead of immediately relinquishing her hold she left her forefinger where it was for a moment, perhaps thirty seconds, so that it lay alongside his own and skin delicately touched skin.

Again he thought, before he abruptly pulled his hand away, of skin waiting to be bruised, of how it would be if he took that white wrist, thin as a child's, blue-veined, in a harsh grip and squeezed, his fingers more than meeting, overlapping and crushing until she cried out. He had never had such thoughts before, never before about anyone, and they made him uncomfortable. Departing from the room, she again gave him one of those over-the-shoulder glances, but this time wistful – disappointed?

Yet she didn't attract him, he insisted on that. He was very honest with me about all of it. She didn't attract him except in a way he didn't wish to be attracted. Oenone, shepherdess and daughter of the river, was how he saw her. Her fragility, her look of utter weakness, as of a girl to be blown over by the wind or felled by a single touch, inspired in him only what he insisted it would inspire in all men, a desire to ravish, to crush, to injure and to conquer.

'Ravish' was his word, not 'rape'. 'You really felt all that?'

'I thought about it afterwards. I don't say I felt that at the time. I thought about it and that's how I felt about her. It didn't make me happy, you know, I wasn't proud of myself. I'm trying to tell you the honest truth.'

'She was –' I hesitated '– offering herself to you?'

'She had been from the first. Every time we encountered each other she was telling me by her looks and her gestures that she was available, that I could have her. And, you know, I'd never come across anything quite like that before.'

Since the separation from his wife he had been celibate. And he could see no end to his celibacy; he thought it would go on for the rest of his life, for the step that must be taken to end it seemed too great for him to consider, let alone take. Now someone else was taking that step for him. He had only to respond, only to return that glance, let his finger lie a little longer against that finger, close his fingers around that wrist.

Any of these responses was also too great to make. Besides, he was afraid. He was afraid of himself, of those horrors that presented themselves to him as his need. His active imagination showed him how it would be with him when he saw her damaged and at his hands, the bruised whiteness, the abraded skin. But her image came into his consciousness many times throughout that day and visited him in the night like a succubus. He stood at the open window listening to the nightingales and felt her come into the room behind him, could have sworn one of those transparent fingers of hers softly brushed his neck. When he spun round no one was there, nothing was there but the faint herby smell of her, left behind from that morning.

That night was the first time he dreamt of the lake and the tower.

The lake was as it was in his conscious hours, a sheet of water that took twenty minutes to walk round, but the tower on Gothic House was immensely large, as high as a church spire. It had absorbed the house, there was no house, only this tall and broad tower with crenellated top and *oeil de boeuf* windows, as might be part of a battlemented castle. He had seen the tower and then he was on the tower, as is the way in dreams, and Lavinia the river god's daughter was walking out of the lake, water streaming from her body and her uplifted arms. She came to the tower and embraced it, pressing her wet body against the stone. But the curious thing, he said, was that by then *he* had become the tower, the tower was himself, stone still but about to be metamorphosed, he felt, into flesh that could respond and act. He woke up before that happened and he was soaking wet as if a real woman had come out from the lake and embraced him.

'Sweat,' he said, 'and – well, you can have wet dreams even at my age.'

'Why not?' I said, though at that time, in those early days, I was still surprised by his openness.

'Henry James uses that imagery, the tower for the man and the lake for the woman. *The Turn of the Screw*, isn't it? I haven't read it for a hundred years but I suppose my unconscious remembered.'

Lavinia didn't come next day. It wasn't one of her days. On the Friday he prepared himself for her coming, nervous, excited, afraid of himself and her, recalling always the dream and the feel against his body of her wet slippery skin, her small soft breasts. He put in the diary that he remembered water trickling down her breasts and spilling from the nipples.

She was due at eight thirty. By twenty to nine when she still hadn't come – she was never late – he knew he must have offended her. His lack of response she saw as rejection. He reminded himself that the woman in the dream was not she but an imagined figment. The real woman knew nothing of his dreams, his fears, his terrible self-reproach.

She didn't come. No one did. He was relieved but at the same time sorry for the hurt he must have done her. Apart from that, he was well content, he preferred his solitude, the silence of the house. Having to make his own mid-morning coffee wasn't a chore but a welcome interruption of the work to which he went back, refreshed. He was translating a passage from Eustathius on Homer that the author cited as early evidence of sexual deviation. Laodameia missed her husband so much when he set sail for the Trojan War that she made a wax statue of him and laid it in the bed beside her.

It was an irony, Ben thought, that the first time he'd been involved since the end of his marriage in any amorous temptation happened to coincide with his translating this disturbingly sexy book. Or did the book disturb him only because of the Lavinia episode? He knew he hadn't been tempted by Lavinia because of the book. And when he went out for his walk that afternoon he understood that he was no longer tempted; the memory of her, even the dream, had no power to stir him. All that was past.

But it – and perhaps the book – had awakened his long-dormant sexuality. He had lingered longer than he needed over the passage where Laodameia's husband, killed in the war, comes back as a ghost and inhabits as her lover the wax image. It had left him a prey to undefined, aimless, undirected desire.

That evening he wrote his diary. It was full of sexual imagery. And when he slept he dreamt flamboyantly, the dreams full of colour, teeming with luscious images, none approximating to anything he'd known in life. Throughout the day he was restless, working automatically, distracted by sounds from outside: bird-song, a car passing along the road, the arrival of Sandy, and then by the noise of the lawnmower. He couldn't bring himself to ask what had happened to Lavinia. He didn't speak to Sandy at all, disregarding the man's waves and smiles and other meaningless signals.

It occurred to him when he was getting up on the Wednesday that Lavinia might come. She might have been ill on Monday or otherwise prevented from coming. Perhaps those signs that Sandy had made to him had indicated a wish to impart some sort of information about Lavinia. It was an unpleasant thought. He dreaded the sight of her.

He had already begun work on the author's analysis of a suggestion that the real Helen fled to Egypt while it was only a simulacrum that Paris took to Troy, when distantly he heard the back door open and close, footsteps cross the tiles. It was not Lavinia's tread, these were not Lavinia's movements. For a moment he feared Sandy's entry into his room, Sandy with an explanation, or worse, Sandy *asking* for an explanation. Somehow he felt that was possible.

Instead, a girl came in, a different girl. She didn't knock. She walked into his room without the least diffidence, confidently, as if it were her right. 'I'm Susannah, I've taken over from Lavinia. You won't mind, will you? We didn't think you'd mind. It's not as if it will make a scrap of difference.'

I know the girl he meant, this Susannah. Or I think I do, though perhaps it's one of her sisters that I know, that I have seen in the village outside her parents' house. Her father was one of those rarities not native to the place, but a newcomer when he married her mother, a man for some reason acceptable and even welcomed. There were a few of such people, perhaps four. As for the girl . . .

'She was so beautiful,' he said.

'There are a lot of good-looking people in the village,' I said. 'In fact, there's no one you could even call ordinarily plain. They're a handsome lot.'

He went on as if I hadn't spoken. Her beauty struck him forcibly from that first moment. She had golden looks, film star looks. If that had a vulgar sound, I was to remember that this particular appearance was only associated with Hollywood *because* it was the archetype, because no greater beauty could be found than the tall blonde with the full lips, straight nose and large blue eyes, the plump breasts and narrow hips and long legs. Susannah had all that and a smile of infinite sweetness.

'And she didn't throw herself at me,' he said. 'She cleaned the house and made me coffee and she wasn't – well, servile, the way Lavinia was. She smiled. She talked to me when she brought the coffee and before she left, and she talked sensibly and simply, just about how she'd cycled to the house and the fine weather and her dad giving her a Walkman for her birthday. It was nice. It was *sweet*. Perhaps one of the best things was that she didn't mention

Sandy. And there was something *curative* about her coming. I didn't dream the dreams again and as for Lavinia – Lavinia vanished. From my thoughts, I mean. That weekend I felt something quite new to me, contentment. I worked. I was satisfied with my rendering of *The Golden Apple*. I was going to be all right. I didn't even mind Sandy turning up on Sunday and cleaning all the windows inside and out.'

'Young Susannah must be a marvel if she could do all that,' I said.

He didn't exactly shiver but he hunched his shoulders as if he was cold. In a low voice he began to read from his diary entries.

3

She seemed very young to him. The next time she came and the next he wanted to ask her how old she was but he had a natural aversion from asking that question of anyone. He looked at her breasts, he couldn't help himself, they were so beautiful, so perfect. The shape of a young woman's breasts was like nothing else on earth, he said, there was nothing they could be compared to and all comparison was vulgar pornography.

At first he told himself he looked at them so because he was curious about her age – was she sixteen or seventeen or more? – but that wasn't the reason, that was self-deception. She dressed in modest clothes, or at least in clothes that covered most of her, a high-necked T-shirt, a long skirt, but he could tell she wore nothing underneath, nothing at all. Her navel showed as a shallow declivity in the clinging cotton of the skirt and the material was lifted by her mount of Venus (his words, not mine). When he thought of these things as well as when he looked the blood pumped loudly in his head and his throat constricted. She wore sandals that were no more than thongs which left her small high-instepped feet virtually bare.

It never occurred to him at that time that he was the object of some definite strategy. His mind was never crossed even by the suspicion that Susannah might have taken Lavinia's place because he'd made it plain he didn't find Lavinia desirable. That it would be most exceptional for two young girls, coming to work for him in succession, both – immediately – to make attempts to fascinate him, indeed to seduce him.

There should have been no doubt in his mind, after all, for all he had said about Susannah not throwing herself at him, that in the ordinary usages of society a girl doesn't come to work for and be alone with a man stark naked under her skirt and top unless she is extending an invitation. But he didn't see it. He saw the movement of her breasts under that thin stuff but he saw only innocence. He saw the cotton stretched across her belly, close as a second skin, and put down her choice of dressing like this to juvenile naivety. The blame for it was his – and Lavinia's. Lavinia, he told himself, had awakened an amorousness in him that he would have been happy never to feel again. Instead, he had lost all peace and contentment; with her stupid coyness, her posturing and her clothes, she had robbed him of that. And now he was in thrall to this beautiful, simple and innocent girl.

She was subtle. Not for her the blatant raising of her arms above her head to reach a high shelf, still less the climbing on to a chair or up a pair of steps, stuff of soft pornography. He asked her to sit and have her coffee with him and she demurred but finally agreed, and she sat so modestly, taking extravagant care to cover not only her knees but her legs almost to those exquisite ankles. She even tucked her skirt round her legs and tucked it tightly, thus revealing – he was sure in utter innocence – as much as she concealed. While she talked about her family, her mother who had been a Kirkman, her father who came from a hundred miles away, from Yorkshire, her big sister and her little sister, she must

165

have seen the direction his eyes took, for she folded her arms across her breasts.

It dismayed him. He wasn't that sort of man. Before his wife he had had girlfriends but there had been nothing casual, no pick-ups, no one-night stands. He might almost have said he had never made love to a woman without being, or in a fair way to being, in love with her. But this feeling he had was lust. He was sure that it had nothing to do with 'being in love', though it was as strong and as powerful as love. And it was her beauty alone that was to blame – he said 'to blame' – he couldn't have said if he liked her, liking didn't come into it. Her appearance, her presence, the aura of her, stunned him but at the same time had him desperately staring. It was an amazement to him that others didn't see that desperation.

Not that there were others, with the exception, of course, of Sandy.

While Ben was working, Sandy, if he was outside, would sometimes appear at the window to smile and point up his thumbs. Ben would be working on some abstruse lining up of Jungian archetypes with Helen and Achilles, and be confronted by Sandy's grinning face. If the weather was fine enough for the window to be open Sandy put his head inside and enquired if everything was all right. 'Things going OK, are they?'

Ben moved upstairs. He took his word processor and his dictionary into a back bedroom with an inaccessible window. And all this time he thought these people were my servants, 'help' paid by me to wait on him. He couldn't dismiss them, he felt, or even protest. I was charging him no rent, he paid only for his electricity and the telephone. It would have seemed to him the deepest ingratitude and impertinence to criticise my choice. Yet if he had been free to do so he would not only have got rid of Sandy but of Susannah also. He could scarcely bear her in his presence. Yet he wondered what greyness and emptiness would replace her.

I must not give the impression all this went on for long. No more than three weeks, perhaps, before the change came and his world was overturned. He thought afterwards that the change was helped along by his taking his work upstairs. She might not have done what she did if he had been in the room on the ground floor with its view of the lake – and affording a view to other people driving by the lake and to window-cleaning, lawn-mowing, flowerbed-weeding Sandy.

She always came into his room to tell him when she was leaving. He had reached a point when the sound of her footsteps ascending the stairs heated his body and set his blood pounding. The screen of the word processor clouded over and his hands shook above the keyboard. That's how bad it was.

One of the things which terrified him was that she might touch him. Playfully, or in simple friendliness, she might lay her hand on his arm or even, briefly, take his hand. She never had, she wasn't a 'toucher'. But if she did he didn't know what he would do, he felt he couldn't be responsible for his own actions, he might do something outrageous or his body, without his volition, something shameful. The strange thing was that in all this it never seems to have occurred to him that she might want *him*, or at least be acquiescent. She came into the room. His desire blazed out of him but he was long beyond controlling it.

'I'll be off then, sir.'

How he hated that 'sir'! It must be stopped and stopped now, whatever I might require from my 'help'.

'Please don't call me that. Call me Ben.'

It came from him like a piteous cry. He might have been crying to her that he had a mortal illness or someone close to him was dead.

'Ben,' she said, 'Ben.' She said it as if it was new to her or distantly exotic instead of, as he put it, the name of half the pet dogs in the district. 'I like it.' And then she said, 'Are you all right?'

'It doesn't matter,' he said. 'Ignore me.'

'Why would I want to do that, Ben?'

The burr in her voice was suddenly more pronounced. She spoke in a radio rustic's accent. Perhaps she had experience of men in Ben's condition, probably it was a common effect of her presence, for she knew exactly what was wrong with him. What was *right* with him?

She said, 'Come here.'

He got up, mesmerised, not yet believing, a long way still from believing. But she took his hands and laid them on her breasts. It was her way to do that, to take his hands to those soft hidden parts of her body where she most liked to feel his touch. She put her mouth up to his mouth, the tip of her tongue on his tongue, she stood on tiptoe, lifting her pelvis against him. Then, with a nod, with a smile, she took him by the hand and led him into his bedroom.

4

Before Ben went to Gothic House it had been arranged that I should go down myself for a weekend in June. I'd decided to put the house on the market as soon as Ben left and there were matters to see to, such as what I was going to do about the furniture, which of it I wanted to keep and which to sell. As the time grew near I felt less and less like going. To have his company would be good – perhaps rather more than that – but I could have his company in London. It was the place I didn't care to be in. In the time I'd been away from it my aversion had grown. If that was possible, I felt even worse about it than when I'd last been there.

At this time, of course, I knew almost nothing of what Ben was doing. We'd spoken on the phone just once after the nightingale conversation and he had said only that the change of air was doing him good and the translation was going well. The girls weren't mentioned and neither was Sandy, so I knew nothing of Susannah beyond what I'd seen of her some two or three years before.

That was when I had my encounters with her parents. Peddar, they were called, and they had three young daughters, Susannah, Carol and another one whose name I couldn't remember. I couldn't even remember which was the eldest and which the youngest. Of course, I have plenty of cause to do so now. I'd been to the village quite a lot by that time and even taken a small part in village life, attended a social in the village hall and gone to Marion Kirkman's daughter's wedding.

The villagers were guarded at first, then gradually friendlier. Just what one would expect. I went to the wedding and to the party afterwards. In spite of all that has happened since, I still think it was the nicest wedding I've ever been to, the best party, the handsomest guests, the best food, the greatest joy. Everyone was tremendously nice to me. If I had the feeling that I was closely watched, rather as if the other people there were studying me for a social survey, I put that down to imagination. They were curious, that was all. They were probably shy of my middle-classness, for I had noticed by that time that there were no professional people in the village: agricultural labourers, mechanics, shopworkers and cleaners – who went to their jobs elsewhere – plumbers, electricians, builders, thatchers and pargeters, a hairdresser and, because even there modern life intruded, a computer technician, but no one who worked otherwise than with his or her hands.

I think, now, I was a fool. I should have kept myself to myself. I should have resisted the seductions of friendliness and warmth. Instead, because I'd accepted hospitality, I decided to give a party. It would be a Sunday morning drinks party, after church. I invited everyone who had invited me and a good many who hadn't but whom I had met at other people's gatherings. Sandy offered to serve the drinks and in the event did so admirably.

They came and the party happened. Everyone was charming, everyone seemed to know that if you go to a party you should endeavour to be entertaining, to talk, to listen, to appear carefree. What was lacking was middle-class sophistication and it was a welcome omission. The party resulted in an invitation, just one, from the Peddars, who delivered it as they were leaving, a written invitation in an envelope, evidently prepared beforehand with great care. Would I come to supper the following Friday? And I need not bother to drive, John Peddar would collect me and take me home.

It must have been about that time that I noticed another oddity – if good manners and friendliness can be called that – about the village and its people. I'd already, of course, observed my own resemblance to the general appearance of them, a sort of look we had in common. I was tall and fair with blue eyes and so were they. Not that they were all the same, not clone-like, I don't mean that, some were shorter, some less slender, eyes varied from midnight-blue through turquoise to palest sky and hair from flaxen to light-brown, but they had a certain look of all belonging to the same tribe. Danes used to look like that, I was once told, before the influx of immigrants and visitors; if you sat outside a café on Strøget you saw all these blue-eyed blondes pass by, all looking like members of a family. Thus it was in the village, as if their gene pool was small and I might have been one of them.

So might Ben, though I didn't think of it then. Why should I?

I wrote a note to the Peddars, saying I'd be pleased to come on Friday.

It sounds very cowardly, what I'm about to say. Well, it will have to sound that way. Although I'd much have preferred to postpone going to Gothic House till the Saturday, I'd told Ben I'd come on the Friday and I kept to that. But I drove down in the evening so as to pass through the village in the dark and since, in June, it didn't start getting dark till after nine thirty, I was late arriving.

I braced myself, even took a deep breath, as I reached the corner where the first house was, some half-mile from the rest, Mark and Kathy Gresham's house. There were lights on but no windows open, though it was a warm night. I drove on quickly. A dozen or so teenagers had assembled with their bikes by the bus shelter, they were the only people about. The light from the single lamp in the village street shone on their fair hair. They turned as one as I passed, recognising the car, but not one of them waved.

An estate agent's 'For Sale' board was up outside the Old Rectory. So the farmer from Lynn hadn't been able to stand it either. Or they hadn't been able to stand him. I slowed and, certain no one was about, stopped. No lights were on in the big, handsome Georgian house. It was in darkness and it was deserted. You can always tell from the outside if a house is empty – no wonder burglars are so successful.

No doubt he spent as little time there as possible. He hadn't been there long, perhaps two years, and I'd known him only by sight, a big, dark man with a pretty blonde wife, much younger than he. As I started the car again I wondered what they had done to him and why.

The sky was clear but moonless. In the dark, glassy lake whole constellations were reflected and a single bright planet shining like a torch held under the water. A little wind had got up and the woodland trees rustled their heavy weight of leaves. In my headlights Gothic House had its fairy-tale castle look, grey but bright, its lighted windows orange oblongs with arched tops, the crenellated crown of the turret the only part of it reflected in the water.

Ben and I had never kissed. But now he took me in his arms and kissed me with great affection. 'Louise, how wonderful that you're here. Welcome to your own house!'

I thought him a changed man.

It was only half an hour since Susannah had left him and gone home to her father's house. He told me that while we sat drinking whisky at the window with its view of the lake. The moon had risen, a bright full moon whose radiance was nearly equal to winter sunshine. Its silver-green light painted the tree trunks like lichen.

'Susannah Peddar?' I was finding an awkwardness in saying it, already remembering.

'Why the surprise?' he said. 'You employ her. And, come to that, Sandy.'

I told him I used to employ Sandy but no longer. As for Susannah . . . She wasn't quite the last person from that village I'd have wanted in my house but nearly. I didn't say that. I said I was glad he'd found someone to look after him. He went on talking about her, already caught up in the lover's need to utter repeatedly the beloved's name, but I didn't know that then. I only wondered why he dwelt so obsessively on the niceness, the cleverness and the beauty of someone I still thought of as a village teenager.

That night he said nothing of what had happened between them but went off to bed in pensive mood, still astonished that Susannah wasn't employed by me. I, who had been relaxed, moving into a quiet, sleepy frame of mind, was now unpleasantly wide awake and I lay sleepless for a long time, thinking of the Peddars and of other things.

The evening with John and Iris Peddar was very much what I'd expected it would be, or the early part was. They lived in one of the newer houses, originally a council house, but they had done a great deal of work on it, building an annexe and turning the two downstairs rooms into one.

I'd calculated, in my middle-class way, my deeply English class-conscious way, that they would dress up for me. He would wear a suit, she a dress with fussy jewellery and the three little girls frilly frocks. So I decided to dress up for them and did that rare thing, wore a dress and stockings and shoes with heels. When John Peddar arrived to collect me I was surprised to see him in jeans and an open-necked check shirt but supposed that he intended to change when we got to his house.

In my opinion, everyone looks better in informal clothes. Something of the absurd is inseparable from gowns and jewels and men's dark suits. But I didn't expect them to feel this. I was astonished when Iris came out to greet me in jeans and striped T-shirt. The children too wore what they'd worn at school that day, or even what they'd changed into after the greater formality of school.

Even now, knowing what I know, I marvel at the psychology of it, at their knowledge of people and taste. They *knew* I wouldn't necessarily be easier with them dressed like that, but that I would unquestionably find one or all of them more attractive. They were a good-looking family, John especially, tall, thin, fair with a fine-featured face and enquiring eyes, eyebrows that went up often, as if commenting with secret laughter on the outrageous. She was pretty with commonplace Barbie doll looks, but the three little girls were all beauties, two of them golden blondes who favoured their father, the third unlike either parent, the image of a Millais child with nut-brown hair and soulful eyes.

We drank sherry before the meal. John drank as much as Iris and I did and as much wine. I think I must have known by that time that in the village you drank as much as you liked before driving. The police who drove their little car round the streets every so often would never stop a villager, still less breath-test him. Two PCs lived here, after all, and one was Jennifer Fowler's brother.

We had avocado with prawns, chicken casserole and chocolate mousse. That, at any rate, was what I'd expected. The children went to bed, the eldest one last as was fair. Iris called me upstairs to see her bedroom that she and John had newly decorated, and I went – it was still light, though dusk, the soft violet dusk that comes to woodland places – and there, while I admired the wallpaper, she tucked her arm into mine and stood close up against me.

It was friendliness, the warm outgoing attitude of one woman to another whom she finds congenial. So I thought as she squeezed my arm and pressed her body against mine. She had had a great deal to drink. Her inhibitions had gone down. I still thought that when she moved her arm to my shoulders and slowly turning me to her, brought her lips to within an inch of mine. I stepped aside, I managed a small laugh. I was anxious, terribly anxious in that moment, to avoid her doing anything she might bitterly regret next morning. We all know the feeling of waking to horrified memory, to the what-have-I-done self-enquiry that sets the blood pounding.

About an hour later he drove me home. She was all pleasantness and charm, begging me to come again, it was delightful that we'd got to know each other at last. This time I had no choice but to allow the kiss, it was no more than a cool pecking of the air around my cheek. John showed no signs of the amount he'd drunk. But neither, then, had she, apart from that bedroom overture I was sure now came from nothing more than a sudden impulse of finding she liked me.

In the car, sitting beside me, he told me I was a beautiful woman. It made me feel uncomfortable. All possible rejoinders were either coy or vulgar, so I said nothing. He drove me home and said he'd come in with me, he wouldn't allow me to go alone into a dark empty house. It was late, I said, I was tired. All the more reason for him to come in with me. Once inside I put on a lot of lights; I offered him a drink. He had seated himself comfortably as if at home.

'Won't Iris wonder where you are?'

He looked at me and those eyebrows rose. 'I don't think she will.'

It was clear what he meant. I was revolted. His intrigues must be so habitual that his wife accepted with resignation that if he was late home he was with a woman. It explained her overture to me, a gesture born of loneliness and rejection.

He began talking about her, how he would never do anything

to hurt her or imperil their marriage. Nothing *could* imperil it, he insisted. Most women have heard that sort of thing from men at some time or other, it is standard philander-speak. Yet if he hadn't said it, if he'd been a little different, less knowing, less confident, and yes, less rustic, I might have felt his attraction, at least the attraction of his looks. I'd have done nothing because of her, but I might have felt like doing something. As it was, I was simply contemptuous. But I didn't want trouble, I didn't want a scene. Was I afraid of him? Perhaps a little. He was a tall, strong man who had had a lot to drink and I was alone with him.

In the end, when he'd had a second whisky, I stood up, said I was desperately tired, I was going to have to turn him out. I know now that physical violence was quite foreign to his nature but I didn't then and I hated it when he put his hand under my chin, lifted my face and kissed me. You could just – only just – have called it a friendly social kiss.

Just as Ben was later to have those dreams, so did I. Something in the air? Or, more subtly, the atmosphere of the place? The first of my dreams was that night. John Peddar was different in the dream, looking the same but more my kind of man. 'Civilised' is the word that comes to mind, yet it's not quite the right one. Gentler, more sensitive, less crude in his approach. I suppose that the I who was dreaming arranged all that, but whatever it was I didn't repulse him, I began to make love with him, I began to enjoy him in a luxuriating way, but the dawn chorus of birds awoke me with their singing.

He came back in the morning, the real man, not the dream image.

It was a dull morning of heavy cloud. I've said the sky was always clear and the sun always shining but of course it wasn't. All that is fantasy, myth and magic. The house was quite dark inside. Before the dream came I had slept badly. That was the beginning of sleeping badly at Gothic House, of bad nights and later total insomnia. I came downstairs in my dressing gown, thinking it must be Sandy at the door. He came in and – I don't know how to put this – took the door out of my hands, took my hands from it and closed it himself, shot the bolt across it.

I was taken aback by this appropriation of actions that should be exclusively mine. I stared. He took me in his arms in a curious caressing gesture, a sweeping of light gentle hands down my arms, my body, my thighs. He drew me close to him, murmuring 'darling' and 'darling' again and 'sweetheart', his voice thick and breathless. Before his mouth could touch mine I pushed him away with a great shove and he staggered back against the wall.

'Please go,' I said. 'I can't stand this. Please go.'

I expected trouble, excuses that I'd invited him, defences that he could sense my desire, accusations finally of frigidity. But there was nothing. For a moment he looked at me enquiringly. Then he nodded as if something suspected had been confirmed. He even smiled. My front door, that he had previously taken possession of, he opened, let himself out, and closed it quietly and very carefully behind him.

Ben told me about Susannah. He told me all those things I have already told you and more than that. We sat out in the garden, there was a stone table, a bench and chairs, on the lawn in front of the house under a mulberry tree, and we sat there in the heat of the day. Its fallen fruit lay about on the grass like spoonfuls of crimson jam.

The tree gave enough shade to make sitting there pleasant. You could no more look at the lake than you could at a mirror with the full sun shining on it. A few cars passed along the road, village people off to shop in the town supermarkets, and the drivers waved. At Ben, of course, they wouldn't wave at me. He told me how his early love-making with Susannah had become a full-blown love affair.

No inhibition held him back from telling me about it. He had to tell someone. I'd never known him so open, so revelatory.

'I'm glad it's making you happy,' I said.

What lies we tell for the sake of social accord!

'It won't last, of course, I know that. It's entirely physical.' (I'm always sceptical when people say that. What do they mean? Do they know what they mean?) 'She's years younger than I am.'

'Yes.' Oh, yes, she was. 'How old *is* she?'

'Eighteen, I suppose.'

'And you wouldn't –' I tried to put it tactfully '– exactly call her an educated person, would you?'

'What does that matter? I'm not going to marry her, I'm not going to settle down with her for life. It's not as if I were in love with her. I'm having with her – oh, something I've never had with anyone in my life before, something I've only read about: pure, uncomplicated, beautiful sex. Sex without questions, without pain, without consequences. It's as if we're mythical beings at the beginning of the world, we're Paris and Helen, mutually exulting in the sweetest and most innocent pleasure known to mankind.'

'My goodness,' I said.

'I suppose you think that very high-flown, but it's an accurate expression of my feelings.'

Why didn't I warn him then? Why didn't I tell him about Susannah's father and Sandy and Roddy Fowler and meetings in the village hall? Or my suspicions about the farmer's wife from Lynn? Quite simply because I thought *the difference of gender made the difference*. He was a man. I thought men would be exempt. But later that day, after I'd made a rough inventory of the furniture I'd keep and noted the few small repairs the house needed before it could be put up for sale, I found myself looking at him, assessing things about him.

I was very fond of him, had started to grow fond after he separated from his wife, but it was very much for his mind and his manner. His gentleness pleased me and his thoughtfulness, his sensitivity and modesty. Pointless to pretend that he was much to look at, though I liked his looks, the intelligence in his face and the perceptiveness, his expressions of understanding and of pondering. But he was somewhat below medium height and very thin with an unfit slack-muscled thinness. He looked older than his age – thirty-seven? Thirty-eight? – his face was lined, as thin fair faces soon become with time, and his hair was fast receding.

I knew what I saw in him but not what Susannah did. The older man, perhaps, a father figure, though she had a perfectly adequate father of her own, very little older than Ben. They marry early in the village. But who can account for love? Even for attraction?

We went out for our dinner that evening to a restaurant ten miles away. During the meal he asked me if he should be paying Sandy. Wasn't there something wrong about Sandy working for him without payment?

'If you don't pay him,' I said, 'maybe he'll get the message and go away. He's a pest and a nuisance.' I said nothing about Sandy's attempts to make love to me after the John Peddar incident and my outrage. I would have if I'd thought it would make a difference.

'But for him,' he said, 'I suppose I'd never have met Susannah.'

He would have but I didn't know it then.

'When are you seeing her again?' I meant this joke question seriously and that was how he took it.

'On Monday morning. It's a bit awkward her going on cleaning the house and paying her is very awkward. I shall have to try and get someone else. Of course, we meet in the evenings – well, she comes here. I can't exactly go to her father's house.'

I had nothing to say to that. But from what I knew of her father's house, an orgy in the front room in broad daylight wouldn't have been unacceptable. I had revised my sympathy for Iris when at a village dance she tried to introduce me, with unmistakable motive, to her younger unattached brother, Roddy. For some reason the Peddar family had done their best to find me a sexual partner and apparently anyone would do, if not either of them or a relation of theirs, some other villager. Sandy, I supposed, had been put up to it by them. After all, I knew him already and in their eyes perhaps that was the only necessary prerequisite.

While showing me something he'd done in the garden he put his arm round me. I told him not to do that. He looked sideways at me and asked why not.

'Because,' I said. 'Because I don't want you to. Isn't that enough?'

'Come on, it's not natural, a nice-looking woman like yourself, never with a man.'

'None of this is any business of yours.' How ridiculous one sounds when offended!

'Is it women that you fancy? You can say, you needn't be shy. I know about those things, I've been around.'

'You needn't be around here any more, that's for sure,' I said. 'I don't want you working for me any longer. Please go and don't come back.'

Ben wouldn't have been interested in any of that, so I didn't tell him. We went home to Gothic House and next day I said I thought of putting it on the market at the end of August.

'You'll have finished your translation by then, won't you?'

'Yes, I'm sure I will.' He looked rather dismayed. 'I said three months, didn't I? It's so beautiful here and the situation of the house, this village – won't you regret getting rid of it?'

'I come here so seldom,' I said, 'it's really not worth keeping it up.'

5

It was strange how infrequently those people went out in the evenings. They visited each other, I know that now, but they hardly ever left the village after six. I spent two weeks there once, when I was trying to teach myself to like the place, and not a single car passed along the road by the lake in the evenings. I might not have seen cars if they had passed but I would have seen the beams from their headlights sweep across my ceilings. They stayed at home. They preferred their isolation.

I believe I was their principal concern at that time. No doubt they had a meeting in the village hall, called especially for the discussion of *me*. I blundered into one of those meetings once, having mistaken it for a teenage cancer fund-raising night. Utter silence prevailed as I walked in, they had heard or sensed my coming. Mark Gresham came down the hall to me, explained my mistake and escorted me out with such care and exquisite politeness that the thinnest-skinned couldn't have taken offence.

Sometimes, in those days, the last of those days, the watchers in the windows waved to me. There was never any question of concealing from me that they *were* watching. They waved or they smiled and nodded. And then, suddenly, all smiles and waving ceased, all friendliness came to an end. When Ben came down for that weekend and we saw the bathers they were still amiably inclined towards me. Next time I came everything had changed and the antagonism was almost palpable.

Ben fell in love with her.

Perhaps he'd really been in love from the first but refused to allow himself to admit it and all that insistence on matters between them being 'entirely physical' was self-deception. Whatever it was, by the middle of July he was in love, 'deeply in, in up to his neck', as he told me, utterly, obsessively, committed to love.

Not that he told me *then*. That came much later. At the time, though I heard from him it was not to mention Susannah. He wrote to ask if I was sincere about selling Gothic House and if I was, would I sell it to him. His former wife had found a buyer for the home they had shared and under the terms of the divorce settlement half the proceeds were to be his. Gothic House might even so be beyond his means and if this was the case he would look for some cottage in the village. In a mysterious oblique sentence he wrote that he thought 'living elsewhere might not be acceptable to everyone concerned'.

Why live there? He was a Londoner. He had lived abroad but never other than in a big city. The answer was that in the short time he'd been there he'd become very attached to the place. He loved it. How could he return to London and its painful memories? As a translator he could live anywhere. The village was a place in which he thought he could be happy as he had never been before.

Perhaps I was slow but I attached no particular significance to any of this. The truth was that I felt it awkward. It was a principle of mine, never before needing to be acted on, that one does not sell a house, a car or any large valuable item or object, maybe anything at all, to a friend. The passing of money will break the friendship, or that was the theory.

I waited a few days before replying. The seriousness of this, the projected sale or refusal to sell, caused me to write rather than phone. If I had phoned I might have learned more. But at last I wrote to say that as I'd told him I wasn't intending to sell yet. Let us wait till the end of August. Didn't he really need more time before committing himself? If by then he still wanted to live in the village and still wanted Gothic House, then we could talk about it.

No answer came to my letter. I found out later that Ben, exasperated by my delaying tactics, had gone next day to an estate agent to enquire about cottages. He didn't much care what he lived in, what roof was over his head, so long as he could live there with Susannah.

When it was all over and we were talking, when he poured out his heart to me, he told me that love had come to him in a moment, with an absolute suddenness. From being a contented man with a beautiful young lover whose body he enjoyed more than perhaps he'd ever enjoyed any woman's, he became lost, at once terrified and exalted, obsessed, alone and desperate. Yet it came to him when she was out of his sight, when she was at home in her father's house.

They had made love in his bed at Gothic House, had eaten a meal and drunk wine and gone back to bed to make love again. And then quite late, but not as late as midnight, he had done what he was now in the habit of doing, had driven her home, discreetly dropping her at the end of the street. Useless, all this secrecy, as I could have told him. Everyone would have known. They would have known from the first kiss that passed between those two. But to him the love affair was a secret that, almost as soon as he recognised his feelings for what they truly were, he wanted everything out in the open, he wanted the world to know.

He walked about the house, putting dishes in the sink, drinking the last of the wine and suddenly he found himself longing for her. A pain caught him in the chest and shoulders. Like a heart attack, he said, or what he imagined a heart attack would be. He hugged himself in his arms. He sat down and said aloud, 'I'm in love and I know I've never been in love before.'

The pain flowed out of him and left him tired and spent. He was filled with what he called 'a glory'. He saw her in his mind's eye, naked and smiling, coming to him so sweetly, so tenderly, to put her arms round him and touch him with her lips. The wrench of it was so bad that he said he didn't know how he continued to sit there, how he resisted jumping in the car and rushing back to her, beating on her father's door to demand her release into his arms. And he did get up but only to pace the room, the house, speaking her name, Susannah, and uttering into that silent place, 'I love you, oh, I love you.'

Next day he told her. She seemed surprised. 'I know,' she said.

'You know?' He gazed at her, holding her hands. 'How clever you are, my love, my sweetheart, to know what I didn't know. Do you love *me*? Can you love me?'

She said with the utmost tranquillity, 'I've always loved you. From the first. Of course I love you.'

'Do you, darling Susannah?'

'Did you think I'd have done those things we've done if I didn't love you?'

He was chastened. He should have known. She was no Lavinia. Yet I suppose some caution, some vestige of prudence or perhaps just his age and the remembrance of his marriage, prevented his asking her there and then to marry him. For that was what he had wanted from the first moment of his realisation, to marry her. It was what you did, he said to me, when you were in love like that, irrevocably, profoundly, you didn't want any trial time, you wanted commitment for life. Besides, she was half his age, she was very young, it wasn't as if he was a fellow teenager and the two of them experimenting with passion. Honourably, he must marry her.

'But you didn't ask her?' I said.

'Not then. I intended to wait a week. She was so sweet that week, Louise, so loving, I can't tell you how giving she was, how passionate. Of course I wouldn't tell you, it's not something I'd speak of. I wrote some of it down in my diary. You can see the diary. Why should I care now?'

She had shown him, when they made love, things he wouldn't have suspected she knew. Things he had hardly known himself. She was adventurous and entirely uninhibited. He was even, once, quite shocked.

'Oh, I wouldn't do it,' she said serenely, 'if I didn't love you so much.'

She still came to clean the house. His suggestion that it was no longer suitable, that he must find someone else, was met with incredulity, with laughter. Of course she would come to clean the house and she had done, regularly, without fail. Only sometimes she came to him away from her work to kiss him or hold her arms round his neck and lay her cheek sweetly against his.

It was a Saturday when she made that remark about loving him so much and he expected her on the Monday morning. No, that is to put it too tamely. He hadn't seen her for thirty hours and he yearned for her. Waiting for the appointed hour, eight thirty, he paced the house, watching for her from window after window.

She didn't come.

After a half-hour of hell in which he speculated every possible disaster, a road accident, her father's wrath, when he at last decided he must phone the Peddars' house, Lavinia came.

She had no explanation to offer him beyond saying Susannah couldn't be there and had sent her as a substitute. Susannah had come round to her mother's very early and asked if she, Lavinia, would do the Gothic House duty that day. Only today? he had asked, and she said as far as she knew. She, at any rate, doubted if she would be coming again herself. But when she said this she gave him one of her coy looks over her thin white shoulder, somehow making him understand that future visits could happen, might be contingent on his response. He was disgusted and angry. He did his best to ignore her, put her money downstairs on the kitchen table and fled to his room upstairs. Susannah would come that evening, they had an arrangement for her to come at seven, and then all would be well, all would be explained.

Soon after Lavinia left the estate agent phoned. A cottage had just been put on to the market. It was in the heart of the village. Would he be interested? If so, the estate agent would meet him outside the cottage at three and show him round. The owner was a Mrs Fowler, an old lady growing infirm, who intended to move in with her son and his wife.

Ben walked to the village. It was a lovely day. The sun was brighter for him than for others, the lake bluer and its waters more sparkling, the flowers in the gardens more scented and more brilliant and the air sweeter – because he was in love. Sometimes 'the glory' came back to him and when that happened he wanted to leap and sing, he wanted to prostrate himself on the ground and cry aloud to whomever or whatever had given him the joy of love, had given him Susannah. All this was in his diary. A phrase from the Bible kept coming back to him: And sorrow and sighing shall flee away. He said it to himself as he walked along – there shall be no more pain, and sorrow and sighing shall flee away. He didn't think the word in the text was 'pain' but he couldn't really remember.

Mrs Fowler's was a tiny cottage, two up and two down, with a thatched roof. The frowsty little bedroom, low-ceilinged, the floor piled with layers of rugs, the bed with layers of dingy whitish covers, fringed or lacy and now inhabited by sleeping cats, he saw as it would be when transformed, when occupied by himself and Susannah. A four-poster they would have, he thought, and he imagined her kneeling up naked on the quilt, drawing back the curtains to disclose herself to him, the two of them sinking embraced into that silky, shadowy, scented warmth . . .

He looked out of the window and faces looked back at him, one in each of the windows opposite. A curtain dropped, another pair of eyes appeared.

Mrs Fowler said comfortably, 'Everyone likes to know your business down here.'

She was a tiny upright woman, still handsome in extreme age, hawk-faced and no doubt hawk-eyed, those eyes a sparkling pale turquoise.

'My granddaughter does for you,' she said.

He thought for some reason she meant Lavinia, but she didn't. 'Susannah Peddar.'

There was the suspicion of a smile at the corners of her mouth when she said the name. She looked conspiratorial. In that moment he longed to tell her. An overpowering desire to tell her seized him, to come out with it. He wanted to say that this was why he needed a house in the village, a home to which he could bring his bride, a bower for Susannah, among her own people, a stone's throw from her mother. How splendid it was, how serendipitous, that the very house in the whole village that might seem almost home to Susannah was the one he could buy.

He managed to suppress that desire, but all ideas of purchasing Gothic House vanished. This was the house for him, the only one. He would have offered her double what she was asking, anything to possess it and present it to Susannah. Probably it was as well he had been cautioned only to make his offer through the estate agents.

'At least I was saved from making a total fool of myself,' he wrote in his diary.

The agent, he discovered, had his own home in the village. He was a villager born and bred. Mrs Fowler would very likely take an offer, he said. Anyway, there would be no harm in trying.

'I wouldn't want to lose it,' Ben said.

The estate agent smiled. 'No fear of that. Think about it and come back to me.'

Rather late in the day Ben reflected that he should have asked Susannah first. She should have been asked if she wanted to live in a house that had belonged to her grandmother. He would ask her that night. He would propose marriage to her and he had no doubt she would accept, since she had told him she loved him. Then he'd tell her about the cottage. She was, he told himself, a simple country girl. Of course she was a goddess, his Helen and Oenone and Aphrodite, an ideal woman, a queen, the perfect paramour, but she was a country girl also, only eighteen, and one who would have no latter-day urban preferences for cohabitation over marriage or any nonsense of that sort.

At seven thirty she still hadn't come. He was mad with worry and terror. He didn't want to phone her father's house, he'd never done so, and he'd got it into his head – without any evidence for so doing – that the Peddars disapproved of him. Perhaps she was ill. He had a moment's comfort from thinking that. (Thus do lovers console themselves, deriving peace of mind from the beloved's incapacity.) He had forgotten for the moment that she had gone out 'very early' to Lavinia's house, hardly the behaviour of someone too ill to go to work. He would phone, he had to.

Her voice was magical to him, soft, sweet, with the lilting accent he had come to hear as pretty and, of course, seductive. He had never heard it on the phone, but somehow he knew that when he did hear it he would be silenced, for seconds he would be unable to reply, he would have to listen, be captured by her voice and feel it run into his blood, and take away his breath. He dialled the number and waited, waited for *her*. It was the first time in his life he had ever suffered the awfulness of hearing the ringing tone repeated and repeated while longing, praying, for an answer.

Someone answered at last. It was a young girl's voice, soft, sweet, with that same accent, but without the power to stir him, a voice immediately recognisable as not hers. One of the sisters, he supposed. She didn't say.

'Sue's gone round to Kim's.'

It sounded like a code to him, a spatter of phonemes. He had to ask her to repeat it.

'Sue', she said more slowly, 'has gone round to Kim's house, OK?'

'Thank you,' he said.

He realised he knew nothing of her friends, nothing of her life away from him. He had supposed her so young and artless as to be satisfied with the company of her parents and her sisters, remaining at home in the evenings until he rescued her from this rustic domesticity. But of course she had friends, girls she had been to school with, the daughters of neighbours. None of that accounted for her failure to come to him and he racked his mind for reasons. Had he inadvertently said something to hurt her feelings?

Could it be that, after taking thought, she found herself offended by his enquiry as to her sexual adventurousness? But she had replied that she would only do these things with someone she loved and she loved him so much. That had been almost the last thing she had said to him when they parted on the previous Friday a hundred yards from her father's house, that she loved him so much. He was driven to think – he *wanted* to think – that it was that father and that mother who, having discovered the truth from Susannah, her heart too full to keep love to herself, had taken a heavy line and sent her to spend the evening not at Gothic House but with a girlfriend.

Night is the enemy of the unhappy lover, for it's then that fearful thoughts come and horrible forebodings. It would have been better if the night had been dull and wet but it was warm, with a yellow moon rising, a moon fattening to the full. He walked out and down to the lake, expecting to hear the nightingales, not knowing that they cease to sing once early June is past. The moonlight was almost golden, laying a pale sheen on the water and on the lilies, closed into buds for the hours of darkness. He wrote about that in his diary, the things he observed and the sounds he heard, a single cry from the woods as of an animal attacked by a fox, a disturbance of lily pads as a roosting moorhen shifted and folded its wings. Above him the sky was a clear bright opal, the stars too weak to show in the light of that moon.

He thought about Susannah, perhaps lying in her bed wakeful and longing for him as he longed for her. He lay down on the dry turf of the shoreline, face downwards, his arms outstretched, and whispered her name into the sand, Susannah, Susannah.

The following morning he tried to work. Over and over he read the last passage he had translated, of Hecabe's dream that she had given birth to a burning brand that split into coils of fiery serpents. The French text swam before his eyes like tadpoles, meaningless black squiggles. He spent the rest of the day trying to reach Susannah.

He phoned and no one answered. He tried again and still there was no reply. Her job at Gothic House wasn't the only one she had, he knew that. She cleaned for someone else somewhere, she minded the children of one of the schoolteachers, she washed hair and swept up for the hairdresser who operated from two rooms over the shop. The irony escaped him that in London, in his old life, he would never have considered taking a woman who earned her living by performing such menial tasks for a living out for a drink, still less been intent on marrying her.

He had very little idea when and where she went to these jobs. The hairdresser's perhaps, he could find that number and try that. Anne Whiteson at the shop gave him the number. It was his imagination, it must be, but he had an uncomfortable sense that she knew something he didn't know or was humouring him, was playing along with him in some indefinable way. A great deal to read into a woman's voice asking after his health and giving him a phone number, but, as he said, his imagination was very active, was pulsating with theories and suspicions and terrors.

Susannah wasn't at the hairdresser's. She wasn't expected there till Wednesday afternoon. He phoned her father's house again and again there was no reply. He imagined phones unplugged by determined parents. Nothing more was done on the translation that day and in the late afternoon he drove down to her home, anxious, very apprehensive, not in the least wanting to confront John Peddar or Iris but seeing no other way.

A little girl came to the door. That was how he described her, Julie, the youngest one, who must have been fourteen or fifteen but whom he saw as a child.

'They've all gone to the seaside. They won't be back till late.'

It wasn't the voice on the phone. He thought she was lying but could hardly tell her so. 'Why didn't you go, then?' This was the nearest to an accusation he could get.

'I was at school, wasn't I?'

By then he had noticed how seldom people left the village but to work or shop. The seaside story strained his credulity, he thought they must all be hidden in the house, Susannah perhaps a prisoner, and that evening, in his misery, he sat in the window watching for the Peddar van to pass along the lake road, that being the way the family would be obliged to return from the coast. But only two cars passed and they were both saloons.

He dreamt of Susannah, naked and chained like Andromeda, who appeared briefly in the preface to *The Golden Apple*, on her dragon-menaced rock. He struck off the chains and they fell from her at a single blow but when he took her into his arms and felt the smooth resilience of her breasts and thighs press against him, the flesh began to melt and pour through his hands in a scented sticky flood like cream or some cosmetic fluid. He woke up crying out, put his head in his hands, then saw the time and knew that Lavinia would soon come. Or would she? Hadn't she said she had no plans to come on Wednesday? Was it possible that after everything *Susannah* would come?

The girl who let herself into the house and came into the kitchen where he stood staring, his fists clenched, his teeth set, was the one whose voice he had heard the only time one of his calls was answered.

'Sue won't be coming today.'

He said rudely, 'Who are you?'

'Carol,' she said. 'I'm the middle one.'

She opened the cupboard where the cleaning things were kept, pulled out the vacuum cleaner, inspected a not very clean duster and sniffed it. He could hardly believe what he was seeing. It was as if the whole family had united and conspired together to control him, keep an eye on him, *handle* him and keep him from Susannah. He was a man of thirty-seven, an intellectual, a highly respected linguist taken over by a bunch of peasants of whom this pert sixteen-year-old blonde was the representative. No doubt we say such things to ourselves when we are desperately unhappy and frightened. Ben wouldn't normally have talked about peasants nor about himself as belonging to an elite. Besides, his Susannah was one of them . . .

'I want an explanation,' he said.

She smiled, about to leave the room. 'Do you?'

He took her by the wrist. 'You have to tell me. I want you to tell me – now. What's going on. Why can't I see Susannah?'

She looked at his hand gripping her wrist. 'Let me go.'

'All right,' he said. 'But you can sit down, sit down here at the table, and tell me.'

'I came to tell you, as a matter of fact,' she said calmly. 'I thought I'd get your bits and pieces done and then I'd tell you over a coffee.'

'Tell me now.'

She smiled comfortably. It was the smile of a woman much

older than she was, a middle-aged smile, as of a mother speaking of some gratifying event, a daughter's wedding, for instance. Yet she was a smooth-faced pink-cheeked adolescent, full-mouthed, her lips as red as lipstick but unpainted, not a line or mark on her velvety skin.

'You can see Sue again, of course you can. There's no question of anything else. But not all the time. You can't –' she brought the word out as if someone had taught it to her that morning '– monopolise her. You can't do that. Don't you see?'

'I don't see anything,' he said. 'I love Susannah and she loves me.' He might as well tell her. It must all come into the open now. 'I want to marry Susannah.'

She shrugged. She said the unbelievable thing. 'Sue's engaged to Kim Gresham.'

His voice almost went. He said hoarsely, 'I don't know what you mean.'

'Sue's been engaged to Kim for a year now. They'll be getting married in the spring.' She got up. 'There are plenty of other girls, you know.'

6

On a warm September evening I saw the bathers in the lake outside my house. Not the woman and the two children who appeared to us when Ben was staying with me for that weekend, but a whole group who arrived to swim from 'my' beach. This was after I'd repulsed John Peddar and after I'd dismissed Sandy but before the really alarming things happened.

They were all women and all good to look at. I suppose it was then that I realised there were no grossly fat women in the village, none who was misshapen, and even as they grew older their bodies seemed not pulled down by gravity or ridged with wrinkles or marked with distorted veins. These things are very much a matter of genes. I had plenty of chance to observe the results of a good gene pool when I watched the women from my front garden in that soft twilight.

It wasn't quite warm enough to bathe. Not strictly. If I'd gone closer I expect I should have seen gooseflesh on limbs but I didn't go closer, though they evidently wanted me to. They waved. Jennifer Fowler called out, 'It's lovely in the water!'

They swam among the lilies. Those lilies were like a Monet painting, red and pink and white cups floating among their flat duck-green leaves on the pale water. One of the women picked a red lily and tucked its brown snaky stem into the knot of yellow hair she had tied up on top of her head. The wife of the farmer from Lynn was there, floating on her back beside Jennifer on the calm gleaming surface, her outstretched hand clasping Jennifer's hand.

Have I said they were naked, every one of them? They swam but mostly they played in the shallow water by the shore, splashing each other, then lying down and submerging themselves but for uplifted laughing faces and long hair spread on rippling water. The farmer's wife, whose name I never knew, stood up and in a gesture at once erotic and innocent – didn't that sum them all up? – lifted her full breasts, one cupped in each hand, while Kathy Gresham splashed her with handfuls of water.

All the time they were glancing at me, smiling at me, giving me smiles of encouragement. It was plain they wanted me to come in too. I didn't disapprove, I didn't mind what they did, the lake was free and as much theirs as anyone's, but I did object to an attitude they all had, unmistakable though hard to define. It was as if they were laughing at me. It was as if they were saying, and probably were saying to each other, that I was a fool, inhibited, shy, perhaps ashamed of my own body. Go in there with them and all that would change. But I didn't want to go in there. It's not an excuse to say that it was really by this time quite cold. I got up and went into the house.

Later I saw them all emerge from the woods where their clothes were, fully dressed, still laughing, slowly dancing homewards along the lake shore, some of them holding hands. It was dusk by then and all I could see as they receded into the distance were shadowy forms, still dancing and no doubt still laughing, coming together and parting as if taking part in some elegant pavane.

If any bathers came to display themselves to Ben he didn't mention them in his diary. But there was a lot he left out. I suppose he couldn't bear to put it down or perhaps look at it on the page after he'd written it. Some of it he told me but there must have been a lot he didn't, a great deal I shall never know.

The actions of others he faithfully recorded. It was his own that he became, for a few days, reticent about. For example, he didn't seem to mind putting on paper that Carol Peddar had offered herself to him. After she said that about there being plenty of other girls, she looked into his eyes and, smiling, said there was herself. Didn't he like her? A lot of men thought she was prettier than her sister. 'Try me,' she said, and then, 'Touch me' and she reached for his hand.

He told her to go, to get out, and never to come back. He still believed, you see, that it was a family conspiracy that was trying to separate him from Susannah, a plot in which every Peddar was involved and Carol with them.

'I even believed the engagement was an arranged thing,' he told me. 'I thought they'd fixed it up. Perhaps that was the way marriages happened in that village. I knew something strange was going on and I thought there must be a tradition of arranged marriages. Susannah and this Kim Gresham had been destined for each other from babyhood, like something in India or among the

Habsburgs. You see, I knew it was me she wanted, I knew it as I know you and I are sitting here together now.'

'You thought you did,' I said.

'Later on, when I really knew, I tried telling myself I'd only known her for a couple of months, it couldn't be real, it must be sex and infatuation, whatever that is. I told myself what you told me that weekend, that she wasn't an educated person and that she was too young for me.'

'Did I say that?'

'You meant it whether you said it or not,' he said. 'I told myself all that and I asked myself what we had in common. Would she even understand what I did for a living, for instance? That sort of thing ought to matter but it didn't. I was in love with her. I'd never felt for anyone what I felt for her, not even for Margaret when we were first married. I'd have given the whole world, I'd have given ten years of my life, for her to have walked in at that moment and said the engagement story was nonsense, made up by her family, and it was me she was going to marry.'

Ten years of his life, in those circumstances, was the last thing he should have thought of giving. Still, he wasn't called on to give anything. He went to the Peddars' house that evening, demanded admittance and got it. John and Iris were at home with Carol and Julie but there was no sign of Susannah. She was out, Iris said. No, she didn't know where, she didn't think a person of eighteen ought to have to account to her parents for everywhere she went.

'Especially in this village,' John said. 'This is a safe place. Horrible things don't happen here, never have and never will.'

He sounded absolutely sure of himself, Ben said. He was smiling. Had I ever noticed how much they smiled in that village? The men always had a grin on their faces and the women sunny smiles.

'Now you mention it,' I said, 'I suppose I have.' Until they changed towards me and all smiles stopped.

Ben was tremendously angry. He thought of himself – and others thought of him – as a quiet, reserved sort of man, but by then he was angry. How did he know she wasn't in the house, that they hadn't got her hidden somewhere?

'You're welcome to look,' Iris said and then, incredibly, the self-conscious housewife: 'It's not very tidy upstairs, I'm afraid.'

Of course he didn't look. They wouldn't have given him the chance if she'd been there. John was looking him up and down as if summing him up for some purpose. Then he asked him why he wanted Susannah. What did he want her *for*?

Carol, no doubt, had reported back their conversation of the morning, so they must know about himself and Susannah, that he wanted to marry her. He told them so then and there, he repeated what he'd said.

'It takes two to agree to that,' Iris said comfortably.

'We are two,' he said. 'She loves me, she's told me often enough. I don't know what you're doing, how you're controlling her or coercing her, but it won't work. She's eighteen, she doesn't need your consent, she can please herself.'

'She has pleased herself, Ben.' It was the first time anyone from the village but Susannah had called him by his given name. 'She's pleased herself and chosen Kim.'

'I don't believe it,' he said. 'I don't believe *you*.'

'That's up to you,' said John. 'You can believe what you like.'

He said it serenely, he was smiling. Ben said then what I'd often thought, that they were so happy in that village, as if they'd found the secret of life, always smiling, never ruffled, calm, forbearing. They were mostly quite poor, a lot of them were unemployed, a few were on the edge of being comfortably off, that was all, but they didn't need material things, they were happy without them.

'As if they were all in love,' Ben said bitterly. 'All in love all the time.'

'Perhaps,' I said, 'in a way they were.'

After he'd told Ben he could believe what he liked and added that that was his privilege, John said why be so set on marrying Susannah. Why not, for instance, Carol?

'This I don't believe,' Ben said.

'Ah, but you'll have to change your way of thinking. That's the point, don't you see? If you're going to live here, if you're going to take on my mother-in-law's place.'

'There are no secrets in this village,' said Iris, 'but you know that.'

John nodded. 'Carol's as lovely in her way as Susannah and she likes you. I wouldn't be saying any of this if she didn't like you. That's not our way. Stand up, Carol.'

The girl stood. She held her head high and slowly turned to show herself in profile, then fully frontal. Like a slave for sale, he thought, and he remembered the bather emerging from the lake. She put up her arms and untied the ribbon that confined her hair in a ponytail. It was thick, shiny hair, the colour of the corn they'd begun cutting that day.

'You could be engaged to Carol if you like,' said Iris.

He got up and walked out of the house, slamming the front door behind him.

At the house next door he rang the bell hard. He didn't know who lived there, that hardly mattered. The woman who answered the door he recognised at once. Later on he found out she was Gillian Atkins but all he knew then was that she was the bather he had seen when with me and had been thinking of only a moment before. It gave him, he said, a horrible feeling of having stumbled into another world, a place of dreams and magic and perhaps science fiction. Or into the French analyst's myths where goddesses appeared out of clouds and where gods, in order to seduce, disguised themselves as swans and bulls and showers of gold.

She was smiling, of course. He stared, then he asked her if she knew where Kim Gresham lived. That made her smile again. As if she wouldn't know that, as if anyone in this place wouldn't know a thing like that. She told him to go to the house on the outskirts of the village.

When he got there the house was shut up. He knew, as one does, that there was no one at home. It was a lovely place, like a cottage on an old-fashioned calendar or chocolate box lid, thatch coming down over eyelid dormers, a pheasant made of straw perched on the roof. Roses climbed over the half-timbering and a white-flowering climber with them that gave off a rich heavy scent. It made him feel sick.

The evening was warm, the sky lilac and pink. Birds flew homewards in flocks as dense as swarms of bees. He walked back to where he'd left his car, passing the cottage he meant to buy, he still at that time meant to buy. Old Mrs Fowler was taking the air, sitting on the wooden bench in the front garden beside an old man. They were holding hands and they waved to him and smiled. He said that though he was in a turmoil, he was profoundly aware of them and that he had never seen such a picture of tranquillity.

He knew where Susannah would be next day. On Wednesday afternoons she went to work for the hairdresser. He expected Lavinia to come in the morning – it surely wouldn't be Carol after what had happened – but instead a stranger arrived, brought to his door by Sandy.

'We didn't want to let you down,' Sandy said, 'did we, Teresa? This is Teresa, she's taking Susannah's place.'

'Teresa what?' he said.

'Gresham,' the woman said. 'Teresa Gresham. It's my husband's nephew that Susannah's engaged to.'

She was probably thirty-five, shorter and plumper than the girls, browner-skinned and with light-brown hair, an exquisitely pretty face, her eyes the bright dark-blue of delphiniums. The summer dress she wore he had learned to think of as an old-fashioned garment. This one was pink with white flowers on it. Her legs were bare and she had white sandals on her strong brown feet.

'They tried everything,' I said when he told me.

'I suppose they did. But she wasn't flirtatious like Lavinia or blatant like Carol. I suppose you could say she was – *maternal*. She talked to me in a soothing way, she was cheerful and comforting –

or she thought she was being comforting. Of course, the whole village knew about Susannah and me by then, and they knew what had happened. Teresa made me coffee and brought it up. I was still working upstairs, still hiding from Sandy's grins and gestures, and she brought the coffee in and said not to be unhappy, life was too short for that. Smiling all the time, of course, need I say? She didn't tell me there were plenty more girls in the village, she said there were more fish in the sea than ever came out of it.'

Sandy knocked on the back door at one to take her home in his van. Ben had suspected there was something between those two, he sensed a close affectionate intimacy, but then Sandy announced he was getting married in ten days' time and would Ben like to come. The village church at twelve noon. He didn't say whom he was marrying but it couldn't be Teresa because she had talked of a husband and Marion Kirkman also was married. Almost anything could have been believed of the villagers by that time, he thought, but no doubt they drew the line at bigamy.

He said he didn't know if he could accept, he didn't know where he'd be on the Saturday week, he'd have to see.

'Oh, you'll come,' Sandy said airily. 'Things'll work out, you'll see. Everything'll be coming up roses by then.'

You had to pass through the shop to get to the hairdresser's, through the shop and up the stairs. Anne Whiteson, behind the counter, detained him too long, smiling, friendly, asking after his health, his work, his opinion of the enduring hot weather. He heard Susannah's voice while he was climbing the steep staircase and, much as he longed to see her, he stood for a moment experiencing the pleasure and the pain, not knowing which predominated, of those soft sweet tones, that rustic burr, the sunny warmth that informed everything she said. Not that she said anything particularly worth hearing, even he knew that, though it was poetry to him. It was something about a kind of shampoo she was discussing and whether it really made a perm last longer but it thrilled him so that he was both shivering and awestruck.

The door was open but as he came to it two hairdryers started up simultaneously. He walked in. All the women had their backs to him: Angela Burns the hairdresser and her assistant Debbie Kirkman – he learned their names later – two older women with their grey hair wound up on to pink plastic curlers, and Gillian Atkins whose long blonde curls were at that moment being liberated from a battery of rollers by Susannah herself. He was beginning to see Gillian Atkins as some kind of evil genius who dogged his steps and appeared at crucial moments of his life. Aphrodite or Hecate.

Although the windows were open the place was very hot and when Susannah turned round her cheeks were flushed and her hair curled into tendrils round her face like one of Botticelli's girls. He thought she had never looked more beautiful. In front of them all she came up to him, put her arms round his neck and kissed him. Over her shoulder he could see five pairs of eyes watching them, heads all turned round to see. In front of them he couldn't speak but she could. 'It's all right,' she said. 'It's going to be fine. Trust me. I'll come to you tomorrow evening.'

Someone laughed. The five women started clapping. They clapped as at a play or a show put on for their benefit. Horribly embarrassed, he muttered something and ran down the stairs and out through the shop. But she'd restored him, he was better now, she had told him to trust her. He could see it all, the arranged marriage, the established engagement, two sets of parents and a bunch of siblings all wanting the marriage, everyone set on it but the promised bride who was set on *him*.

That evening he managed to do some good work. The French was about sacrifice as propitiation of the gods, Agamemnon's killing of Iphigenia and the sacrifice of Polyxena on Achilles' tomb, and the subject demanded a similarly elegant grave prose. He worked upstairs in that room that had a view of the forest, not the lake, and when he reached Polyxena's burial, a wind sprang up like that which had risen while the Greeks waited to embark from

Rhoetea. The forest trees bent and fluttered in this freakish wind that blew and howled and died after half an hour.

Once he had the Greeks embarked for Thrace, he abandoned the translation and turned to write in his diary instead, the diary that had been untouched for almost a week. He wrote about Susannah and how she had reassured him and about the dark forest too and the strange sounds he could hear as he sat there with the dark closing in. 'A yelping like a puppy,' he wrote, unaware that what he heard must have been the cry of the Little Owl out hunting.

He slept soundly that night and next day, at lunchtime, on a whim, he walked down to the pub. Have I mentioned there was a pub? I don't think I have but there was one and it was kept by Jean and David Stamford. It should have been called by some suitable name in that village, the Cupid's Bow perhaps or the Maiden's Prayer, Ben said, but it wasn't, it was called the Red Lion. Like almost every house along the village street and round the green, it was a pretty building, half-timbered, with flowers climbing over it and flowers in tubs outside. Ben went in there to lunch off a beer and a sandwich for no better reason than that he was happy.

You could always tell strangers from the village people. They looked different. Ben said brutally that strangers were fat or dark or ugly or all those things together. There were several couples like that in the bar. He had noticed their cars parked outside. They were passing through, all they would be permitted to do, he said, though in fact the Red Lion did have rooms available and visitors had been known to stay a few nights or even a week.

The farmer from Lynn was sitting by himself up at the bar. It's a measure of the way the village people regarded him and had for quite a long time regarded him that no one ever uttered his name or called him by it, which is why even now I don't know what it was. He sat in miserable solitude while the rest of the clientele enjoyed themselves, greeting Ben enthusiastically, the old man he had seen holding hands with Mrs Fowler actually slapping him on the back. No doubt the farmer had come in there out of defiance, refusing to be browbeaten. He drank his beer and after sitting there a further five minutes, staring at the bottles behind the bar, got down from his stool and left.

To Ben's astonishment everyone laughed and clapped. It was like the scene in the hairdresser's all over again. When the applause died down Jean Stamford announced to the assembled company that a little bird had told her the Old Rectory was sold. Everyone seemed to know that the little bird was the village's resident agent and her brother-in-law. Mrs Fowler's friend asked how much the farmer had got for it and Jean Stamford named a sum so large that the customers could only shake their heads in silence.

'Who's bought it?' Ben asked.

They seemed to like his intervention. There was a kind of hum of approval. It was apparently the right enquiry put at the right time. But no one knew who had bought the Old Rectory, only that it was nobody from the village.

'More's the pity,' said the old man.

'And a pity for them,' David Stamford said strangely, 'if they don't suit.'

Ben walked home. All this talk of houses as well as the prospect of his reunion with Susannah prompted him to ring up the estate agent and make an offer for Mrs Fowler's house. The agent assured him it would be accepted, no doubt about it.

The combination of the beer, the walk and the sunshine sent him to sleep. It was gone five before he woke and he immediately set about putting wine in the fridge and preparing a meal for Susannah and himself, avocados and chicken salad and ice cream. He wrote all this down in his diary next morning while she still slept. It was the first time she had ever stayed a whole night with him.

From his bedroom window he'd watched for her to come. She hadn't said a time and he watched for her for an hour, quietly going mad, unable to remain still. When at last she arrived it was in her father's van which she was driving herself. The sight of it filled him with joy, with enormous exhilaration. All the suspense and terrors of the past hour were forgotten. If she could come in her father's own car this must mean that, miraculously, her parents had given their approval, minds had changed and he was to be received, the accredited lover.

She was wearing nothing underneath her thin silk almost transparent trousers and a loose top of lilac-coloured silk. He had never been so aware of the beauty of her young body, her long legs and very slightly rounded belly in which the navel was a shallow well. Her loose hair covered her breasts as if spread there from modesty. She lifted to him warm red lips and her tongue darted against the roof of his mouth.

'Susannah, I love you so. Tell me you love me.'

'I love you, dear Ben.'

He was utterly consoled. Those were the words he wrote down next morning. She shared the wine with him, she ate. She talked excitedly of Sandy Clements's wedding to Rosalind Wantage, the present her parents had bought, the dress she would wear to the ceremony. And Ben must come with her, they would go together. He would, wouldn't he? Ben laughed. He'd have gone to the ends of the earth with her, let alone to the village church.

His laughter died and he asked her about Kim Gresham. She was to tell him there was nothing in it or at least that it was over. He could bear an old love, a love from the past.

She said seriously, 'Let's not talk about other people' and, as if repeating a rule, 'We don't. Not here. You'll soon learn, darling Ben.'

They made love many times that night. Ben wrote that there had never been such a night in all his life. He didn't know it could be like that, he had read of such things and thought they existed only in the writer's imagination. And one of the strange things was that those actions of hers he had previously thought of as adventurous, even as shocking, weren't indulged in, or if they were they became *unmemorable*, for something else had happened. It was as if in the midst of this bodily rapture they had somehow become detached from their physical selves, it was sex made spirit and all the stuff of sex transcended. They were taken from themselves to be made angels or gods and everything they did took on the aspect of acts of grace or sacred rituals, yet at the same time made a continuum of pleasure.

He wrote that in his diary in the morning. He couldn't have brought himself to tell it to me in words.

She slept with her head on his pillow and her hair spread out, 'rayed' out, was how he put it, 'like the sun in splendour'. He watched her sleeping and he remembered her telling him to trust her. He couldn't therefore account for his terror, his awful fear. What was he afraid of?

Teresa Gresham came at eight thirty to clean the house and at nine Susannah woke up.

7

Dodging Teresa, avoiding knowing glances, he made coffee for Susannah and set a tray with orange juice, toast and fruit. But when he took it up to her she was already dressed, sitting on the edge of the bed combing her hair. She smiled at him and held out her arms. They held each other and kissed and he asked her when they could be married.

She gave him a sidelong look. 'You've never asked me to marry you.'

'Haven't I?' he said. 'I've told almost everyone else it's what I want.'

'Anyway, darling Ben . . .' She always called him that, 'dear Ben' or 'darling Ben' and it sat oddly – charmingly to him – with her rustic accent. But what she had to say wasn't charming. 'Anyway, darling Ben, I can't because I'm going to marry Kim.'

He didn't believe he'd heard that, he literally didn't believe his ears. She must have asked if he'd thought she was marrying Kim.

He asked her what she'd said and she repeated it. She said, 'You know I'm engaged to Kim. Carol said she'd told you.'

'This is a joke, isn't it?' he said.

She took his hand, kissed it and held it between her breasts. 'It's nice that you want to marry me. Marriage is very important, you only do it once, so I think it's lovely that you want to be with me like that for ever and ever. But that's the way I'm going to be with Kim. Live in the same house and share the same bed and bring up children together. It can't be changed, darling Ben. But I can still see you, we can be like we were last night. No one will mind. Did you think they would mind?'

She was his dear love, his adored Susannah, but she was a madwoman too. Or a child who understood nothing of life. But he knew that wasn't so. She was eighteen but the depths of her eyes weren't, they were as old as her grandmother's, as knowledgeable, in her own way as sophisticated.

He took his hand away. It didn't belong there. She picked up her coffee cup and repeated what she'd said. She was patient with him but she didn't know what it was he failed to understand. It seemed as clear as glass to her. 'Look, I'm not good at this,' she said. 'Ask Teresa.'

The last person he wanted at that moment was Teresa Gresham but Susannah went to the door and called her, and Teresa came upstairs.

She looked quite unembarrassed, she wasn't even surprised. 'We all do as we please here,' she said. 'Marriage is for life, of course, just the once. But love-making, that's another matter. Men go with who they like and so do women. There's only been one divorce in this village in thirty years,' she said. 'And before that no one got divorced, anyway. No one outside here – in the world, that is.'

It made him shudder to hear the village talked of as if it were heaven or some utopian planet. 'In the world', out there, two miles away . . .

'I couldn't believe it,' he said to me. 'Human beings wouldn't stand for it, not as a theory of life. It may be all right in a commune, a temporary thing, but for everyone of all ages, a whole village community in *England*? I asked her about jealousy. Teresa, I mean. I asked her. She said they used to say jealousy wasn't in their blood but now they thought it was rather that a gene of jealousy had been left out of them. After all, they were all more or less the same stock, they came out of the same gene pool.' He asked me, 'Did you know about all this?'

'I? No, I didn't know.'

'Not the green-eyed monster,' he said, 'but the blue-eyed fairy. You didn't know when you came down for that weekend?'

'I knew there was something. I thought it was because I was a woman and it wouldn't happen to a man.'

'We sat in that bedroom, Susannah and Teresa and I, and Teresa told me all about it. She'd known it all her life, it was part of everyone's life, and as far as they knew it had always been so, perhaps for hundreds of years. When new people tried to live in the village they judged whether they'd be acceptable or not, did they have the right physical appearance, would they *join in*.'

'You mean take part in this sexual free-for-all?'

'They tested them. John Peddar passed the test. If they didn't pass they – got rid of them. Like they were getting rid of the man from Lynn. He wouldn't, Teresa said, but she would, and naturally the poor man didn't want her to.'

'And I wouldn't,' I said, 'and you wouldn't.'

'They knew enough to be aware that new genes ought to be introduced sometimes, though no defects ever appeared in the children. As to who their fathers were it just as often wasn't the mother's husband but he'd have children elsewhere so no one minded. If a man's children weren't his they were very likely a brother's or a cousin's.'

'How about accidental brother and sister incest?'

'Perhaps they didn't care,' he said, and then he added, 'I've told you all this as if I believed it when I was first told. But I didn't believe it. I thought Susannah had been brainwashed by her parents and Teresa roped in because she was articulate, a suitable spokeswoman. You see, it wasn't possible for me to take this in after – well, after the way Susannah had been with me and the things she'd said. Teresa hadn't been there, thank God – what did she know? I thought the Peddar family had instructed Susannah in what to say and they and Teresa concocted this tale to make me back off.'

'It was true, though, wasn't it?'

He said, 'Even the Olympian gods were jealous. Hera persecuted the lovers of Zeus. Persephone was jealous of the King of the Underworld.' Then he answered me. 'Oh, yes, it was true.'

After Susannah had gone and Teresa had followed her, for he had told Teresa to get out of the house and never to come back, he shifted the blame from the Peddar family on to her and on to Kim Gresham. Wasn't she, after all, Kim Gresham's aunt? (Or cousin or second cousin or even sister.) Kim Gresham was holding Susannah to her engagement even though she loved him, Ben. In the light of what he'd just heard this wasn't a logical assumption, but he was beyond logic.

He would go to the Greshams' house and see Kim, have it out with him, drive down to the village and find out where he worked. But something strange happened while he was locking up, getting the car out. It was another beautiful day, sunny and warm, the blue sky flecked with tiny clouds like down. A pair of swans had appeared on the lake to swim on the calm glassy water among the lily pads. The forest was a rich velvety green and for a moment he stood staring at the green reflected in the blue.

He found himself thinking that if, as he put it, 'all things had been equal', if he hadn't been in love with Susannah, how idyllic

206

would be the life Teresa had presented to him: unlimited love and pleasure without jealousy or recrimination, without fear or risk, free love in all senses, something to look forward to all day and look back on every morning. Love of which one never wearied because if one did it could without pain or damage be changed. An endless series of love affairs in this beautiful place where everyone was kind and warm and liked you, where people clapped at the sight of kisses. He thought of his wife whom he hated because she had been unfaithful to him. Here he would have given her his blessing and they would still be together.

If he believed what Teresa said. But he didn't. The sun didn't always shine. Jealousy hadn't been left out of his genetic make-up nor, he was sure, out of Susannah's. It hadn't occurred to him before this that she might have slept with Kim Gresham but now it did and the green of the forest turned red, the sky blazed with a hard yellow light, passion roared inside his head, and he forgot about idylls and blessings and unlimited love.

He drove to the village, parked the car and went into the shop, source of all his supplies of food and information. Anne Whiteson was less friendly than usual and it occurred to him that Teresa might already have begun spreading the tale of her expulsion from Gothic House. She was less friendly but it was no worse than that and she was quite willing to tell him where Kim Gresham was to be found: at home with his parents in their house on the village outskirts. He had lost his job as a mechanic in a garage four miles away and was, until he found another, on the dole.

Scorn was now added to Ben's rage against Kim. Those Peddars were willing for their daughter to marry an unemployed man who couldn't support her. They preferred that man to him. He made his way to the Greshams' house, that pretty house a little way outside the village with the roses round the door. Kathy opened it and let him in, and he found Kim sprawled in the front room in front of the television. In his eyes that compounded the offence.

Kim got up when Ben came in and, all unsuspecting, smiling – how they all smiled and smiled! – held out his hand. He was a tall, well-built young man, very young, perhaps twenty, several inches taller than Ben and probably two stone heavier. Ben ignored the hand. It suddenly came to him that it wouldn't do to have a row in Kim's parents' house, he had no particular quarrel with the parents, and he told Kim to come outside.

Though obviously in the dark about all this, Kim followed Ben out into the front garden. I suppose he thought Ben wanted to show him something, possibly there was something wrong with his car. After all, he was a motor mechanic. Outside, among the flowers, standing on a lawn with a bird bath in the middle of it, Ben told him he was in love with Susannah and she with him, there was no room for Kim in that relationship, he'd been replaced, his time with Susannah was past. Did he understand?

Kim said he didn't know what Ben was talking about. 'I'm going to marry Susannah,' he said, and he said it with no show of emotion, in the tone he might have used to say he was going bowling or down to the pub. 'The wedding's been fixed for September. Second Saturday in September. You can come if you want. I know you like her, she's said, and that's OK with me. She's told me all about it, we don't have secrets.'

Ben hit him. He said it was the first time in his life he'd ever hit anyone and it wasn't a very successful blow. He had lashed out and struck Kim on the neck below the jawbone and he hit him again with the other fist, this time striking his head, but neither seemed to have much effect. Unlike adversaries in films, Kim didn't reel back or fall over. He got hold of Ben round his neck, in that armlock the police are advised not to use on people they arrest, propelled him down the path and out of the gate, where Ben collapsed and sat down heavily on the ground. Ben told me all this quite openly. He said he was utterly humiliated.

Kim Gresham, who probably watched a lot of television, said to Ben not to try anything further or he might 'be obliged to hurt him'. Then he asked him if he was all right and when Ben didn't answer, went back into the house and closed the front door quietly behind him.

Because the Gresham house stood alone with fields on either side of it – Greshams, someone had told me, always liked to live a little way away from the village – there were no witnesses. Ben got up and rubbed his neck and thought that, with luck, no one else would know of his defeat and humiliation. His ignorance of the village and its ways was still sublime. He still thought there were things he could do outside his own four walls and no one would know.

He walked back to the village to where he had parked. In his absence his car had received attention. Someone had printed on the windscreen in a shiny red substance, probably nail varnish: *Go away*. Even then he knew they didn't just mean go away for now, don't park here. The village street was empty. It often was but if people were about this was the time they would be, eleven in the morning. There was no one to be seen. Even the front gardens were empty and on this fine August day all the front doors and windows were closed. Eyes watched him. No one made any pretence that those eyes weren't watching.

Back at Gothic House he cleaned the printed letters off with nail varnish remover he found in the bathroom cabinet. Deterred by what had happened but willing himself to be strong, he phoned the Peddars. A woman answered, Iris, he supposed, for the voice didn't belong to Susannah or her sisters.

He said, 'This is Ben Powell.'

Without another word, she put the receiver down. In the afternoon he phoned the hairdresser. Before the horrible things began to happen, on the previous evening when he and Susannah had been so happy, she'd told him she worked for the hairdresser on Friday afternoons as well. He phoned at two. Angela Burns answered and, when he said who it was, she put the receiver down.

That shook him because it seemed to him to prove that Kim

Gresham or his mother had talked of what had happened. Teresa had talked. It was one thing telling the Peddars but the news had spread to the hairdresser's. His defeat of the morning made him feel he had to be brave. If he was to achieve anything, overcome these people and secure Susannah for himself exclusively, he had to have courage now. He drove back to the village but this time he parked the car directly outside the shop.

When Anne Whiteson saw him she said straight out she wasn't going to serve him. Then she walked into the room at the back and shut the door behind her. Ben went to the staircase but before he'd gone up half a dozen stairs Susannah appeared at the top. She came down and met him halfway. Or, rather, she stood two stairs above him. He put out his hand to her. She shook her head and said very softly so that no one else should hear, 'It's over, Ben.'

'What do you mean?' he said. 'What do you mean, over? Because of what these people say and do? The rest of the world isn't like this, Susannah. You don't know that but I do, I've seen, believe me.'

'It's over,' she said and now she was whispering. 'I thought it needn't be, I thought it could go on, because I do love you, but it has to be over because of what you've done and, Ben, because of what you *are*.'

'What I am?'

'You're not like my dad, not many are. You're like the man who lives in the rectory, you're like the lady Gothic House belongs to. I didn't think you were but you are.'

'This is all nonsense.' He wasn't going to whisper, no matter what she might do. 'It's rubbish, it's irrelevant. Listen, Susannah, I want us to go away. Come away with me.' He forgot about her grandmother's cottage. 'I've got a place in London, we can go there tonight, we can go there *now*.'

'You must go, Ben. I'm not going anywhere. This is where I live and I always will, you know. The people who live here never want to go away.' She reached down from her higher stair and touched him on the arm. It was electric, that touch, he felt the shock of it run up his arm and rattle his body. 'But you must go,' she said.

'Of course I'm not going,' he shouted. 'I'm staying here and I'm going to get you away from these people.'

He meant it. He thought he could. He ran back to his car and drove home to Gothic House where he began composing a letter to Susannah's parents and another, for good measure I suppose, to Susannah's grandmother. Perhaps he was thinking of her in the capacity of a village elder. Then, by one of those coincidences, just as he was writing 'Dear Mrs Fowler . . .' the phone rang and it was the estate agent to tell him Susannah's grandmother had received a better offer than his for her house.

'What is it?' he said. 'I'll match it.' Recklessness, that can be as much the effect of terror as of happiness, made him say, 'I'll top it.'

'Mrs Fowler has already accepted the offer.'

He tore up the letter he'd started writing. The one he'd written to the Peddars remained on his desk. But he intended to send it. He intended to fight. This time he refused to allow himself to become despondent. He pushed away the longings for her that came, the desire that was an inevitable concomitant of thinking of her. He would fight for her, he would think of that. What did the loss of the cottage matter? They couldn't live in this village anyway.

He refused to let her become part of what he saw as an exceptionally large commune, where wife-swapping was the norm and husbands couldn't tell which were their own offspring. For a moment he had seen it, very briefly he'd seen it, as the ideal that all men, and women too perhaps, would want. But that had been a moment of madness. These people had made a reality out of a common fantasy but he was not going to be drawn into it and nor was Susannah. Nor was he going to leave the village until it was to take her with him.

8

They got rid of me. I had no idea of the reason for my expulsion – no, that's not true, I did have ideas, they just weren't the right ones. I did have explanations of a kind. I was a 'foreigner', so to speak, born and bred a long way off with most of my life lived elsewhere. I'd sacked Sandy. When I asked myself if it also had something to do with my repudiation of John Peddar I was getting near the truth but I thought it too far-fetched. Aware that I had somehow offended, I could never believe that I had done anything reprehensible enough to deserve the treatment I got.

The day after the bathers had extended their invitation to me – the final overture, as it happened, from any of them – I went to church. I tried to go to church. It was St John's day and the church's dedication was to St John, and I had noticed that a special service was always held on that day, whether it fell during the week or on a Sunday. They had a wonderful organist at St John's, a Burns who came from a village some miles away but was, I suppose, a cousin of that Angela, the hairdresser. The visiting clergyman preached a good sermon and everyone sang the hymns lustily.

One of the sidesmen or wardens, I don't know what he was but he was a Stamford, I knew that, met me in the church porch. He was waiting for me. They knew I'd come and they despatched him to wait for me.

'The service is private this morning,' he said.

'What do you mean, private?'

'I'm not obliged to explain to you,' he said and he stood with his back against the heavy old door, barring my way.

There wasn't much I could do. There was nothing I could do. I couldn't get involved in a struggle with him. I went back to my car and drove home, indignant and humiliated. I wasn't frightened then, not yet, not by then.

A week later I came down again. I came on the Friday evening as I often did when I could make it. Of course, I'd thought a lot about what had happened when I tried to get into the church but the incident became less a cause for rage and indignation the more I considered it. Perhaps I'd asked my question aggressively and Stamford, also being inclined to belligerence, had answered in kind. Perhaps he was having a bad day, was already angry. It was nonsense, I decided, to suppose 'they' had sent him, it was paranoia. He happened to be there, was probably just arriving himself, when I arrived.

All this, somewhat recycled and much reviewed, was passing through my mind as I reached the village at dusk that Friday evening. They knew I would come, knew too approximately what time I'd come and besides that, I had to pass the Greshams' house two minutes before I entered the village proper. They used the phone and their own grapevine.

It was like pictures that one sees of streets that royalty or some other celebrity is about to pass through. They were all outside, standing in front of their houses. They stood in front gardens if they had them, on the road itself if they didn't. But those waiting to welcome someone famous are preparing to smile and wave, even to cheer. These people, these Kirkmans and Burnses, Stamfords and Wantages, Clementses and Atkinses and Fowlers, all of them, some with children in their arms, tall, fair, handsome people, stood and stared.

As I approached I saw their eyes all turned in my direction and as I passed I've no doubt their eyes followed, for in my driving mirror I could see them staring after me. All down that village street they were outside their houses, waiting for me. Not one of them smiled. Not one of them even moved beyond turning their eyes to follow me. Outside the last house three old people stood, a woman between two men, all holding hands. I don't know why this hand-holding particularly unnerved me. Perhaps it was the implication of total solidarity it conveyed. Now I think it symbolised what I had rejected, diffused love.

A little way down the road I slowed and saw in the mirror the three of them turn and go back into the house. I drove to Gothic House and when I got out of the car I found that I was trembling. They had done very little but they had frightened me. I hadn't much food in the house and I'd meant to go to the village shop in the morning, but now I wouldn't go, I'd take the road that didn't pass through the village to the town four miles away.

I've since wondered if they approached every newcomer to the village or if they applied some system of selection. Would they, for instance, tolerate someone for the sake of a spouse, as in the case of the farmer from Lynn? Would elderly retired people be welcome? I thought not, since their principal motivation was to draw in new genes to their pool and the old were past breeding.

I should therefore, I suppose, have been flattered, for I was getting on for forty. Did they hope I would settle there, would *live* there, *marry* some selected man? I shall never know. I shall never know why they wanted Ben, although it has occurred to me that it might have been for his intellect. He had a good mind and perhaps they thought that brains too might be passed on. Perhaps whoever decided these things – all of them in concert? Like a parliament? – discerned a falling intelligence quotient in the village.

He too tried to go to church. It was Sandy's wedding and Susannah had said they would go to it together. His mind had magnified her invitation to a firm promise and he still believed she'd honour it. He stuck for a long while to his belief that, having said and said many times that she loved him, she would come to him and stay with him.

He wasn't, then, frightened of the village the way I was. He walked there boldly and knocked on the Peddars' door. Carol opened it. When she saw who it was she tried to shut the door but he put his foot in the way. He pushed past her into the house and she came after him as he kicked the door open and burst into their living room. There was nobody there, all the Peddars but Carol had already gone to the wedding. He didn't believe her and he ran upstairs, going into all the rooms.

'Where's Susannah?'

'Gone,' she said. 'Gone to the church. You'll never get her, you might as well give up. Why don't you go away?'

Leave the house, was what he thought she meant. He didn't, then, take in the wider implication. Sandy was just arriving at the church when he got there, Sandy in a morning coat and carrying a topper, looking completely different from the handyman and window cleaner Ben knew. His best man was one of the Kirkmans, similarly dressed, red-faced, very blond, self-conscious. Ben stood by the gate and let them go in. Then he tried to get in himself and his way was barred by two tall men who came out of the porch and simply marched at him. Ben didn't recognise them, though they sounded from his description like George Whiteson and Roger Atkins. They marched at him and he stood his ground.

For a moment. It's hard to do that when you're being borne down upon but Ben did his best. He walked at them and there was an impasse as he struggled to break through the high wall their bodies made and they pushed at him with the flats of their hands. They were determined not to assault him directly, Ben was sure of that. He, however, was indifferent as to whether he assaulted them or not. He said he beat at them with his fists and that was when other men joined in, John Peddar who came out of the church, Philip Wantage who had just arrived with his daughter, the bride. They pinned Ben's arms behind him, lifted him up and dropped him on to the grass on the other side of the wall.

With these indignities heaped on him, he sat up in time to see Rosalind Wantage in white lace and streaming veil proceed up the path with a bevy of pink-clad Kirkman and Atkins and Clements girls behind her. He tried to go after them but was once more stopped at the porch. Another tall, straight-backed guardian gave him a heavy push, which sent him sprawling, and retreated into the church. Ben sprang at the door in time to hear a heavy bolt pushed across it on the inside.

The more of this they did the more he believed that they might be acting on Susannah's behalf but not with her consent. It was a conspiracy to keep her from him. He sat on the grass outside the church gate and waited for the wedding to be over. It was a fine, sunny day and such windows in the church as could be opened were open. Hymns, swelling from the throats of almost the entire village, floated out to him, 'Love divine, all loves excelling' and 'The voice that breathed o'er Eden'.

> For dower of blessed children,
> For love and faith's sweet sake,
> For high mysterious union
> Which nought on earth may break.

No one should break the union he had with Susannah and, sitting out there in the sunshine, perhaps he thought of the night they had spent, of transcendence and sex made spirit, that he had written of in his diary. It didn't occur to him then, though it did later, that a high mysterious union was what that village had, what those village people had.

They began coming out of the church, bride and bridegroom first, bridesmaids, parents. Susannah came out with her parents and Carol. He said that when he saw her he saw no one else. Everyone else became shadows, gradually became invisible, when she was there. She came down the path, let herself out of the gate. What the others did he said he didn't know, if they stared after her or made to follow her, he had no eyes for them.

Susannah was in a pale-blue dress. If she had stood against the sky, he said, it would have disappeared into the blueness, it was like a thin, scanty slip of sky. She pushed back her hair with long pale fingers. He wanted to fall at her feet, her beautiful white feet, and worship her.

'You must go away, Ben,' she said to him. 'I've told you that before but you didn't hear me.'

'They've put you up to this,' he said. 'You're wrong to listen. Why do you listen? You're old enough to make up your own mind. Don't you understand that away from here you can have a great life? You can do anything.'

'I don't want us to have to hurt you, Ben.' She didn't say 'them' she said 'us'. She said 'we'. 'We needn't do that if you go. You can have a day, you don't have to go till Monday, but you must go on Monday.'

'You and I will go on Monday.' But her use of that 'us' and that 'we' had shaken him. 'You're coming with me, Susannah,' he said, but his doubts had begun.

'No, Ben, you'll go. You'll have to.' She added, as if inconsequentially, but it was a consequence, it was an absolute corollary, 'Sandy's buying the cottage, grandma's cottage, for him and Roz to live in.'

I haven't said much about the forest.

The forest surrounded the lake in a horseshoe shape with a gap on the side where the road left its shores and turned towards the village. Behind the arms of the horseshoe it extended for many miles, dense and intersected only by rides or as a scattered sprinkling of trees with heathy clearings between them. It was protected and parts of it were a nature reserve, the habitat of the Little Owl and the Greater Spotted Woodpecker. If I haven't mentioned it much, if I've avoided referring to it, it's because of the experience I had within its depths, the event that drove me from the village and made me decide to sell Gothic House.

Already, by then, the place was losing its charms for me. I avoided it for a whole month after that Friday night drive through the village, confronted as I'd been by the silent staring inhabitants. But I still liked the house and its situation, I loved the lake and walking in the forest, the nightingales in spring and the owl calling in winter, the great skies and the swans and water lilies. Unwilling to face that silent hostility again, I drove down very late. I passed through half an hour before midnight.

No one was about but every light was on. They had turned on the lights in every room in the front of their houses, upstairs and down. The village was ablaze. And yet not a face showed at any of those bright windows. It was if they had turned on their lights and left, departed somewhere, perhaps to be swallowed up by the forest. I think those lights were more frightening than the hostile stares had been, and then and there I resolved not to pass through the village again, for, as I slowed and turned to look, the lights were one after another turned off, all died into darkness. No one had departed, they were there and they had done their work.

I wouldn't pass through the village again, not, at least, until they had got over whatever it was, had come to accept me once more. I really believed, then, that this would happen. But not passing through hardly meant I had to stay indoors. There is, after all, little point in a weekend retreat in the country if you never go out of it.

On Saturday afternoons I was in the habit of going for a walk in the forest. If I had a guest I asked that guest to go with me, if I was alone I went alone. They knew I was alone that weekend. If I hadn't seen them behind their lights they had seen me, alone at the wheel in an otherwise empty car.

At three in the afternoon I set out into the forest. It was May, just one year before Ben went there, not a glorious day but fine enough, the sun coming out for half an hour, then retreating behind white fluffy cloud. A little wind was blowing, not then much more than a breeze. Ten minutes in and I saw the first of them. I was walking on the wide path that ran for several miles into the forest's heart. He stood close to the silver-grey trunk of a beech tree; I recognised him as George Whiteson, but if he recognised me – and of course he did, I was why he was there – he gave no sign of it. He wasn't staring this time, but looking at the ground around his feet.

A hundred yards on three of them were sitting on a log, Kirkmans or Kirkmans and an Atkins, I forget and it doesn't matter, but I saw them and they affected not to see me, and almost immediately there were more, a man and a woman on the ground embraced – a demonstration for my benefit, I suppose – two children in the branches of a tree, a knot of women, those bathers, standing in a ring, holding hands.

The sun was shining on to a clearing and it was beautiful in there, all the tiny wild flowers in blossom in the close heathy turf, crabapple trees flowering and the sunlight flitting, as the wind drove clouds across it and bared it again. But it was terrible too, with those people, the whole village it seemed, there waiting for me but making no sign they'd seen me. They were everywhere, near at hand or in the depths of the forest, close to the path or just discernible at the distant end of a green ride, Burnses and Whitesons, Atkinses and Fowlers and Stamfords, men and women, young and old. And as I walked on, as I tried to stick it out and keep on, I became aware that they were following me. As I passed they fell into silent step behind, so that when I turned round – it was quite a long time before I turned round – I saw behind me this stream of people padding along quietly on the sandy path, on last year's dry fallen leaves.

It was as if I were the Pied Piper. But the children I led were not in happy thrall to me, not following me to some paradise, but dogging my steps with silent menace, driving me ahead of them. To what end? To what confrontation in the forest depths?

I was terribly afraid. It's not an exaggeration to say I feared for my life. The whole tribe of them, as one, had gone mad, had succumbed to spontaneous psychopathy, had conceived some fearful paranoiac hatred of me. They would surround me in some dark green grove and murder me. In their high mysterious union. In silence.

But I never quite came to believe that. If I wanted to crouch on the ground and cover my head and whimper to them to let me go, to leave me alone, I didn't do that either. By some sort of effort of will that I achieved, God knows how, I turned, clenched my fists, set one foot before the other and began walking back the way I'd come.

This brought me face to face with the vanguard of them, with John Peddar and one of his daughters, Susannah herself for all I know. They fell back out of my path. It was gracefully done, one by one they all yielded, half bowing, as if this were some complicated ritual dance and they were giving place to the principal dancer who must now pass with prescribed steps down the space between them. Only I had no partner in this minuet, I was alone.

No one spoke. I didn't speak. I wanted to, I wanted to challenge them, to ask why, but I couldn't. I suppose I knew I wouldn't get an answer or perhaps that no voice would come when I tried to speak. The speechlessness was one of the worst things, that and the closed faces and the silent movements. Another was the sound of the rising wind.

They followed me all the way back. While I was in the forest the wind could be heard but not much felt. It met me as I emerged on to the lake shore and even held me back for a moment as if pushing me with its hands. The surface of the lake was ruffled into waves and the tree branches were pulled and stretched and beaten. By the shore the people who followed me let me go and turned aside, two hundred of them I suppose, at least two hundred.

From having been perfectly silent, they broke into talk and laughter as soon as they were separated from me and, buffeted by the wind, made their way homewards. I ran into my house. I shut myself inside but I could still hear their voices, raised in conversation, in laughter, and at last in song. It would be something to chronicle, wouldn't it, if they'd sung an ancient ballad, a treasure for an anthropologist, something whose words had come down unbroken from the time of Langland or Chaucer? But they didn't. The tune I heard carried by the wind, receding, at last dying into silence, was 'Over the Rainbow'.

That evening the gale became a storm. Trees went down on the edge of the woodland and four tiles blew off the roof of Gothic House. The people of the village weren't to blame but that was not how it seemed to me at the time, as I cowered in my house, as I lay in bed listening to the storm, the crying of the wind and the crash of falling tree branches. It was just a lucky happening for them that this gale blew up immediately after their slow dramatic pursuit of me in the forest. But that night I could have believed them all witches and magicians, Wicca people who could control the elements and raise a wind.

9

They had something else in store for Ben.

'I was determined not to go,' he said. 'I would have gone immediately if Susannah had come too but without her I was going to stay put. On the Sunday I went back to the village to try to find her but no one would answer the door to me, not just the Peddars, no one.'

'It was brave of you to try,' I said and that was when I told him what had happened to me, the silent starers, the blazing lights, the pursuit through the forest.

'I'd stopped being a coward – well, I thought I had.'

Next morning someone was due to come and clean the house. Which girl would they send? Or was it possible Susannah might come? Of course, he hadn't slept much, he hadn't really slept for four nights and exhaustion was beginning to tell on him. If he managed to doze off it would be to plunge into dreams of Susannah, always erotic dreams, but deeply unsatisfying. In them she was always naked. She began making love with him, kissing him, placing his hands on her body as was her habit, kissing his fingers and taking them to the places she loved to be touched. Then, suddenly, she would spring out of his arms and run to whomsoever had come into the room, Kim Gresham or George Whiteson or Tom Kirkman, it could be any of them, and in a frenzy begin stripping off their clothes, nuzzling them, gasping with excitement. He'd reached a point where he didn't want to sleep for fear of those dreams.

By eight thirty next morning he'd been up for more than two hours. He'd made himself a pot of coffee and drunk it. His head was banging and he felt sick. The time went by, nine o'clock went by, and no one came. No one would come now, he knew that.

The weather had changed and become dull and cool. He went outside for a while and walked about, he couldn't say why. There wasn't anyone to be seen, there seldom was, but he had a feeling that he was being watched. He took his work into the ground-floor front room because he knew it would be impossible for him to stay upstairs in the back. If he did that, sat up there where he could only see the rear garden and the forest, something terrible might happen in the front, by the lake, some awful event take place that he ought to witness. It was an unreasonable feeling but he gave in to it and moved into the living room.

The author of *The Golden Apple* was analysing Helen, her narcissism, her choice of Menelaus declared by hanging a wreath round his neck, her elopement with Paris. Ben tried to concentrate on translating this, firstly to understand which events stemmed in the writer's estimation from destiny and which from character, but he couldn't stop himself constantly glancing up at the window. Half an hour had passed, and he had translated only two lines, when a car came along the road from the village. It parked by the lake in front of Gothic House.

I suppose there were about a hundred yards between the house and the little beach, and it was on the grass just above the beach. He watched and waited for the driver or the driver and passenger to get out of it and come up to the house. No one did. Nothing moved. Then, about ten minutes later, the car windows were wound down. He saw that the driver was Kim Gresham and his passenger an unknown woman.

He tried to work. He translated the lines about Helen taking one of her children on the elopement with her, read what he had written and saw that the prose was barely comprehensible and the sense lost. There was no point in working in these conditions. He wondered what would happen if he tried to go out and felt sure that if he attempted a walk to the village those two would stop him. They would seize hold of him and frogmarch him back to the house. 'I thought of calling the police,' he said.

'Why didn't you?'

'The man they'd have sent lived in the police house in the village. He's one of them, he's called Michael Wantage. If anyone else had come, what could I have said? That two men were sitting in a parked car admiring the view? I didn't call the police. I got my car out of the garage.'

He put his work aside and decided to drive to the town four miles away and do his weekly shopping. He watched them watching him as he backed the car out.

'I think they were hoping I'd fetch out suitcases and the word processor and my books. Then they'd know I was being obedient and leaving. They'd just have let me go, I'm sure of that. A sigh of relief would have been heaved and they'd have gone back to the village.'

As it was, they followed him. He saw the car behind him all the way. They made no attempt at secrecy. In the town he left his car and went to the supermarket but, as far as he knew, they remained in theirs. When he got back they were still sitting in their car and when he drove home they were behind him.

In the early afternoon a second car arrived and the first one left. They were operating a shift system. From Ben's description it seemed as if Marion Kirkman was driving the second car. He had no doubt as to the identity of her passenger. It was Iris Peddar. Later on another car replaced it and was still there when darkness came.

Perhaps a car was there all night. He didn't know. By then he didn't want to know, he just desperately hoped this surveillance would have ceased by morning. Just after sunrise he pulled back the curtains and looked out. A car was there. He couldn't see who was inside it. It was then that he told himself he could be as strong and as resolute as they. He could stick it out. He simply wouldn't look, he'd do what seemed impossible the day before, work in the back, not look, ignore them. They meant him no harm, they only mounted this guard to stop him going to the village to find Susannah. But there must be other ways of reaching Susannah. He could do a huge circular detour via the town and come into the village from the other direction. He could park *his* car outside her father's house. But if he did that, all that, any of that, they would follow him . . .

All that day he stayed indoors. He couldn't work, he couldn't read, he didn't want to eat. At one point he lay down and slept, only to dream of Susannah. This time he was in a tower, tall and narrow with a winding stair inside like a windmill, and he was watching her from above, through a hole in the floor. He heard her footsteps climbing the stairs, hers and another's, and when she came into the room below she was with Sandy Clements. Sandy began to undress her, taking the bracelet from her arm and the necklace from her neck, and held one finger of her right hand as she stepped naked out of the blue dress. She looked up to the ceiling and smiled, stretching out her hands, one to him, one to Sandy, turning her body languorously for them to gaze at and worship. He awoke with a cry and, forgetting his resolve, stumbled into the front room to look for the car. A red one this time, Teresa Gresham's. She was alone in it.

At about seven in the evening, long before dark, she got out of the car and came up to the house. He'd forgotten he'd left the back door unlocked. She walked in. He asked her what the hell she thought she was doing.

'You asked me to come up and do your ironing,' she said.

'That's rubbish,' he said. 'I asked you nothing. Now get out.'

She had apparently been gone five minutes when he saw, in the far distance, a bicycle approaching. The very first time she came Susannah had been on a bicycle and that was who he thought it was. The surveillance was over, she had persuaded them to end it, and she was coming to him. She had told them they couldn't prevent her being with him, she was over age, she loved him. He opened the front door and stood on the doorstep waiting for her.

It wasn't Susannah. It was the younger of her two sisters, the fourteen-year-old Julie. Disappointment turned inside his body as love does, with a wrench, an apparent lurching of the heart. But he called out a greeting to her. She rested her bicycle against the garden wall, fastened chain and padlock to its front wheel, the good girl, the responsible teenager. Who did she think would steal it out here? He let her into the house, certain she must have a message for him, perhaps a message from Susannah who was allowed to reach him in no other way.

She was a pretty little girl – his words – who was much shorter than her sisters, who clearly would never reach Susannah's height, with a very slight childish figure. She wore a short skirt and a white sweatshirt, ankle socks and white trainers. Her straw-coloured hair was shoulder-length and she had a fringe.

'She looked exactly like the girl in the Millais painting, the one who's sitting up in bed and looking surprised but not unhappy.'

'I know the one,' I said. 'It's called *Just Awake*.'

'Is it?' he said. 'I wonder what Millais meant by "awake". D'you think a double meaning was intended?'

Julie sat down sedately in my living room. He asked her if she had a message for him from Susannah and she shook her head. 'You asked me to come,' she said. 'You phoned up an hour ago and said if I'd come over you'd let me have those books you told Susannah I could have.'

'What books?' He had no idea what she meant.

'For my schoolwork. For my English homework.'

It was at this point that he had the dreadful feeling they had sent her as the next in progression. They'd decided it was still worth trying to keep him and make him one of them. He didn't want Lavinia or Carol, stubbornly he still wanted monogamy with Susannah, but since he'd rejected the more mature Teresa, wasn't it possible he'd be attracted by her antithesis, by this child?

Of course, he was wrong there. They weren't perverse. In their peculiar way they were innocent. But by this time he'd have believed anything of them and he did, for a few minutes, believe they'd sent her to tempt him. He'd been sitting down but he jumped up and she too got up.

'Why are you really here?'

She forgot about the books. 'I'm to tell you to go away,' she said. 'I'm to say it's your last chance.'

'This is ridiculous,' he said. 'I'm not listening to this.'

'You can stay here tonight.' She said it airily, as if it were absolutely her province to give him permission. 'You can stay here tonight but you must go tomorrow. Or we'll make you go.'

He didn't once touch her. She didn't touch him. She left the house, unlocked the padlock on her bicycle chain and got on the bicycle. It's almost impossible for a practised cyclist to fall off a bicycle, but she did. She fell off in the road and the machine fell on her. He lifted the bicycle off her, put out his hand to help her up, pulled her to her feet. She jumped on the bicycle and rode off, turning round to call something after him but he didn't hear what it was. He returned to the house and thought that in the morning he'd go to the village and get into her parents' house, even if that meant breaking a window or kicking the door in.

In the morning the car was back. It was parked at the lake shore, the driver was David Stamford and the passenger Gillian Atkins.

If he went to the town and from there by the back way into the village, they would follow him. He had no doubt that they would physically prevent him from driving or walking along the lake shore road. It was harassment, their simply being there was harassment, but imagine telling this tale to the police, imagine proving anything.

Working on his translation was impossible. Attempting to find Susannah would be difficult, but he tried. He phoned the Peddars, Sandy Clements, the shop, the pub, Angela Burns. One after the other, when they heard his voice, they put down the phone. It was deeply unnerving and after Angela's silence and the click of the receiver going into its rest, he stopped trying.

But there was some comfort to be drawn from these abortive phone calls. He'd been able to make them. They hadn't cut his phone line. It's some measure of the state he was getting into that he even considered they might. This negativity, this absence of some hypothetical action, told him there would be no violence used against him. He hadn't exactly been afraid of violence but he'd been apprehensive about it.

He sat down, in the back of the house where he couldn't see that car, and thought about what they'd done. Not so very much, really. They'd stopped him going to a wedding and followed his car and sent him to Coventry. Surely he could stick it out if that was all that was going to happen? If he had Susannah he could. He had to stay at Gothic House for her sake, he had to stay until he got her away.

'I thought of going out to them,' he said to me, 'to those two, Stamford and the Atkins woman, and later on to the people who replaced them, the Wantages, Rosalind's parents, of going out to them and asking what they wanted of me. Of course I knew, really, I knew they wanted me to leave, but I wanted to hear someone say it, and not a child of fourteen. And then I thought I'd say, OK, I'll leave but I'm taking Susannah with me.'

By now he couldn't bear to leave his observers unobserved and he sat in the front window watching them while they watched him. He still hadn't been able to bring himself to carry out his intention. He just sat there watching and thinking of how to put his question and what words to choose to frame his resolution. In the middle of the afternoon a terrible thing happened. He had calculated that the Wantages' shift would end at four – that was the state he had got into, that he was measuring his watchers' shifts – and sure enough at five to four another car arrived. The driver was an unknown man, his passenger Susannah.

The car was parked so that its nearside, and therefore the passenger's seat, was towards Gothic House. He looked out into Susannah's eyes and she looked back, her face quite expressionless. There are times when thinking is dismissed as useless, when one stops thinking and just acts. He had thought enough. He walked, marched, out there, calling her name.

She wound down the window. The face she presented to him, he said, was that of a woman in a car of whom a stranger has asked the way. It was as if she had never seen him before. The man in the driving seat didn't even turn round. He was staring at the lake with rapt attention. He looked, Ben said, as if he'd seen the Loch Ness monster.

'Please get out of the car and come inside, Susannah,' he said to her.

She was silent. She went on staring as if he really was that stranger and she was considering what directions to give him.

'We can talk about all this, Susannah. Come inside and talk, will you please? I know you don't want to leave this place but that's because you don't know anywhere else. Won't you come with me and try?'

Slowly she shook her head. 'You have to go,' she said.

'Not without you.'

'I'm not coming. You have to go alone.'

She touched her companion's arm and he turned his head. From that touch, intimate but relaxed, Ben somehow knew this young fair-haired man was her lover as he had been her lover, and for a moment the sky went black and a sharp pain pierced his chest.

She watched him as if calculating all this. Then she said, 'Why don't you go now? You'll go if you've any sense.'

The young man beside her said, 'I'd advise you to leave before dark.'

'We'll follow you through the village,' said Susannah. 'Then you'll be safe. Pack your bags and put them in the car.'

'Shall we say an hour?' That was the young man, in his coarse rustic voice.

Ben went back into the house. He had no intention of packing but at the same time he didn't know what to do next. The idea came to him that if he could only get Susannah alone all would be well. He could talk to her, remind her, persuade her. The question was how to do that. Not at the hairdresser's, he'd tried that. She baby-sat for Jennifer Fowler one evening a week, an evening she'd never been able to come to him, a Wednesday – those few Wednesdays, how bereft and lonely he'd felt. Tomorrow, then, he'd somehow get to the village and Jennifer Fowler's house. They'd only kept up their surveillance till dark the night before and it would be dark by nine . . .

He sat inside the window watching Susannah for a long time. It was marginally better to see her, he'd decided, than to be in some other part of the house, not seeing her but knowing she was there. To gaze and gaze was both pleasure and pain. The strange thing was, he told me, that watching her was never boring and he couldn't imagine that applying to any other person or object on earth.

He also watched, in sick dread, to see if she and the man with her touched each other or moved towards each other or gave any sign of the relationship he had at first been sure was theirs. But they didn't. As far as he could tell, they didn't. They talked and of course he wondered what they said. He saw Susannah's head go back against the headrest on the seat and her eyes close.

The afternoon was calm and dull, white-skied. Because there was no wind the surface of the water was quite smooth and the forest trees were still. He went into the back of the house to watch the sunset, a bronze and red spectacular sunset striped with black-rimmed thin cloud. These signs of time going by seemed to bring tomorrow night closer, Wednesday night when he could be alone with her. He began planning how to do it.

When he went back to the front window the car was moving, turning round prior to leaving. And no other had come to replace it. He began to feel a lightness, something that was almost excitement. They couldn't keep her from him if they both wanted to be together and if they could influence her, how much more could he? Any relationship between her and her companion in the car had been in his imagination. Probably, at some time or other, she had slept with Kim Gresham, but that was only to be expected. He had never had any ideas of being the first with her or even desired to be.

After a little while he poured himself a drink. Never much of a drinker, he had nevertheless had to stop himself having recourse to whisky these past few days. But at eight o'clock at night he could indulge himself. He began thinking of getting something to eat but he hadn't been outside all day except to speak those few brief words to Susannah and at about nine, when the twilight was deepening, he walked down to the lake.

Flies swarmed a few inches above its surface and fish were jumping for them. The water bubbled and broke as a slippery body leapt, twisted, gleaming silver in the last of the light. He watched, growing calm and almost fatalistic, resigning himself to the hard struggle ahead, but knowing that anyone as determined as he would be bound to win.

Because their lights were off and dusk had by now fallen, because they drove quietly and in convoy, he didn't see the cars until the first of them was almost upon him.

10

He went back into the house. He didn't quite know what else to do. They parked the cars on the little beach and on the grass, there were about twenty of them, and he said it was like people going to some function in a village hall and parking on the green outside. Only they didn't get out of their cars until he was indoors and then not immediately.

You have to understand that it was all in darkness, or absence of light, for it wasn't quite dark. The cars were unlit and so was the house. Once he was inside he tried putting lights on but then he couldn't see what they meant to do. He put on the light in the hall and watched them through the front room window.

They sat inside their cars. He recognised the Wantages' car and Sandy Clements's and of course John Peddar's white van. There was just enough light left to see that. He thought then of phoning the police, he often had that thought, and he always came to the same conclusion, that there was nothing he could say. They had a right to be there. For all he knew, they'd explain their presence by saying they'd come fishing or owl-watching. But by now he was frightened. He was also determined not to show his fear whatever they did.

The doors of the white van opened and the four people inside it got out, Susannah and her parents and one of the sisters. He stepped back from the window and moved into the hall. One after the other he heard car doors slamming. It seemed as if an hour passed before the front doorbell rang, though it was probably less than a minute. He breathed in slowly and out slowly and opened the door.

John Peddar pushed his way into the house, or rather, he pushed his daughter Julie into the house and followed behind her. Next came his wife and Susannah. Ben saw about forty people in the front garden, and on the path and the doorstep, and once he had let Susannah in he tried to shut the door but his effort was useless against the steady but entirely non-violent onslaught. They simply pushed their way in, close together, a body of men and women, a relentless shoving crowd. He retreated before them into the living room where the Peddars already were. He backed against the fireplace and stood there with his elbows on the mantelpiece, because there was nowhere further that he could go, and faced them, feeling that now he knew how it was to be an animal at bay.

My small front room was full of people. He thought at this moment literally that they meant to kill him, that as one they had gone mad. He thought, as I had thought in the wood, that the collective unconscious they seemed to share had taken a turn into madness and they had come there to do him to death. And the worst thing was, one of the worst things, that he grouped Susannah with them. Suddenly he lost his feeling for her, she became one of them and his passion evaporated with his fear. He could look at her, and did, without desire or tenderness or even nostalgia, but with distaste and the same fear as he had for her family and her neighbours.

At first he couldn't speak. He swallowed, he cleared his throat. 'What do you want?'

John Peddar answered him. He said something Ben couldn't believe he'd heard aright.

'*What?*'

'You heard but I'll say it again. I told you you could have my Carol, not my little girl, not my Julie.'

Ben said, his voice strengthening, 'I don't know what you mean.'

'Yes, you do. D'you know how old she is? She's not fourteen.' He was still holding the girl in front of him and now he pushed her forward, displaying her. 'See the bruises on her? See her leg? Look at that blue all up her arms.'

There was a murmur that seemed to swell all round him, like the buzzing of angry bees. His eyes went to Susannah and he thought he saw on that face that was no longer lovely to him the hint of a tiny malicious smile. 'Your daughter fell off her bicycle,' he said. 'She hurt her leg falling off her bicycle. The bruises on her arm I may have made, I don't know. I may have made them when I helped her to her feet, that's all.'

The child said in a harsh unchildish voice, 'You were going to rape me.'

'Is that why you've come here?' he said. 'To accuse me of that?'

'You tried to rape me.' The accusation, slightly differently phrased, was repeated. 'I fell over when I ran out of the house. Because you were trying to do it.'

'This is rubbish,' he said. 'Will you please go.' He looked at Susannah. 'All of you, please leave.'

'We've a witness,' said Iris. 'Teresa saw it all.'

'Teresa wasn't in the house,' he said.

'That's not true,' Teresa Gresham said. 'I'd been there an hour when Julie came. I expect you'd forgotten, there was a lot you forgot once you got to touch her.' She said to the Peddars, 'I came out of the kitchen and I saw it all.'

'What do you want of me?' he said again.

'We don't want to go to the police,' John Peddar said.

His wife said, 'It's humiliating for our little girl.'

'Not that it's in any way her fault. But we'll go to them if you don't go. You go tonight and this'll be the last you hear of it. Go now or we get the police. Me and Julie and her mother and Teresa. You can phone them on his phone, Iris.'

He imagined the police coming and his having absolutely no defence except the truth, which would collapse in the face of Julie's evidence and the Peddars' and Teresa's. If that weren't enough they'd no doubt produce Sandy Clements who would also have been there watching, cleaning the windows, perhaps, or weeding the garden. Sandy he could pick out of the crowd packed into the room, just squeezed in, leaning against the closed door beside his new wife.

'None of this is true,' he said. 'It's lies and you know it.'

They didn't try to deny it. They weren't interested in whether something was true or not, only in their power to control him. None of them smiled now or looked anything but grim. One of the strangest things, he said, was that they were all perfectly calm. There was no anxiety. They knew he'd do as they asked.

'This is a false accusation, entirely fabricated,' he said.

'Iris,' said John Peddar, 'phone the police.'

'Where's the phone?'

Teresa Gresham said, 'It's in the back room. I'll come with you.'

Sandy moved away from the door and opened it for them. The crowd made a passage, squeezing back against each other in a curiously intimate way, not seeming to resist the pressure of other bodies. Breasts pushed against arms, hips rested against bellies, without inhibition, without awkwardness. But perhaps that wasn't curious, perhaps it wasn't curious at all. They stood close together, crushed together, as if in some collective embrace, cheek to cheek, hand to shoulder, thigh to thigh.

Then Teresa went out of the room. Iris, following her, had reached the door when Ben said, 'All right. I'll go.'

He was deeply humiliated. He kept his head lowered so that he couldn't meet Susannah's eyes. His shame was so great that he felt a burning flush spread across his neck and face. But what else could he have done? One man is helpless against many. In those moments he knew every one of those people and those left behind in the village would stand by the Peddars. No doubt, if need was, they would produce other evidence of his proclivities and he remembered how, once, he had taken hold of Carol Peddar by the wrist.

'I'll go now,' he said.

They didn't leave. They helped his departure. He went upstairs and they followed him, pushed their way into his bedroom, one of them found his suitcases, another set them on the bed and opened their lids. Teresa Gresham opened the wardrobe and took out his clothes. Kathy Gresham and Angela Burns folded them and packed them in the cases. No one touched him, but once he was in that bedroom he was their prisoner. They packed his hairbrush and his shoes. John Peddar came out of the bathroom with his sponge bag and his razor and toothbrush. All the time Julie, the injured one, sat on the bed and stared at him.

Sandy Clements and George Whiteson carried the cases out of the room. One of the women produced a carrier bag and asked him if they'd got everything of his. When he said they had but for his dressing gown and the book he'd been reading in bed, she put those items in the bag, and then they let him leave the room.

If they were enjoying themselves there was no sign of it. They were calm, unsmiling, mostly silent. Teresa led them into the back room where he had worked on his translation, admitted him and closed the door behind him. Gillian Atkins – she was bound to be there, his nemesis – brought two plastic bags with her and into these they cleared his table of books and papers. They did it carefully, lining up the pages, clipping them together, careful not to crease or crumple. A man Ben didn't recognise, though his colouring, height and manner were consistent with the village people, unplugged his word processor and put it into its case. Then his dictionary went into the second bag.

Again he was asked if there was anything they'd forgotten. He shook his head and they let him go downstairs. Gillian Atkins went into the kitchen and came back with a bag containing the contents of the fridge.

'Now give me the door key,' Mark Gresham said.

Ben asked why. Why should he?

'You won't need it. I'll send it back to the present owner.'

Ben gave him the key. He really had no choice. He left the house in the midst of them. Their bodies pressed against him, warm, shapely, herbal-smelling. They eased him out, nudging and elbowing him, and when the last of them had left and turned out the hall light, closed the door behind them. His cases and bags were already in the boot of his car, his word processor in its case carefully placed on the floor in front of the back seat. He looked for Susannah to say goodbye but she had already left, he could see the red tail lights of the car she was in receding into the distance along the shore road.

They accompanied him in convoy through the village, two cars ahead of him and all the rest behind. Every light was on and some of the older people, the ones who hadn't come to Gothic House, were in their front gardens to see him go. Not all the cars came on, some fell away when their owners' homes were reached, but the Peddars and the Clementses continued to precede him, Gillian Atkins with Angela Burns continued to follow him and he thought the Greshams but he wasn't sure of that because he couldn't see the car colour in the dark.

After ten miles, almost at the approach to an A road, Gillian Atkins cut off his further progress the way a police car does, by overtaking him and pulling sharply ahead of him. He was forced to stop. The car behind stopped. Those in front already had. Gillian Atkins came round to his window, which he refused to open. But he'd forgotten to lock the door and she opened it.

'Don't come back,' was all she said.

They let him go on alone.

He had to stop for a while on the A road in a lay-by because his hands were shaking and his breathing erratic. He thought he might choke. But after a while things improved and he was able to drive on to London.

11

My key came home before he did.

There was no note to accompany it. I knew where it had come from only by the postmark. No one answered the phone, either at Gothic House or Ben's London flat. I drove to Gothic House, making the detour through the town to reach it, and found it empty, all Ben's possessions gone.

I phoned the estate agent and put the house up for sale.

A month passed before Ben surfaced. He asked if he could come over and, once with me, he stayed. The translation was done, he had worked on it unremittingly, thinking of nothing else, closing off his mind, until it was finished.

'Helen went back to her husband,' he said. 'He took her home to Sparta and she brought the heroes nepenthe in a golden dish, which made them forget their sorrows. My author got a lot of analytical insights out of that.'

'What was nepenthe?' I said.

'No one knows. Opium? Cannabis maybe?' He was silent for a while, then suddenly vociferous. 'Do you know what I'd like? I've thought a lot about this. I'd like them to build a road right through that village, one of those bypasses there are all these protests about. They never work, the protests, do they? The road gets built. And that's what I'd like to hear, that some town nearby has to be bypassed and the village is in the way, the village has to be cut in half, split up, destroyed.'

'It doesn't seem very likely,' I said, thinking of the forest, the empty arable landscape.

After that he never mentioned the place, so when I heard, as I did from time to time, how my efforts to sell Gothic House were proceeding I said nothing to him. I didn't tell him when I heard, from the same source, that old Mrs Fowler had died and had left, in excess of all expectations, rather a large sum.

By then he'd shown me the diary and told me his story. In the details he told me far more than I often cared to hear. He was still sharing my house, though he often talked of buying a new flat for himself, and one evening, when we were alone and warm and I felt very close to him, when the story was long told, I asked him – more or less – if we should make it permanent, if we should change the sharing to a living together, with its subtle difference of meaning.

I took his hand and he leaned towards me to kiss me absently. It was the sort of kiss that told me everything: that I shouldn't have asked or even suggested, that he regretted I had, that we must forget it ever happened.

'You see,' he said, after a few moments in which I tried to conquer my humiliation, 'it sounds foolish, it sounds absurd, but it's not only that I've never got over what happened, though that's part of it. The sad, dreadful thing is that I want to be back there, I want to be with them. Not just Susannah, of course I want *her*, I've never stopped wanting her for more than a few minutes, but it's to be with all of them that I want, and in that place. Sometimes I have a dream that I am – back there, I mean. I said yes to the offers, I was accepted and I stayed.'

'You mean you regret saying no?'

'Oh, no. Of course not. It wouldn't have worked. I suppose I mean I wish I were that different person it might have worked for. And then sometimes I think it never happened, I only dreamt that it happened.'

'In that case, I dreamt it too.'

He said some more, about knowing that the sun didn't always shine there, it wasn't always summer, it couldn't be eternally happy, not with human nature the way it was, and then he said he'd be moving out soon to live by himself.

'Did you manage to sell Gothic House?'

I shook my head. I couldn't tell him the truth, that I'd heard the day before that I had a buyer, or rather a couple of buyers with an inheritance to spend, Kim Gresham and his wife. Greshams have always liked to live a little way outside the village.

Myth

It was a map of the Garden of Eden. The monk, who was also their guide, pointed it out to them under its protective glass and said something in Greek. The interpreter interpreted. Made in the eighth century AD by one Alexander of Philae, the map had been in this monastery for a thousand years, had been stolen, retrieved, threatened by fire and flood, defaced, patched up and finally restored to its present near-perfect condition.

The tour party crowded around to look at it. Rosemary Meacher, standing in front of her much taller husband, saw a sheet of yellowish parchment that looked as if coffee had been spilt over it, spindly-legged insects died on it and a child experimented on its mottled surface with a new paintbox. The monk made another short speech in Greek. The interpreter said that, if they were interested, on their way out they could buy postcards of the map at the shop.

'Or tea towels perhaps,' whispered Rosemary to her husband, 'or tablecloths with matching napkins.'

David Meacher made no reply. He had moved to a position beside her and was peering closely at the map. For the first time since their holiday began, for the first time, really, since he was made redundant, his face wore an expression that was neither bitter nor indifferent. He was looking at the map as if it interested him.

The monk and the interpreter moved on; through the library, through the refectory, out into the cloisters. The party followed. Flaking frescos and faded murals were pointed out, their provenance explained. The hot sun was white and trembling on the stone flags, the shadows black. Thankfully the party surged into the shop.

There were no tea towels or tablecloths or aprons or even calendars of the map of the Garden of Eden, but there were the postcards and life-size facsimiles. Framed or unframed.

'You don't really want one, do you?' Rosemary said.

'Yes, of course I do.' David had taken to barking at her lately, especially if, as now, she seemed even mildly to oppose his wishes. 'I think it's very beautiful, a marvellous piece of history.'

'As you wish.'

He bought a framed map and then, on second thoughts, an unframed map as well and four postcards. Back at the hotel he got her to pack the framed map, parcelled in bubble-wrap and their clothes, into their carry-on bag. The unframed map he spread out on the desk top, weighting down its corners with the ashtray, two glasses and the stand that held the room service menu. He sat down with his elbows on the desk and studied the map. After dinner, instead of going to the bar, he went back to their room and she found him there later, crouched over the desk. From somewhere or other he had procured a magnifying glass.

She was pleased. He had found something to take him out of himself. These were probably early days to think of a hobby developing from it, that he might begin collecting old maps, antiquarian books, something like that. But surely this was how such things began. She vaguely remembered hearing that an uncle of hers had started collecting stamps because a friend sent him a letter from Outer Mongolia. If only David would find an interest!

Since the loss of his job he had been a changed man, sullen, bad-tempered, sometimes savage in his manner towards her. And he had been very unhappy. The large sum of money he received in compensation, the golden handshake, had done nothing to

240

mitigate his misery. He still spoke daily of the Chief Executive, a young woman, walking into his office, telling him to clear his desk and go.

'I'll never forget it,' he said. 'Her face, that red mouth like a slice of raw beef, and that tight bright-blue suit showing her fat knees. And her voice, not a word of excuse or apology, not a hint of shame.'

Rosemary saw to her horror that he had tears in his eyes. She thought it would help when the cheque that came was twice what he expected. She thought he might put those humiliating events behind him once she had found the beautiful house in Wiltshire and driven him there and shown him. But apathy had succeeded rage, and then rage came back alternating with periods of deep depression. He sat about all day or he paced. In the evenings he watched television indiscriminately. His doctor suggested this holiday, two weeks in the Aegean before the move.

'I don't care,' he said. 'If you like. It's all one to me. I'll never get her voice out of my head, not a word of apology, no shame.'

He rolled up the map of the Garden of Eden and she packed it in his suitcase. What became of the postcards she didn't know until she saw him studying one of them on the plane.

They moved house two weeks after their return. It was only his second visit to the house, only the second time he had walked through these spacious rooms and down the steps from the terrace on to the lawn to look across at the seven acres which were now his. Wasn't this better than living in a north London terrace, taking the Northern Line daily to a Docklands office? She wasn't so tactless as to ask him directly. It put heart into her to see him explore the place, pronounce later that evening that it wasn't so bad, that it was a relief to breathe fresh air.

She busied herself getting the place straight, unpacking the boxes, deciding where this piece of furniture and that should go. Two men arrived to hang the new curtains. Another brought the chandelier, holland-wrapped, tied up with string. He hung it in the drawing room and he hung the pictures. David hung up his framed map of the Garden of Eden in the room that was going to be his study. Then he asked the man to hang a much bigger picture he had and which he wanted in the dining room. Rosemary saw, to her surprise, that it was the map again, but blown up to three times its size (and therefore rather vague and blurred) in an ornate gilt frame.

'I had it done,' David said. 'Last week. I found a place where they photocopy things to any size you want.'

She was overjoyed. If she felt a tremor of unease it was a tiny thing, brought about surely by her heightened nervousness and sensitivity to his moods. If she was ever so slightly disturbed by the spectacle of a man of fifty engrossed in a cheap copy of a map of some mythical place . . . But no, it was wonderful to see him returning to his old self, to interest and occupation. He even arranged the furniture in his study, put his books out on the shelves. By nine next morning he was out in the garden and later in the day off in the car to a nursery where there was a chance of finding some particular shrub he wanted.

After they had been in the new place a week she realised he hadn't once mentioned the Chief Executive or her mouth or her blue suit or her voice. So this, apparently, was the solution. Not the holiday or the doctor's drugs or even kindness but the move to somewhere new and different. His days, which had been empty, gradually became busy and filled. He followed a pattern, gardening in the morning and in the afternoon going out in the car and returning with books. Some came from a library, some he bought. She paid them very little attention. It was enough to know that he was reading again after not opening a book of any kind for months. Then one day he asked her if they had a Bible in the house.

She was astonished. Neither of them had religious leanings. 'Your old school Bible is somewhere. Shall I look for it?'

'I will,' he said, and then, 'I want to look something up.'

He found the Bible and was soon immersed in it. Perhaps he was about to undergo some sort of conversion. This house was his road to Damascus. Disquiet returned in a small niggling way and when he was outside mowing the lawn next day she looked at the library books and the books he had bought. Every one of them was concerned in some respect or other with the Garden of Eden. There was a scholarly examination of the book of Genesis, an American Fundamentalist work, a modern novel called *Rib into Woman*, Milton's *Paradise Lost* and several others. Well, she had hoped he would take up a hobby, that he would study something or collect something, and what it appeared he was studying was evidently – paradise.

Presumably, he would tell her about it sooner or later. He would say what the purpose of it was, what he meant to do with it, what he expected to accomplish. They had enough to live on comfortably, he had no need of an earned income, but perhaps he intended to write a book for his own pleasure. She watched him. She didn't ask. Her own life was less busy than it had been in London and it took concentration to find enough to do. She must become involved with village life, she thought, find charity work, develop her own interests. He didn't seem to want her to help in the garden. Meanwhile, she cooked more than she ever had, baked their bread, made jam from the soft fruit. She admitted to herself that she was lonely.

But when, at last, he did tell her, it came as a shock. She said, 'I don't understand. I don't know what you mean.'

'Just what I say.' He had stopped barking at her. He habitually spoke gently now, even dreamily. 'It's here. The Garden is here. This is where it is. It's taken me a few weeks to be sure, that's why I've said nothing till now. But now I am absolutely certain. The Garden of Eden is there, outside our windows.'

'David,' she said, 'the Garden of Eden doesn't exist. It never did exist. It is a myth. You know that as well as I do.'

He looked at her with narrowed eyes, as if he suspected her mental equilibrium. 'Why do you say that?'

'Believing in it as a real place is like saying Adam and Eve really existed.'

'Why not?' he said.

'David, I'm not hearing this. You can't be saying this. Listen, people used to believe in it. Then Darwin came along and his theory of evolution, you know that. You know that God, if there is a God, didn't make a man out of whatever it is . . .'

'Dust.'

'Well, dust, all right. He didn't take out one of his ribs and make a woman. I mean, it's laughable. Only crazy sects believe that stuff.' She stopped, thought. 'You're joking, aren't you, you're having me on?'

In a rapt, dreamy tone, as if she hadn't spoken, he said, 'It's always been believed that the site of the Garden was somewhere in the Middle East because Genesis mentions the river Euphrates and Ethiopia and Assyria. But, seriously, how could a garden be in Syria and Ethiopia and Iraq all at the same time? The truth is that it was far away, in a place they knew nothing of, a distant place beyond the confines of the known world . . .'

'Wiltshire,' she said.

'Please don't mock,' he said. 'Cynicism doesn't suit you. Come outside and I'll show you.'

He took the Bible with him and one of the postcards. The area of their land he led her to comprised the old orchard, a lawn and the water garden, through which two spring-fed streams flowed. She saw that the lawn had been mown and the banks of the streams tidied up. It was very pretty, a lush mature garden in which unusual plants grew and where fruit trees against the old wall bore ripening plums and pears.

'There, you see,' he said, referring to his Bible, 'is the river called Pison, that is it which compasseth the whole land of Havilah, where there is gold.' His eyes flashed. There was sweat on his upper lip. 'And the name of the second river is Gihon, and the third Hiddekel and the fourth river is Euphrates.'

She could only see two, not much more than trickles, flowing over English stones among English water buttercups. He turned and beckoned to her in his old peremptory way but his voice was still measured and gentle. His voice was as if he was explaining something obvious to a slow-witted child.

'There,' he said, 'the Tree of Life. Sometimes we call it the tree of the knowledge of good and evil.'

He pointed to it and led her up under its branches, a big old apple tree, laden with small green apples. When first she saw the house she remembered it had been in blossom.

'Mustn't eat those, eh?'

His smile and his short bark of laughter frightened her. She felt entirely at a loss. This was the man she had been married to for twenty years, the practical, clever businessman. How had he known those words, how had he known where to look for this – this web of nonsense? She put out her hand and touched the tree. She hung on to it, leaned against it, for she was afraid she might faint.

'I wondered, when I first discovered it,' he said, 'if we were being given a second chance.'

She didn't know what he meant. She closed her eyes, bowed her head. When she felt she could breathe again and that strength was returning she looked for him but he was gone. She made her way back to the house. Later, after he had gone to bed, she sat downstairs, wondering what to do. It couldn't be right for him to be left to go on like this. But in the morning when she woke and he woke, when they encountered each other on adjoining pillows, then across the breakfast table, he seemed his normal self. He talked about taking on a gardener, the place was too much for him alone. Would she like the dining room redecorated? She had said she disliked the wallpaper. And perhaps it was time to invite the neighbours in – if you could call people living half a mile away neighbours – have a small drinks party, acquaint themselves with the village.

She summoned up all the courage she had. 'That was a game you were playing last evening, wasn't it? You weren't serious?'

He laughed. 'You evidently didn't think I was.' It was hardly an answer. 'I dreamt of that bitch,' he said. 'She came in wearing that ghastly blue suit that showed her fat knees and told me to clear my desk. She was eating an apple – did I tell you that?'

'In your dream, do you mean?'

He was instantly angry. 'No, I don't mean that. In reality is what I mean. She came into my office with an apple in her hand, she was eating an apple. I *told* you.'

She shook her head. He had never told her that, she would have remembered. Next day the new gardener started. She was afraid David would say something to him about the Garden of Eden. When neighbours came in for drinks a week later she was afraid David would say something to them. He didn't. It seemed that conversation on this subject was reserved to her alone. With other people he was genial, bland, civilised. In the evenings, alone with her, he spent his time compiling a list of the plants indigenous to Eden, balm and pomegranate, coriander and hyssop. He took her into the fruit garden and showed her the fig tree that grew up against the wall, pointing out its hand-shaped leathery leaves and saying that they could stitch the leaves together and make themselves aprons.

She looked that up in Genesis and found the reference. Then she went to seek advice.

The doctor didn't take her seriously. Or he didn't take David's obsession seriously. He said he would review the tranquillisers he was already prescribing for David and this he did – with startling effect. David's enthusiasm seemed to wane, he became quiet and preoccupied, busied himself in other areas of the grounds, returned to his old interest of reading biographies. He joined the golf club. He no longer spoke of the Chief Executive and her blue suit and her apple. The only thing to disquiet Rosemary was the snake.

'I've just seen an adder,' he told her when he came in for his lunch. 'Curled up under the fig tree.'

She said nothing, just looked at him.

'It might have been a grass snake, I'm not sure, but it was certainly a snake.'

'Is it still there?'

There came a flash of the bad temper she hadn't seen for weeks. 'How do I know if it's still there? Come and see.'

Not a snake, but a shed snake skin. Nothing could have made Rosemary happier. She was so certain the snake was part of his delusion, but he had seen a real snake, or a real snake's skin. He was well again, it was over, whatever it had been.

The summer had been long and hot, and the fruit crop was spectacular. First the raspberries and gooseberries, then peaches and plums. Rosemary made jam and jelly, she even bottled fruit the way her mother used to. None of it must be wasted. David picked the pears before they were ripe, wrapped each one individually in tissue paper and stored them in boxes. The days were long and golden, the evenings mild and the air scented with ripe fruit. David often walked round the grounds at dusk but that was the merest coincidence, it had nothing to do with the Lord God walking in the garden at the cool of the day.

The big tree was a Cox, David thought, a Cox's Orange Pippin, considered by many even today to be the finest English apple. It was laden with fruit. They used an apple picker with a ten-foot handle but they had to put a ladder up into the highest branches. Rosemary went up it because she was the lighter of them and the more agile. He held the ladder and she picked.

If her fears hadn't been allayed, if she hadn't put the whole business of the map and the Garden of Eden behind her – and, come to that, the Chief Executive in her bright-blue suit – she might have been more cautious. She might have been wary. She had forgotten that cryptic remark of his when he said that they – meaning mankind? – might have been given a second chance. She had come to see his delusion as the temporary madness of a man humiliated and driven beyond endurance. So she climbed down the ladder with her basket of shiny red and gold fruit and, taking one in her hand, a flawless ripe apple, held it out to him and said, 'Look at that, isn't that absolutely perfect? Try it, have a bite.'

His face grew dark-red and swollen. He shouted, 'You won't do it a second time, woman, you won't bring evil into the world a second time!'

He lashed out at her with the apple picker, struck her on the side of the head, on the shoulder, again on her head. She fell to the ground and the apples spilled out and rolled everywhere. Her screams fetched the gardener who got there just in time, pulled David off, wrested the bloodstained apple picker out of his hands.

Rosemary was in hospital for a long time but not so long as David. When she was better she went to see him. He was in the day room, quiet and subdued, watching a game show on television. When he saw her he picked up the first weapon that came to hand, a table lamp, brandished it and flung himself upon her, cursing her and crying that he would multiply her sorrow. They advised her not to go back and she never did.

She stayed in the house on her own, she liked it. After all, she had chosen it in the first place. But she took the maps of the Garden of Eden out of their frames and gave the frames to the village jumble sale. In the spring she had the apple tree cut down and made a big fishpond where it had stood. Fed by the streams he had called Pison and Gihon, Hiddekel and Euphrates, it was an ideal home for her Koi carp which became the envy of the county.